BITTER PAST

CAROLINE FARDIG

SEVERN RIVER

PUBLISHING

Severn River Publishing
www.SevernRiverBooks.com

ISBN: 978-1-64875-469-2 (Paperback)

ALSO BY CAROLINE FARDIG

Ellie Matthews Novels

Bitter Past

An Eye for an Eye

Dead Sprint

Parted by Death

Relative Harm

To find out more about Caroline Fardig and her books, visit

severnriverbooks.com/authors/caroline-fardig

PROLOGUE

A laughing clown with disturbing red eyes stared down from a sign reading "Welcome to Carnival Cove." With intermittent clouds blocking the full moon, the warm autumn evening was particularly dark at that moment. A gust of wind whirled the fallen leaves and discarded trash littering the entrance to the old water park, sending an eerie chill down his spine.

"This place is creepy as hell," he muttered, shining his flashlight on the weathered sign. "You sure you want to do this?"

She ripped the lid from the plastic bucket she was holding. "Dr. Cooper needs to take notice that the students of Ashmore College are not going to stand for him going ahead with his new research facility. You heard how smug he sounded at the protest tonight. He thinks he can get away with anything because his mother is president of the college. Someone has to put him in his place." She dipped her fingers into the red liquid and wrote "Death to the Body Farm" across the sign.

He shook his head, chuckling. "I never thought I'd see you touch pig's blood, much less vandalize a property belonging to our school."

She set down the bucket and picked up a pair of bolt cutters. "This dump doesn't belong to the school yet. Dr. Cooper bought it himself so he could skip some red tape." She snipped the padlock securing a chain around the bars of the gate, then removed the chain and tossed it onto the ground. "Typical that he expects everything to be handed to him when he wants it. And if things don't go exactly his way, he changes the rules."

Frowning, he watched her push open the gate and barge into the park, which was now a gloomy and deserted eyesore. Once a happy place where families came to play on hot summer days, Carnival Cove had fallen into disrepair after being shut down years ago. As they explored the park, their flashlights cast shadows of the broken-down tables and chairs against the cracked concrete and retaining walls, where vegetation had begun to creep back. The tall trees above them swayed as another blast of wind whipped through.

He joked, "Maybe we're doing the forensics majors a favor by trying to block this thing from happening. I can't imagine this place being any freakier than it already is. I also can't get my head around the fact that the forensics profs are seriously going to leave dead bodies out here and let them decompose so students can study them."

"They are unless we stop them," she said, coming to a halt in front of what used to be a snack bar. "Can you imagine donating your body to science only to have some demented professor throw it out here to be ravaged by the elements and vermin of every kind? It's unconscionable."

Shivering at the thought, he approached a painted statue of a portly clown and gave its peeling red nose a honk, only to have the nose crumble off into his hand. "Sick. This place has horror movie written all over it." Appraising the message she was painting across the outer wall of the snack bar, he said, "And you're making it worse. Although 'Dr. Death Sucks' is pretty hilarious—and fitting."

She walked over and handed him the bucket of blood. "I thought you came here to help me—not to stand around and crack jokes."

"I think enough blood has been spilled tonight." Setting down the bucket, he put his arms around her waist. "Why don't we go get a drink or something?"

She shook her head and pushed away from him. "I'm just getting started. Dr. Cooper is never going to know what hit him. Now get to work."

Sighing, he replied, "Yes, ma'am."

He began painting "Say No to the Body Farm" on a nearby retaining wall while she wandered into a section of the park marked "Kiddie Land."

The clouds parted, allowing the full moon to shine down on her. As she gazed up at it and relaxed for a moment, she began to have second thoughts, knowing this destructive vandalism wasn't her style. She hated to stoop to this level. However, the rage she felt against Dr. Cooper and his horrific body farm had overtaken her. She wouldn't allow this research facility to go forward, no matter the cost.

As she stood staring up at the sky, she felt a force slam into her gut and an all-encompassing, searing pain rip through her body. A loud crack shattered the quiet of the night. Crying out, she clutched her stomach. Something warm and wet oozed onto her shaking hands. When she looked down, her breath caught at the sight of the blood. She felt another blast, this one exploding through the center of her chest. Falling backward, the last thing she saw was the moon overhead fading from her vision.

1

Earlier that evening

"Cooper, you need to relax that death grip you have on the steering wheel," I said to my colleague as he weaved through traffic on a congested stretch of North Meridian Street in Indianapolis.

Dr. Dudley Cooper grimaced. "I would like to get to my aunt's home as soon as possible so that we might defuse the situation before resorting to calling the police. According to my father, the sidewalks are already teeming with student protestors, and the fundraiser isn't supposed to start for another hour."

I appreciated Cooper's concern. This was his big night. The fundraiser gala at his aunt's mansion was to raise money to fund his plan to establish a new research facility for Ashmore College, where we were both professors.

"True, your patrons might get nervous if they find out how much the Ashmore students oppose your body fa—I mean, outdoor forensic anthropology research facility." I hoped he had missed my slip. He hated it when I called his baby a "body farm," although that was essentially what it was.

He zoomed around a slow driver in front of us. "Well, not *all* of them oppose it. For every student protestor, there are a dozen students who are either in favor of or at least not against the facility. Unfortunately, they're not the ones who are making their feelings known." Flicking worried eyes at me, he said, "Ellie, how in the world do you get them to listen to you when you talk about the facility instead of complain and...and attack your integrity?" he asked.

Even though every professor in the forensics department had been doing his or her part to sell the students on the idea of a body farm, Cooper, as head of the proposed facility, had taken most of the flak. After he had made the official announcement last week, it hadn't taken long for a few opinionated, outspoken students to whip up some righteous indignation and feel the need to cause a stir. There had already been a thrown-together picket march in front of the science building and an organized protest on the campus front lawn that managed to gain local news attention.

Students seemed to have myriad reasons for protesting the facility. Some were grossed out, some were scared, and some were worried about the environmental impact. A number of others were protesting because that's what they did—their interest in hot-button issues often came across as more of a hobby than a crusade. Still, Cooper took every negative comment as a personal attack.

Smiling, I said, "It helps that I haven't been branded 'Dr. Death.' I'm only his lovely assistant."

That got a chuckle out of him. "That you are. But you're still much better at talking to these kids than I am."

"I'm not a fancy-schmancy PhD like you, and they know it. Plus, I live with a college kid. I speak the language."

"I'm sure it's quite helpful that your sister can keep you in the loop of what our students are doing and thinking."

Smiling, I said, "True, but sometimes when Rachel overshares, I wish I were out of the loop."

When we got close to Cooper's aunt's home, a sprawling red brick Colonial estate in an old money neighborhood, the surrounding area was crawling with young people. I recognized most of them as Ashmore College students. They lined the sidewalks on either side of the street, likely breaking a few dozen neighborhood association rules, but no laws—yet.

Cooper wiped a hand down his face. "Ellie, I'm sick about this. I'm appalled at the overwhelming negativity of our students. I thought this would be a grand opportunity for their study."

I put my hand on his arm. "Don't worry. I checked out your not-so-angry mob. It's mainly composed of the usual loudmouthed tree-huggers who protest everything. They'll be onto the next popular cause soon enough. The body farm—"

"Outdoor forensic anthropology research facility," he corrected me.

"Yes, that. It's your dream. If you can make them understand why it's important to you, they'll respect you for it," I said, hoping to build his confidence. He needed to be on his game tonight during the fundraiser, not worrying about the idiot protestors.

"You think so?" he asked, a hopeful expression lighting his face.

I lied, "Of course." They would eat him alive if given the chance. "But maybe let's not get into a debate with them tonight. Is there a back way into your aunt's house?"

"I'm afraid not."

I grimaced upon spotting the editor of the school newspaper, Eli Vanover, taking photographs and videos and jotting down notes as he spoke with the protestors. This would be front-page news in the next edition of the *Ashmore Voice*. The protestors' hand-lettered signs read "Peace for the Dead," "Say No to the Body Farm," "The Human Body Is a Temple," and one that made me chuckle in spite of my loyalty to Cooper, "Dr. Death Sucks." Among the students, hired security guards were stationed at intervals on the sidewalk, making me wonder if someone thought things had the potential to get dicey out here.

Cooper pulled to a stop in front of the home. A valet attendant appeared to help me out of the car while another got in and drove the car away. I didn't know it was possible to hire a valet service for an event at a private residence, but then again, I'd never been to a party like this before.

Before Cooper and I could hurry to the front door, one of the girls stepped out into the street and let out a piercing whistle, quieting the other students. "Dr. Cooper," called Vasti Marais, holding up a hand to silence the leftover grumbling in the crowd.

He turned around to face Vasti, almost as if he couldn't look away. There was something about this girl that commanded immediate attention. An international student from South Africa, Vasti had been president of practically every organization on campus at one time or another. Her striking beauty, lovely lilting accent, and unabashed blind ambition set her apart from her fellow students.

I hissed, "Don't engage, Coop. Not tonight. Especially her." Grabbing his arm, I tried to pull him with me up the sidewalk, but he was rooted in place.

She zeroed her gaze in on him. "What do you have to say about the negative impact your research facility is going to create both environmentally and ethically?"

Cooper became flustered, for some reason unable to get his thoughts together. "I... There is no... There will be *no* negative impact. This facility will help to assist law enforcement across the country and across the world in better understanding—"

"You've been saying that all week in the canned speeches you've been giving us," Vasti interrupted. "We want to know what you *personally* are going to do to preserve the dignity of the people whose bodies you're going to allow to be desecrated."

The crowd shouted a semi-unison "Yeah!" in support, causing the security guards to tense their posture.

Cooper walked out into the street and shouted over the noise, "This is not the venue I wish to use to speak about the new facility. If you'd please disperse, we can talk about it next—"

Vasti wasn't backing down. "No, Dr. Cooper, we want to know *now*! This morbid experiment of yours is a violation of human rights!"

Cooper held his hands up in an effort to quiet the crowd so he could be heard. After he had regained their attention, he said, "As I've said before, these cadavers will be no different than any that we already use at the school for study. Faculty and students alike are expected to treat our deceased research subjects with the respect they deserve. Most of you should already be aware of this."

Vasti frowned. "And what about the safety of the people living in the area around your body farm? Decaying human bodies left out in the open will attract predators, especially vultures and rodents, not to mention feral animals. It would be a big temptation even for household pets. How do you plan to deal with that?"

"The facility isn't going to be in the middle of campus, Ms. Marais. The site I have chosen is in a rural area a few miles away. Don't worry. You'll all be perfectly safe from vultures and feral animals. If you want to know the particulars, please consult the article in last week's *Ashmore Voice*. The article they ran was surprisingly informational."

His condescending comments seemed to incense the students, especially Eli Vanover, whose expression darkened as he stepped out into the street and trained his phone on Vasti and the protestors, who all looked ready to explode. The security guards came out into the street as well, hands at the ready on the pepper spray cans clipped to their belts. This was fast becoming a disaster, and I'd bet anything the video Eli was taking would go viral before the gala was over.

Thrusting the sign she was holding in the air, Vasti turned to her fellow protestors and cried, "No body farm, no way! Not ever, not today!" They joined in her chant, causing her expression to turn to one of haughty satisfaction.

It was evident from the change in Cooper's posture that he knew he'd been bested. He returned to where I'd been waiting on the sidewalk. Running his hands through his sandy hair, he lamented as much to himself as to me, "I don't know what went wrong. I didn't think this facility was going to meet with such opposition. Sure, my father wasn't convinced, but I didn't think I'd run into *this*."

I hated seeing him like this. "Cooper, come on. It's not the end of the world. We can call in some noise complaints to the cops, and they'll come over here and make the protestors leave."

He shook his head. "It's over. The board is going to pull their support. I'm certain of it."

"Come on. No offense, since your family owns the place, but you know as well as I do that the Ashmore administration doesn't care what the students think. If you've already been promised the board's backing and you finish securing your funding tonight, it's a done deal. Screw the protestors." I reached up and straightened his black bow tie. "Now go in there and rub elbows with your parents' rich friends and get the support you need—financial and moral."

My pep talk seemed to help him a bit. Heaving a heavy sigh and trying to paste on a smile, Cooper turned his back on the protestors. He politely motioned for me to go ahead of him up the sidewalk toward his aunt's home and trudged along behind me.

A man in all black—suit, shirt, tie, and sunglasses—blocked our entry to the front door. As we approached him, he slipped his sunglasses off to focus his piercing blue eyes on me.

Cooper said, "Good evening, Rob."

"Dr. Cooper," the man replied, his voice low and scratchy as he shook Cooper's hand. "Good to see you."

Cooper turned to me. "Ellie, this is Rob Larson, my father's head of security."

My eyebrows shot up. Cooper's father was the former mayor of Indianapolis who was now running for US Senate, but I didn't realize that made him so important he needed a security detail. I couldn't help but flick my eyes across Rob Larson's broad, muscular shoulders. He looked more than capable of protecting anyone from pretty much anything.

Before Cooper could make my introduction, I extended my hand, and Rob clasped it. "Ellie Matthews. I teach at Ashmore College with Dr. Cooper. Nice to meet you." I said, smiling up at him.

He held my hand for an extra moment before releasing it. "It's my pleasure, Ms. Matthews." He smiled back at me. "Have a good time tonight."

I wasn't quite ready to leave Rob Larson when Cooper took my arm.

He said, "Let me introduce you to my father and my aunt."

Steeling myself for a long night of useless introductions to people I'd never see again, I let Cooper lead me into the home's cavernous entry hall. We were early to the event, but the band had already begun playing and the drinks were flowing—perhaps in an attempt to focus people's attention away from the protestors outside.

Cooper led me to a group of older people talking and sipping champagne. "Mother, Father, Aunt Vivian," he said.

The three of them turned in our direction. It wasn't difficult to see the family resemblance. Cooper's father was merely an older version of him, down to the trimmed beard, dimpled chin, and designer tuxedo. The two women could have been twins, the only difference being their hair color. Both were dressed, coiffed, plucked, nipped, and tucked to perfection. The two ladies beamed at Cooper and gave me the once over. His father smiled at me, but seemed disinterested in Cooper.

Cooper leaned in to kiss his aunt. "I can't thank you enough for throwing this fundraiser, Aunt Vivian. My research facility wouldn't be possible without you."

She gave him a demure smile. "Oh, you flatterer."

Placing his hand on my shoulder, he said, "And it also wouldn't be possible without Ellie. This is Professor Ellie Matthews, my Head of Operations. Ellie, of course you know my mother." His mother, Judith Ashmore Cooper, was the president of Ashmore College and therefore my boss. He continued, "This is my father, former Indianapolis Mayor George Cooper, and my aunt, Mrs. Vivian Ashmore Harris."

We exchanged pleasantries, but my head wasn't in it. I was busy pondering his use of the title "Head of Operations," a term he hadn't mentioned before. In reality, I didn't expect to be much more than a glorified assistant, but I wasn't surprised Cooper was trying to make the facility sound fancier and more appealing to his family. He seemed overwhelmingly occupied with what they thought of him, which was a foreign concept to me. I'd left home the night of my high school graduation and never looked back.

A young man elbowed his way into our group, pushing Cooper aside in an effort to make a grand show of giving Vivian a big hug and kiss. "Hello, Mother," he said enthusiastically. He couldn't have been much older than my college students, and he was no taller than I was.

"Oh, hello, Tyler my dear," replied Vivian.

I had noticed Cooper and his dad stiffen when Tyler appeared. Tyler didn't seem to notice, or else didn't care, because he went on with his glad-handing. "Aunt Judith! You're looking as beautiful as ever." He gave her a kiss on the cheek and shook hands with George. "Uncle George, your campaign seems to be going along without a hitch. Good for you."

George said between gritted teeth, "Yes, thank you."

Tyler turned to Cooper and gave him a punch in the shoulder. "And

Dudley! Long time no see, cousin." He pretended to think for a moment. "I guess the last time we got to hang out together was in Alaska during our hunting trip. Has it really been a month since we've seen each other? You know, my dad is still going on about the moose I shot. He was so impressed with my kill that he had the head mounted. Just got it back yesterday. It's in his study if you'd like to see it." Tyler was awfully proud of himself, but Cooper and his father didn't seem to share his opinion.

Cooper replied, "Maybe another time."

Clapping Cooper on the back, Tyler joked, "Oh, don't pout, Dudders. You'll get your first kill eventually. There's always next year."

Ignoring his cousin's jab, Cooper said, "Tyler, I'd like to introduce you to Ellie Matthews, Head of Operations for the new research facility. Ellie, this is my cousin, Tyler Harris."

"Hi, Tyler," I said.

"Hel-*lo*," he said, leering at me. "Cooper, why aren't you dancing with this gorgeous creature? If you're not going to, I am."

Before I could object, Tyler whisked me into the great room. No one else had started dancing yet, but that didn't stop Tyler. He clasped my right hand and put his other hand at my waist. He wasn't a bad dance partner, but having to talk to him was utter hell.

"So, Ellie," he began, his face much too close to mine. "You're going to be working alongside my cousin and his disgusting dead bodies at that old water park he bought. What's a sweet girl like you doing working in a place like that?"

In the three minutes since I'd met him, I'd decided I didn't like Tyler. "Well, for one thing, I'm not all that sweet. I used to work for Hamilton County's crime scene unit, so I'm not squeamish, if that's what you're asking."

"Wow. Were you a real-life CSI?"

I hated that question. "I guess you could say that." Years ago, I'd been a criminalist for the county sheriff's office, but after a particularly heinous and deeply personal case, I had resigned and joined the faculty at Ashmore College. For no other reason than to keep the topic off myself, I asked, "What do you do, Tyler, besides excel at hunting wild game?"

He puffed out his tiny little chest. "I am the soon-to-be Senator Powell's campaign manager."

My jaw dropped. "You're the campaign manager for your uncle's opponent?" No wonder Cooper and his dad couldn't stand Tyler.

He shrugged. "I'm a Republican. He's a Democrat. It's not like I could have managed his campaign."

"But he's family."

"Not really. He's only my uncle by marriage."

"I see."

Leering at me again, he asked, "So are you and Dudley a thing? Or are you a free agent?"

I groaned inwardly and looked away, happening to lock eyes with Rob Larson, who had just entered the room. He seemed to be smirking at me. I started to flash him a smile, but Tyler chose that moment to step on my toe, and instead I winced in pain.

Instead of apologizing, Tyler said, "Looks like someone isn't paying attention to where her feet should be."

Before I could return a biting remark, Rob came up to us. "Ms. Matthews," he said, his voice serious, "I'm sorry to interrupt your dance, but I need to speak with you immediately."

Tyler released me and made a big show of giving me a wink. "Catch you later, pretty lady."

I didn't reply, because if I had, it would have been inappropriate.

Rob took my elbow and walked me purposely down a hallway, away from the crowd. He opened a door and ushered me into a study. He was wearing a stern expression and hadn't said a word, so I was beginning to become wary of the situation. He closed the door behind us and turned to face me.

"Am I in trouble here?" I asked.

"Yes, I'm afraid so."

My heart rate increased. "What's going on?"

Crossing his muscular arms, he replied, "I assessed the situation and determined that you were in danger of being hit on by a loser." He broke into a brilliant smile.

Relieved, I smiled back. "That was very observant of you. Thanks for saving me."

"Just doing my job, Ms. Matthews," he said, opening the door for me.

Disappointed that our private chat was over, I set off in search of Cooper. The shoes that went with the recycled yet beautiful bridesmaid's gown I was wearing were starting to hurt my feet, and being stomped on by Tyler surely hadn't helped.

I found Cooper speaking to a man I recognized as a member of Ashmore's Board of Trustees. They looked as though they were in the middle of a serious conversation, so I decided to wait until they were finished before approaching them. A waiter came by offering a tray of pastries, so I chose one. After taking a bite, I nearly gagged. I'd assumed the thing was going to be filled with something sweet, but instead it was hiding a slimy mixture that tasted distantly familiar. Liver. One of the few memories I had of my grandmother was when I had stayed with her once when my mother was off on a bender. I was four or five years old at the time, and all she had to feed me was liver and onions. I remember choking it down only for it to come back up all over her hideous flowered couch. I had never eaten liver since.

Another waiter came by with a tray of champagne flutes, so I snatched one of them and washed down the offending flavor. As I was scanning the room for a trash can to dispose of the rest of the nasty little pastry, I noticed Rob staring at me again with the same smirk on his face. Realizing he must have witnessed the liver incident, I blushed and looked away. He probably thought I was a fool. I downed the rest of my champagne, then discreetly stuffed the pastry into the empty glass and deposited it onto the table behind me. I should have known I could never pull off an elegant party like this.

2

After another agonizing round of introductions to snooty people I hoped I'd never meet again, I was tired of Cooper, this party, and especially my shoes. I grabbed another glass of champagne and slipped out onto the patio alone. Sinking down onto the low stone wall surrounding the slate patio, I glanced at my watch and grimaced. I had only been here for two hours, but it seemed like an eternity. I chugged the champagne and removed my shoes. I was just about to start rubbing my tired feet when the door opened. Hastily shifting my long chiffon dress to cover my bare feet, I looked up to find Rob Larson smiling down at me.

"Rough night?" he asked.

"What gave me away?"

"The expression you had on your face after you looked at your watch. That, and you downing an entire glass of champagne in one gulp."

"These kind of parties aren't quite my style," I admitted.

"Mine either."

Grinning, I said, "Is it wrong that I would actually kill for a beer and a half dozen White Castles right now?"

"I'd be happy to have one of my guys run out and get that for you. I can't have you killing anyone on my watch."

I laughed. "I appreciate your offer, but I'll settle for getting my backup pair of shoes out of Cooper's car."

"I can help you with that. Come with me."

Placing his hand on the small of my back, Rob guided me around the side of the house. When we got near the driveway, I noticed considerably fewer protestors milling around on the sidewalk on the other side of the street. There were still enough to cause trouble, though.

"Those kids are still here?" I complained.

He frowned. "Yes. After the last of the guests arrived and went inside, the protestors got bored and all but a handful of them left." He shook his head. "Pain in the ass. But we can't forcibly remove them if they don't set foot on anyone's property."

"They know that. They're smart little buggers."

"Unfortunately. I'll have Dr. Cooper's car brought around for you."

I waited at the end of the driveway while Rob conferred with the valet attendant several yards away. While I was standing there, two of the protestors left the group and wandered to a car parked down the street. This seemed to enrage one of the young men, who shouted, "Deserters!" at them as they pulled away. He began to pace back and forth angrily, and that was when he spotted me. Striding over to a small bucket sitting on the ground, he picked it up and took off at a run straight toward me. By the time I realized what was about to happen, it was too late. He yelled, "Death to the Body Farm!" and chucked the contents of the bucket at me. A wave of dark red liquid came splashing out of the bucket, hitting me in the torso and running sickly down the front of my pale pink gown.

Everyone on the street froze, staring in horror at what had just happened. Even the boy in front of me had his mouth agape as realization crossed his face.

"Professor...Professor Matthews," he breathed. "I—I had no idea...I didn't think...I didn't know it was you!"

Something snapped inside me. I reached the kid in two strides and had a fistful of his collar before he could get away. Out of the corner of my eye, I saw Rob hurrying over, but he stopped short when I started my tirade.

"What in the *hell* do you think you're doing?" I exploded.

"I...I didn't..." the kid whined.

"Do you think this is a friggin' joke? You threw an entire bucket of *blood* on me!"

Another boy hurried over to us, his eyes wide in disbelief. "Justin, you dumbass! I told you we weren't using the blood to throw on *people!*" I recognized the kid when he turned to speak to me. His name was Tristan Sellers, a student in one of my classes a couple of years ago. He said to me, "I'm so sorry. It's just pig's blood, Professor Matthews."

"*Just* pig's blood? My dress, which cost me a week's worth of pay, is ruined!" I took a look at the boys' cronies, noticing that Vasti Marais was among them. Judging from her expression, she seemed scared. I said to all of them, "For as smart as you kids are, you can be really stupid sometimes. And Vasti, I would think you of all people would have a little more sense than to be a part of this. You all think everything is about you. Well, let me tell you, the real world won't coddle you pretentious, entitled little shits like college does." I turned my wrath back to the kid I was still holding by the collar. "And *you* are going to get a taste of what happens to people in the real world after pulling a dick move like this."

Jerking the empty bucket out of his hand with my free hand, I shoved it down onto his head. He started crying and screaming, so I slapped the side of the bucket for good measure before releasing him. The protestors who were left decided at once that it was time to get the hell out of here.

"Yeah, that's right! You'd better run, you little bitches!" I yelled as they scattered and sprinted to their vehicles.

His expression wary, Rob came over to me and gently touched my shoulder. "It looks like you took care of this yourself, but do you want to press charges? I can call the police..."

I shook my head. "Nah, I don't want to have to stick around and talk to the police. Those kids will get a slap on the wrist at best. It's not worth my time."

I heard murmuring behind me and turned toward the house. Several guests, including Cooper and his parents, were congregated on the porch. My heart sank.

Whirling around so my back was to them, I said to Rob, "Did all those people back there see me lose my shit?"

He hesitated. "Yes."

"Including Mrs. Cooper?" She probably didn't appreciate one of her faculty members going off on students like that, no matter the situation.

"Yes."

I nodded. "Right. So I'm probably no longer welcome at the party, and maybe even out of a job. I'm going to need to find a way home now, aren't I?"

"I think it would be best."

I slapped my forehead in frustration. "You can take the girl out of the trailer park...but you can't take the trailer park out of the girl. And you should *never* let her go to a fancy party."

Before Rob could respond, Cooper rushed up to me and got between us. He stared down at my dress, aghast. "Ellie, are you all right? What happened out here?"

"Some of Ashmore's finest were causing trouble again," I replied.

"Was Vasti a part of this?"

"She was here. Why?"

He grimaced. "I think she has it out for me."

"So why am *I* the one who looks like Carrie?"

At my comment, a smile pulled at the corner of Rob's mouth, but he fought it.

Cooper sighed. "I'm so sorry. I didn't mean for you to—"

"Dudley," Cooper's father snapped, stalking toward us. "What in the world is going on?" He gave me a distasteful glance and continued his tirade. "I told you before that this ridiculous project of yours was a bad idea. The press has been circling you since you bought that property and announced your morbid plan, and it's starting to reflect badly on me. They're going to have a field day with this. Any other incidents and I'm going to have to officially pull my support. You'd better put a lid on this, son." He barked at Rob, "Larson, I'm leaving. Have my car brought up immediately."

"Yes, sir," Rob replied, heading to the valet stand.

George Cooper turned on his heel and marched back to the house, leaving Cooper and me alone.

I shook my head. "I'm sorry for losing it there. I'm sure I embarrassed you in front of your family."

"It's fine. I'm not worried about that." He spoke kindly, but his eyes belied his words.

"I need to go home and get out of this dress." Even though the night was warm, I was starting to get chilly in my now soaking wet clothing.

"I think that would be best. I'm so sorry, Ellie, but I feel it's my duty to stay here at the fundraiser. I'll be happy to call you a cab." I didn't expect him to want to leave the party early on my account, but the thought of riding home alone and covered in blood didn't appeal to me much.

"Yes, thank you."

"Thank you for accompanying me tonight. Tomorrow I'd like to take you to the site for the facility and get your thoughts on which structures should be torn down and which could be of use. May I pick you up at noon?"

I wasn't thrilled about spending my Sunday afternoon at the abandoned clown park, but it had to be done at some point. "Sure. That would be fine."

Smiling, he replied, "I'll see you then," as he headed back to the party.

Suddenly I was exhausted. And freezing. In my uncomfortable shoes, I hobbled to move out of the way for a shiny new Mercedes to pull into the driveway. It was followed by a massive black SUV with tinted windows. The SUV stopped next to me, and Rob stepped out of the driver's seat.

He had a blanket in his hands. "I thought you looked cold," he said, going behind me and wrapping the blanket around me. Leaving his hands on my shoulders, he murmured in my ear, "It was nice to meet you, Ms. Matthews. Maybe we'll run into each other again sometime."

"I'd like that. But you're going to have to start calling me Ellie."

Releasing me, he climbed back into his vehicle. "See you around, Ellie," he said, flashing me one last smile.

"You never told me why you chose this particular location for your research facility," I said to Cooper as we were nearing Carnival Cove, the former water park with the unfortunate clown theme.

For as long as I could remember, I'd always been scared to death of clowns. It was an issue I for some reason could never overcome. Even though I knew there was nothing to be afraid of, I was apprehensive about touring the future location of the body farm. I felt silly for letting it bother me. After all, it was broad daylight, and Cooper and I would be the only people there.

He shrugged. "The location is ideal, and the price was right. Plus, there are enclosed buildings, pools, sheltered areas, and wide-open spaces—basically any type of physical circumstances you can imagine. For example, we can study how a specimen decomposes on a paved area versus a grassy area, or in a body of water versus dry ground. The possibilities are endless."

He had a point, but I still didn't like it. I had decided we would have to tear down and cart away every clown statue, mural, and sign in the entire park if I were going to be able to go out there on a regular basis, especially after dark.

When we pulled up to the entrance to the park, Cooper pounded his fist on the steering wheel. "Damn it!"

That sort of outburst was unlike him, so I followed his gaze to see what he was upset about. On the "Welcome to Carnival Cove" sign next to the front gate, someone had written "Death to the Body Farm" in what looked like blood. It didn't take a genius to figure out who was responsible.

"I see our favorite students have struck again," I muttered, getting out of the car.

Cooper slammed his door. "This is an outrage! I'm calling the police this time. This is vandalism, and someone is going to answer for it." He got out his cell phone and tapped angrily at the screen.

I walked over to the sign for a closer look. The message in blood appeared to me to have been finger-painted. The chain lock on the gate had been cut, and the gate was standing open a couple of inches. I studied the bars on the gate and was delighted to find several partial fingerprints in the blood. Pushing the gate open with my sleeve, I continued my inspection on the back side of the gate. And there it was. A perfect, complete, unsmudged fingerprint—a patent print made in blood. I got out my phone and snapped a close-up photo of the print and also a wider shot of the gate to show the location of the print. I couldn't help but feel a twinge of excitement at the opportunity to poke around at an actual crime scene—the mock scenes I fabricated for my classes weren't nearly as interesting as the real deal.

Cooper finished his call and stomped over to me. "The police are on their way. I don't understand this, Ellie. I don't know why we're being targeted so harshly. Isn't protesting enough?"

"Who knows?" I replied, itching to get inside and search for more evidence. "It looks like someone broke the lock. We should see if there's any more damage inside."

Exasperated, he pushed past me and entered the park. I followed. I hadn't been here since I was a teenager, shortly before it closed. The place was an absolute disaster. Anything that hadn't been nailed down was either broken or missing—metal picnic tables were overturned and rusting, and beach chairs that once had been lined up in neat rows were threadbare and mangled, scattered haphazardly across the ground. Tufts of crabgrass grew out of every crack in the pavement all over the park, and heaps of fallen, dried leaves congregated in every corner. Vines were overtaking the graffiti-tagged waterslides like parasites. Disfigured clown faces grinned evilly down at me from crumbling statues and peeling signs.

Shuddering, I hurried to catch up with Cooper. He was staring at one of the former snack bars, which now said "Dr. Death Sucks" across the front of it.

"Oh, Coop, don't get bent out of shape. I think a visit from the police is all these kids need to scare them into leaving us alone."

"It better be," he growled.

A sudden gust of wind caused the leaves to swirl around us, and I caught a whiff of a pungent aroma I hadn't smelled for a long time. "Do you smell that?" I asked.

Cooper sniffed the air. "Smell what?"

As I started walking in the direction from which the wind had come, the odor became more pronounced. "Over here," I said. "Stand here and take a breath."

He did as I instructed and made a face. "It smells like the facility already has its first guest."

"It's probably some poor animal that crawled in here to die."

Judging from the odor, it wasn't a small animal, which meant it would need to be removed for our safety before we did much more out here. Working with relatively healthy decomposing human cadavers was one thing, but decomposing animal carcasses were another story. They could carry disease and pose serious health threats. I kept walking in the direction of the stench until it was nearly unbearable, but still didn't see anything.

I turned around when I heard Cooper muttering. He was several yards away, losing his cool over yet another bit of vandalism he had found. I soldiered on, determined to find the source. Once I rounded the corner into the "Kiddie Land" section, I found it.

Lying flat on her back in a shallow wading pool was Vasti Marais.

3

I let out a slow breath. I hadn't been to a real crime scene in three years. A few minutes ago, I'd been thrilled about searching for evidence as to who had vandalized the park. But faced with a serious crime, a murder no less, my glee evaporated in an instant.

Vasti was lying face up in a pool of her own blood and bodily waste. The front of her yellow tank top was saturated with blood that had flowed out of what appeared to be two gunshot wounds to her torso. Her dark skin had taken on a purplish cast. Blowflies buzzed around her, greedily feeding and depositing their eggs in the moist openings of her face and wounds. The bright, commanding personality that had defined her in life was heart-breakingly absent in death. She lay there staring straight up at the sky with dead eyes that would never regain their vibrant sparkle.

I shuddered at the thought of her young life being cut short by such a violent and tragic death. Before I started getting emotional, I shoved my feelings aside and put my head into criminalist mode, a practice that had saved my sanity during many of my tougher crime scene investigations. I concentrated my thoughts on the science of the situation to disconnect myself from the gruesome reality.

I had seen Vasti around 7:30 PM the previous night, so she couldn't have been dead more than sixteen or seventeen hours. I was somewhat surprised that the odor of death was already so strong, but several factors were contributing to a speed-up in the decomposition process. Although it was September, the weather had been unseasonably hot, reaching the mid-nineties by day and only dipping into the upper seventies at night. Central Indiana was always high in humidity in the warmer months as well. Between the weather conditions and the body lying in full sunlight, the bacteria inside the body were nice and warm and hard at work. On top of that, her fresh wounds created an attractive place for insects to start their jobs. An open-casket viewing was out of the question at this point.

I wondered who would have done this to her. There were several bloody shoeprints around the body, which could be of help to the police. From eyeballing it, I guessed that the print had been made by a man's shoe, medium-sized, around a size ten or so. The diamond-shaped tread pattern looked like that of a Converse, which was a popular brand of shoe. The prints could belong to the killer, or they could belong to someone who had been here with Vasti. If I were investigating this, I'd start with my pig blood-throwing friend from last night. I didn't happen to notice his shoes, but judging from his hipster-type appearance, I would be willing to bet he had a pair or two of Converse sneakers in his closet. However, most of the protestors were dressed in a similar way, so maybe the shoeprint didn't narrow anything down.

I plucked my phone out of my pocket and called dispatch, explaining to them what I found. After I was done, I went in search of Cooper. He wasn't going to take the news well. I found him snapping photos of the vandalism.

"Coop," I said, my voice cracking.

"Yes," he replied, keeping his attention on his photography.

He was going to blow a gasket over this situation. The police would close off the park for days while their investigation took place. With the property being in Cooper's name, he would be investigated simply because of procedure. It was difficult to imagine how the student protestors would react to Vasti's death—would they be too devastated to continue their protesting, or would this news incite a riot? I felt as if I held Pandora's box in my hands. Everything was calm now, but as soon as the box was opened, all hell would break loose.

I couldn't wait any longer. I walked over to Cooper and stood in front of him. "That odor we smelled is human. There's a dead body in the park."

His face turned bright red. "WHAT?" he exploded. "If this is some sick joke, Ellie..."

"I wish it were. Cooper...it's Vasti Marais. She's been shot."

Cooper's jaw went slack and his phone clattered to the ground. "Are you...are you sure?" he choked out as he stumbled back from me, his face contorted in pain and despair. "Not her..." he whispered to himself. Dropping to his knees, he put his head in his hands.

This was not the reaction I was expecting. Of course I expected him to be upset, but I didn't expect him to be sobbing over the loss of a student he barely knew. Not that her passing wasn't tragic and heartbreaking, but this spectacular show of grief, in my opinion, was usually reserved for family members and close friends. With being a business major, Vasti probably hadn't taken any classes from Cooper, although they could have been acquainted some other way. I had never spoken to the girl before last night, only knowing her by her flawless reputation.

I put my hand on his shoulder and said gently, "I didn't realize you knew her that well."

Taking several deep breaths, he tried to control himself. "I...she... I was the...faculty advisor last year for...for the Student Leadership Council..." He broke down again. Vasti had been a part of the Student Leadership Council her entire college career. That explained the connection, at least.

I heard the crunch of gravel as a vehicle pulled up near the entrance to the park. It was likely a deputy out on patrol responding to the vandalism call. The homicide detectives and crime scene unit wouldn't be here for a while. The park was at the far west end of Hamilton County, and they'd have to drive all the way from the sheriff's office in Noblesville.

"Cooper, we should probably compose ourselves here. I think the police may have just arrived," I said.

Sniffling and wiping his eyes, Cooper got up and followed me to the entrance.

A young sheriff's deputy met us at the gate, his eyes wide. "I'm Deputy Martin. I got a call about some vandalism out here, and then I heard something about a homicide over the radio. Did both of those things happen here?" Judging from his age and reaction, he must have been new to the force. I didn't recognize him from before.

"Yes, Dr. Cooper called in the vandalism, and while we were assessing the damage, I found the deceased victim," I explained.

The deputy let out a low whistle. "Okay, well, I'll get your statement about the vandalism and leave the rest for homicide to deal with." He got out a small notebook. "Let me get your names…"

We gave him our full names and took him on a quick tour of the vandalized areas. Cooper was still agitated and kept looking over his shoulder toward the entrance to Kiddie Land. After his outburst over the news about Vasti, I didn't want him to get anywhere near her body. If the news of her death disturbed him that much, he didn't need to see her like that. It didn't take us long to give our statements to Deputy Martin about the vandalism. I also included an account of my pig blood incident from last night since it was likely to be connected to the vandalism. By the time we were finishing up, several police vehicles rolled in.

Since my abrupt departure from the Investigations Division, I hadn't seen or been in contact with any of my former colleagues except the sheriff herself, a longtime friend and mentor who had been a guest speaker in many of my classes. I felt a bit nervous about seeing some of the others again, worrying that a few were of the opinion that I fled to the classroom because I couldn't hack the real world. There was some truth to that, which was probably why it bothered me.

The person I was least interested in seeing got out of his vehicle first—Jason Sterling, homicide detective and all-around asshole. He was good at his job, but cocky as hell. He spotted me immediately. I could have sworn I saw him flexing his pecs as he approached me.

"Ellie Matthews! Long time no see," he drawled, taking off his sunglasses so that he could look me up and down.

"Not long enough, Sterling," I replied, frowning. Sterling was easy on the eyes—tall, dark, and handsome—but not so easy on my nerves.

"Oh, admit it. You missed me."

The detective who got out of the passenger side of Sterling's SUV came up to me and extended his hand. His smile lit up his entire boyish face. "Hi, I'm Nick Baxter, Sterling's partner. Is this knucklehead giving you trouble?"

"Always," I said, smiling back at him. Maybe with Detective Baxter around, Sterling wouldn't give me too much grief. I shook his hand. "Ellie Matthews."

"You're kind of a local legend around the department."

"How so?" I asked, shooting a wary glance at Sterling.

"I hear you can coax a fingerprint off damn near anything."

"Oh," I said, relieved I wasn't legendary for something embarrassing. "Yes, fingerprinting was a specialty of mine."

"Until she decided she was too good for us and joined the eggheads of that hoity-toity college," Sterling jeered.

"Are you here to solve a murder or work my last nerve?" I asked him, crossing my arms.

Out of the corner of my eye, I saw Detective Baxter cover up a snicker.

An older man guiding a gurney approached us. It was Dr. Everett Berg, the coroner. "Ellie, my dear," he greeted me kindly. "Good to see you again. I've missed you around the department. No one can get Detective Sterling's panties in a twist quite like you can."

Sterling grunted, but otherwise kept quiet.

Grinning, I replied, "Thanks, Doc. I've missed you, too."

"I hear you had the bad fortune of finding a body this time," he said, his face etched with concern. Dr. Berg was a retired doctor, needing something to keep him busy after his wife passed. He'd always had a soft spot for me, insisting I was the cosmic twin of his youngest daughter.

"Yes, I'm afraid I did."

"Lead the way," he said.

I nodded, heading toward the gate. Several deputies had arrived with the detectives, and they were working to cordon off and secure the entrance and perimeter of Carnival Cove. One vehicle had been missing from their caravan—the SUV belonging to the crime scene unit. Not that it was surprising that they were running late, especially if Beck Durant was still the head criminalist. He had been my assistant when I was the head criminalist, and he was a total waste of oxygen, at least at a crime scene. He was a decent lab tech, but the best lab tech in the world couldn't help solve a case if he'd overlooked key evidence at the scene. Unfortunately for Hamilton County, Beck moved up to my job when I quit. I couldn't imagine he would have suddenly become competent, so Detectives Sterling and Baxter would have their work cut out for them if they wanted to solve this murder based solely on the evidence Beck managed to collect at the scene.

Cooper was busy speaking to one of the deputies. I wasn't at all surprised that they were interviewing us separately. It was always better if witnesses didn't listen to each other's statements, otherwise they would tend to tell the same story without even being conscious of it. I led the detectives and coroner toward the entrance to Kiddie Land.

"Whew," said Sterling wrinkling his nose. "There's something dead out here all right."

"I guess the heat got to her—she's only been dead for seventeen hours at most. I saw the girl last night around seven-thirty," I said.

He smirked at me. "Was it when you were killing her?"

"No, assclown. I didn't kill her."

Detective Baxter, whose face had become pale, threw us an odd glance. When we got to the entrance to Kiddie Land, Dr. Berg and Detective Baxter went in to look at Vasti. Sterling stayed behind to keep me company. Lucky me.

"Aren't you supposed to be detecting, Detective?" I asked, hoping to get rid of him.

"It's safer to watch from over here." He nodded toward Detective Baxter.

Baxter was standing several feet away from Vasti as Dr. Berg kneeled down next to her and began his preliminary examination. The detective's hand was over his mouth and nose, and he was hunched over, looking unwell.

Sterling said, "He's gonna puke. He does it every time."

"A homicide detective who pukes at the sight of a dead body? How does that work? This isn't even a bad scene, as they go," I said, thinking Baxter might have been in the wrong line of work.

"Just watch. It's coming—oh, there he goes."

Baxter went running for some nearby bushes and vomited into them.

Sterling continued, "And now he'll be perfectly fine. It's the damnedest thing."

Taking out a handkerchief to wipe his mouth, Baxter began to look better instantly. He marched straight back over to Vasti's body and squatted down beside Dr. Berg like nothing had happened.

Sterling said, "That's my cue. After we get a look at her, we'll take your statement. But you probably know the drill."

He approached the other two men, and they all began conferring and gesturing at Vasti's body. While Dr. Berg and Baxter continued examining the body, Sterling made a wide circle around them, taking in the entire scene. He came to an abrupt halt and put his hands on his hips, shooting me a glare.

"Damn it, Matthews! Did you step in blood and leave these shoeprints? You of all people should know better than that!" he barked at me.

I stalked toward him, making sure not to get too close to the scene. If there was one thing law enforcement hated, it was civilians mucking up a crime scene. "It wasn't me," I fired back, put out over having to defend myself again from Sterling's ridiculous accusations. "Those shoeprints were there when I got here, and besides, they're like a men's size ten, genius."

"I see you two love birds are still at it," sneered Beck Durant, who had slithered up beside me unnoticed.

"Hi, Beck," I said, not at all happy to see him.

Sterling snapped, "Becky! It's about time you showed up. Get your ass over here and make yourself useful."

Beck obeyed, muttering under his breath that his name wasn't "Becky." His assistant, a young woman laden down with her field kit as well as Beck's, hurried after him. Detective Baxter headed my way, with Sterling staying behind to boss around the criminalists.

Baxter said, "Ms. Matthews, how about I take your statement and give you a break from Sterling?"

"That would be great."

"Let's find a place to sit down and talk."

He led me away from Kiddie Land, and we managed to find one picnic table that was still upright and in one piece. We both sat down, and he got out a notebook and a recorder.

"I guess we should start at the beginning. Why were you out here today?" he asked.

"Dr. Cooper and I are in charge of Ashmore College's new forensic

anthropology research facility, and Carnival Cove is its unfortunate location. The plan is for us to be able to study how human bodies decompose
in a variety of outdoor settings. We were out here trying to decide which
structures would be beneficial to our research and should stay and which
ones should be torn down. We didn't expect to already have our first
subject."

He made a face. "You're going to leave bodies all around the park and let
them decompose so you can study them?"

"Yes, that's the plan."

Getting a little green, he said, "That's disgusting."

I leaned away from him. "You're not going to throw up again, are you?"

He shook his head, but I wasn't convinced.

Hoping to steer the conversation away from the gore, I said, "Our
facility could help the Sheriff's Department and the coroner quite a bit. We
could replicate crime scenes to help solve the more difficult cases. We could
recreate certain conditions to help better pinpoint time since death. There's
a lot of good that can be done here."

"I hope I won't ever need help like that. Let's keep going. Did you see
anyone else here besides yourself and Dr. Cooper?"

"No, I didn't."

"And you mentioned that you saw the victim last night. Was that here or
somewhere else?"

I was interested to find out Detective Baxter's take on how the events of
last night and the aftermath today were intertwined. "I saw her at a
fundraiser for this facility that was held at Dr. Cooper's aunt and uncle's
home. By the way, you should know that some of the students at Ashmore
are not in favor of the new facility and have been protesting."

"I know. I saw it on the news."

"Right. Well, there were around two dozen students protesting the
fundraiser last night. The girl who was murdered, Vasti Marais, seemed to
be their fearless leader. After the guests all arrived, most of the protestors
left. But when I went outside, one of the diehards ran up and threw a
bucket of pig's blood on my evening gown, shouting, 'Death to the body
farm.' "

"Someone threw pig's blood all over you?" he asked, dumbfounded. "Are you positive it was pig's blood and not...any other type?"

"I think so. One of the other protestors assured me it was, and I have no reason not to believe him. I'm going to my lab to test it later to be sure."

"Who threw the blood?"

"An Ashmore student. Justin something. I don't know his last name. Now, I'm not trying to put thoughts into your head, Detective, but it would seem that my incident last night and the vandalism here are related, since the phrase 'Death to the body farm' is written in blood on the sign out front and the same girl was in both places."

"You're right. It's no coincidence."

"And one of the kids said 'the blood isn't for throwing on people' or something like that. He didn't say what it was intended for, though, but I can guess."

"Did you recognize any of the other protestors?" he asked.

"They all looked familiar, but the only ones I know by name besides Vasti are Tristan Sellers and Eli Vanover. But Eli seemed to be covering it for the school newspaper rather than participating."

"That helps. Thanks. And I take it you didn't press charges if the student in question was likely out here vandalizing the place after your encounter with him?"

Shrugging, I said, "I figured it would be more trouble that it was worth. You cops make everything so difficult and ask way too many questions."

He smiled. "I'm just getting started."

I groaned. Detective Baxter fired question after question at me, ranging from minute details about last night to my opinion of the condition of the body to why Cooper seemed so upset about this whole mess. After a while, I was getting tired of talking, but I could tell that the detective was close to wrapping things up.

"How did Dr. Cooper know Ms. Marais?" he asked.

"He said he was the faculty advisor last year for a student group she belonged to."

He nodded, jotting down a note. "And what time did he leave the fundraiser last night?"

"I don't know. I left early because of the blood incident. The last time I saw him was at seven-thirty PM."

"And did you go straight home from the fundraiser? Any detours on the way?"

I smiled. "A cab took me straight to my home in Noblesville. No stops. I stayed at home the rest of the night."

"Can anyone corroborate that?"

"My sister and my alarm system."

His eyebrows shot up. "An alarm system. Do you live in one of those fancy McMansions this county is so famous for?"

"Not even close. But it's only my sister, her little boy, and me, so we're cautious. I've seen way too much not to be cautious."

"That's smart. I take it you're already in CODIS and AFIS, so we don't have to swab you or print you."

He was referring to the Combined DNA Index System and the Automated Fingerprint Identification System, databases used to match DNA and fingerprints at crime scenes to persons in the systems. All criminal justice workers' information goes into both systems for the purposes of both background checks and ease in distinguishing possible suspects from inadvertent crime scene contamination by the workers themselves.

"I am," I replied.

"Well, then I guess the only thing I need now is what you were wearing last night when you got hit with the pig blood."

"Aw, really?" I was hoping he wasn't going to take my gown for evidence, but I wasn't surprised he asked for it. "Damn. I was going to cut my gown up and use it for a lab project in my classes."

He laughed. "Only a hard-core criminalist would be more worried about her precious evidence being taken away than about losing a fancy dress." He got up from the picnic table. "I'll drive you to your house. Meet me out front."

"Will do," I replied.

4

When I reached the front gate, a deputy lifted the caution tape stretched across the entrance so I could duck under it. I spotted Cooper sitting on the curb, head in his hands. His reaction bothered me. Usually he was so reserved and calm about everything, but between the protesting, vandalism, and Vasti's murder, he was a wreck.

Going over and sitting down next to him, I placed my hand on his shoulder. "Are you okay?"

Cooper shook his head. "No. On top of everything, I'm a person of interest in Vasti's murder since I own the park and also because I had a disagreement with her at the fundraiser last night. Of course the video recording of it is the top story on the *Ashmore Voice's* website."

"If it makes you feel any better, I'm a person of interest, too. I found the body."

He didn't respond.

"You don't need to take me home, because I have to go with the detective to turn over my gown from last night as evidence. Looks like they may be trying to tie that kid who threw the blood on me to the vandalism here."

Again, he didn't reply.

At a loss for what else to say to him, I said, "So I'll see you later?"

Looking over at me with anguished eyes, he whispered, "Ellie, I—"

"Well, young lady. You've had quite a day." Shielding my eyes from the sun, I looked up to find Sheriff Jayne Walsh smiling down at me. I hopped up, and she embraced me in a motherly hug. She was a middle-aged woman in a man's world, and she was tough as nails, except with me. She continued, "It's a little different when you're on the other side, huh?"

Her kind empathy giving me a lump in my throat, I dropped my arms and stepped back. "It's good to see you, Jayne."

"And you as well. Have my detectives questioned and harassed you thoroughly?"

"Yes, on both counts."

"Ah, I take it you've run into Detective Sterling, then," she said, chuckling.

"Unfortunately."

Detective Baxter approached us, keys in hand. "Hello, Sheriff. Ready to go, Ms. Matthews?"

"Yes, I think I'd like to go home now," I said, happy it was time to get away from this place.

Jayne winked at me. "Don't leave town." She ambled off toward the gate.

The detective was waiting for me, but I felt as though I needed another moment with Cooper. I said, "I'll be just a second, okay?"

"Take your time," Baxter replied, heading toward his vehicle.

I looked down at Cooper, who had his head bowed again. "Coop?"

He squinted up at me. "Yes?"

"If you need anything, call me. Even if it's just to talk."

A hint of relief in his eyes, he took my hand. "Thank you, Ellie. I will."

I hurried over to Detective Baxter's SUV and climbed into the passenger seat.

He asked, "You said you live in Noblesville?"

"Yes, on Pleasant Street."

Pulling out of the parking lot, he said, "I don't know of anyone who's on a first-name basis with the Sheriff. What makes you so special?"

As a rule, I didn't share the details of my personal life with someone I'd just met, but Detective Baxter seemed trustworthy, and he was easy to talk to. "Are you bound by detective/civilian confidentiality rules here?"

He laughed. "I don't think that's a thing. But if you're afraid I'll tell Sterling, don't be. I can keep a secret like it's my job."

"Well, it's not a secret, but it's something I don't want broadcast to the department. When I was a kid, I was a serious hell-raiser. And I was good at not getting caught until I ran up against an off-duty beat cop named Jayne Walsh. She saw me shoplifting at Castleton Square Mall. Before I even knew what was happening, she had my face smashed against a jewelry counter and my hands tied behind my back with the ugliest paisley scarf I'd ever seen."

"She's quite a badass."

"No kidding. I was mortified. Even worse, she took me down to the station, booked me, and threw me in a cell with two crack whores who were jonesing for their next high. They were nuts." I shook my head and smiled at the memory. "I honestly thought they were going to kill me. After I was sufficiently scared out of my wits, she let me out, got my charges dropped, and had a heart-to-heart with me. It literally changed my life. After that, I ditched my delinquent friends, started studying, and decided to make something of myself."

"That's a great story. I had no idea the Sheriff had a soft side."

"Jayne is a good woman. She's the reason I became a criminalist. She took me under her wing—she knew my home life was horrible, so she made it a point to take me to dinner once a week and make sure I was doing okay. She helped me get into a good college, and then she hired me when an opening came up in Hamilton County. The rest is history."

"After all that, though, why did you quit investigations and become a teacher?"

I lowered my eyes and gave my stock answer. "I had a case that really got to me. I lost my stomach for dealing with violence."

His voice kind, he said, "Don't feel bad. That happens. It's unfortunate for the department, though. Our crime lab could really use someone in charge who knows what the hell they're doing."

"Don't get me started on Beck."

"I don't mind so much that he's incompetent, but he's such an ass." He shot me a look and winced. "I probably shouldn't have said that to you. Can I invoke civilian/detective confidentiality?"

Smiling, I replied, "Sure, but it's not a big secret that Beck is an ass."

We both laughed. We were already on Pleasant Street, so I directed him to my house. When I got out, he accompanied me to my door, entering my home right behind me. My faithful Golden Retriever, Trixie, greeted us at the door, and Detective Baxter kneeled down to pet her and let her give him kisses. After Trixie had cleared him for entry, he followed me down the hall to my bedroom, which I found a little strange, but I didn't say anything. He had the good sense to stop at my bedroom door.

I retrieved the bag with my ruined dress from my closet and grudgingly handed it over to Detective Baxter.

"I'm sorry to be the one to take away your lab experiment, but it's evidence," he said.

My half-sister Rachel opened her bedroom door and poked her head out. She whispered, "Shh. Nate is trying to take a nap." She eyed the detective and gave me a meaningful look. "Sis, did you forget our little pact about bringing *friends* home?"

I smiled. Rachel, at twenty-one, was mom to the light of my life, my nephew Nathan. Although she was young, single, and a full-time college student, she took better care of her son than most parents, even after having terrible role models. Her only weakness was that she had poor taste in men, not that I was one to judge. Since we knew we both had that problem, for Nate's sake we had made a pact never to bring any of the men we dated into our home.

"He's a cop, Rach," I explained. "He's collecting my dress from last night for evidence."

"And I was just leaving," said Baxter, heading back down the hallway.

Rachel disappeared into her room, and I followed him out.

Stopping at the door to study the bag, he said, "Nice. It's very nerdy of you to tag your own evidence. Thanks."

Old habits died hard. After taping the bag shut, I had scrawled my name, the date, a brief description of my dress, and the word "biohazard" onto the bag before I'd even realized it. "No problem," I said.

He handed me a business card. "If you remember anything else about today or last night you'd like to add to your statement, give me a call."

"I will."

"Take care, Ms. Matthews. Try to stay out of trouble."

Grinning, I said, "I'll certainly try."

The moment I closed the door, Rachel descended on me. "Who was that guy? He was cute!"

"His name is Detective Nick Baxter. He works for the Sheriff's Department." I hesitated. "Um...Rachel...you'd better sit down. I have something to tell you." She sat down, and I said as gently as I could, "One of your classmates is dead. Vasti Marais."

Her hand flew to her mouth, and her eyes filled with tears. "Vasti? How? What happened?" she whispered. She and Vasti hadn't been especially close, but they were acquaintances who'd been in classes and campus organizations together.

"I can't tell you much, because...I'm sort of mixed up in the situation."

"You? How? I don't understand."

"I found her body when Cooper and I were out at Carnival Cove. She was murdered."

Rachel's mouth gaped open. "Why would anyone want to kill Vasti? Everyone loved her."

Sighing, I replied, "It's a tragedy. And since I found her and I...saw things, I feel like I need to treat it like my cases when I worked for the crime lab. Aside from what I've already told you, I shouldn't talk about it at all. I know you would never blab the details, but I don't want any information about the crime scene leaking out because of me."

She wiped her eyes. "I understand. Are you okay, though? Finding a dead body has to be—"

Rachel was interrupted by a knock at the door. An excited Trixie made a beeline to the front window to get the first glimpse of whoever was outside. When I opened the door, a woman dressed in a pantsuit thrust a microphone in my face.

She asked, "Are you Ellie Matthews, the person who found the body of Vasti Marais, Ashmore College student, at Carnival Cove this afternoon?"

I froze. Behind her stood a cameraman with a large news camera trained on me. The thought hadn't yet crossed my mind that I would be pestered by reporters over this. What troubled me most was that there were already two news vans parked in front of my house, with a third one pulling in. I was about to be the center of a full-blown media circus.

Once I got over the initial shock, I was able to compose myself. I had handled this kind of relentless, invasive media questioning many times before when news crews would congregate around a crime scene I was investigating. I could do it again. The only problem was that I was out of practice.

Digging up my professional tone from years ago, I said, "I'm sorry, but I am unable to answer any of your questions. Any questions you have should be addressed to the Hamilton County Sheriff's office." My voice shook, but I managed to give a firm answer.

As I was closing my door, the reporter shouted, "What type of relationship did the victim have with the suspect, Dr. Dudley Cooper? Is this murder a teacher-student tryst gone bad?"

My jaw dropped, and before I could stop myself I blurted out, "The *suspect*? What? No!" As soon as the words were out of my mouth, I admonished myself for letting them goad me into responding. I slammed the door and collapsed against it. The woman was still shouting questions at me through the closed door.

Wide-eyed, Rachel demanded, "What the hell is going on out there?"

I ran my hands through my hair. "A shitstorm. I hope we have some food for dinner, because we're not going anywhere tonight."

My phone rang, startling me. I plucked it out of my pocket and groaned. The caller ID said the call was coming from a local newspaper. They had already found my name and address, and now they'd found my cell phone number. Needless to say, I didn't answer the call.

To Trixie's dismay, Rachel went to the front window and drew the blinds so no one could see into the house. She said, "Why don't you call that hunky cop and have him come back over? Maybe he can get these guys to piss off and go bother someone else."

"You know, that's not a bad idea."

"I don't want a bunch of strangers milling around outside. I have a child to think of."

"I'll call him right now." Taking out Baxter's card, I dialed his cell number.

"Baxter," was his greeting.

"Hi, Detective. This is Ellie Matthews."

"I didn't think you'd be calling so soon. What's up?"

I sighed. "This is probably more of a Noblesville police issue, but I thought you should know there's a mob of news crews on my front lawn."

"Shit," he said under his breath. "Sorry. I'll send someone out to take care of that right away. You didn't talk to them, did you?"

"I told them to direct their questions to the Sheriff's office."

"Good job. Now, if you feel uneasy or feel like you're being watched or followed, you call me. Day or night."

"Thanks. I will." After we ended our call, I turned to Rachel. "Detective Baxter is going to send someone over to shoo away the vultures out there. I'm going to self-medicate with a couple of shots of vodka, and then I'm going to bed."

"It's not even dinnertime yet, Grandma."

"I don't care. I'm done adulting for today."

―――――――――

Awaking with a start, I shivered as I tried to shake off the haunting image of Vasti Marais that had been pervading my dreams. I looked at my phone. It was only 9:07 PM. And I had twenty-seven missed calls—eight of them from Cooper.

I dialed his number, and he picked up on the first ring. "Ellie?" he said, his voice tight.

"Did you call me? Eight times?"

"I need to talk to you. Can I come over?" he pleaded.

I thought the "no men in the house" rule to be especially important in this case since this particular man was a murder suspect, according to the nosy TV reporter. I didn't believe that my friend would have done such a thing, but there was clearly something troubling him. I glanced out my window and didn't see any people or news vans, so Detective Baxter had made good on his promise. I wasn't a prisoner in my own home anymore.

"Meet me at the Starbucks on 116th in Fishers in fifteen minutes."

Cooper beat me there and already had a cup of coffee waiting for me.

Ever the gentleman, he stood as I approached him, but he was so weary, he sunk back down into his chair before I reached him. If it was possible, he looked even more haggard than he did earlier today. I sat down in the leather armchair next to his.

"What's going on, Coop?" I asked.

He threaded his hands through his hair. "I... This is bad. Very bad."

"What? Did something happen tonight?" I took a sip of my coffee.

He sighed and lowered his voice, although we were the only customers in the store. "I had to go to the Sheriff's station for further questioning. It seems that they...found some emails between Vasti and myself."

"Unless they said 'I'm going to kill you,' that's not exactly damning evidence."

"They found out..." He paused, a pained expression marring his face. "They found out about my...relationship with Vasti."

"Your *what*?" I exploded. A couple of the workers turned their heads in my direction, so I whispered, "You're in a relationship with a *student*? Are you nuts?"

His eyes grew wide. "No, no. Not any longer. It was last semester. Things went too far, and I broke it off."

"Still not okay to have sex with a student, Cooper," I hissed.

Wiping a hand down his face, he said, "I know."

The pieces of this were coming together for me. "Is that why she's been so vocal against the facility? Is she—was she angry with you?"

"Yes, she was angry, and I believe she organized the protests as yet another way of getting back at me. I did a poor job of ending our relationship. I didn't want either of us to get into trouble, so I told her we shouldn't see each other at all, in public or in private. She didn't take the news well and has been hostile toward me ever since. She made quite a nuisance of herself, especially at first. She'd come to my large lecture classes and stand in the back and stare daggers at me. She called me at all hours of the night. When I wouldn't return her calls, she began slipping notes under my office door." He stopped to rub his eyes. "They said horrible things. She went so far as to fabricate lies about having an affair with my father to try to hurt me. I don't even know if she was actually against the facility or if she was only trying to make my life miserable."

"This doesn't look good. You had an inappropriate relationship with a student, which ended badly. She openly opposed your new project and even organized protests against it. And now she's been found dead on a property you own. That's *two* sufficient motives for you to have killed her." I hesitated, not quite sure how to continue. "You didn't kill her, did you?"

He regarded me as if I'd slapped him. "No! How could you think I would be capable of such a thing? Even after everything she's done to me, I still cared about her."

I hated to have asked such a nasty question of my friend. "I don't think you did it. I just needed to hear it from you. Do you have an alibi for last night?"

"Sort of. After you left, the news of what happened between you and Justin spread like wildfire. Everyone at the gala insisted on hearing every detail from me personally. I got so weary of answering questions, I had to get some air. I drove around for a while, returning after I had pulled myself together. The party broke up shortly thereafter, and I went home alone."

I blew out a breath. "Shit. I'd bet anything your little drive coincides with Vasti's time of death window. I'm sorry for causing a scene at the fundraiser. I lost my cool."

Cooper slouched in his chair and rested his head against the back of the seat. "It's not your fault. I made this mess, and now I have to deal with it."

I was disgusted with Cooper after finding out about his affair with Vasti, but I still didn't want to see him hang for her murder. "Look, if you didn't kill her, there won't be any evidence at the crime scene to tie you to the murder. They can't charge you without evidence. They can probably hold you for seventy-two hours, though, on suspicion."

Eyes bulging out, he breathed, "Seventy-two hours? In *jail*?"

"Sorry to be the bearer of bad news."

A few hours in lockup would certainly make him think twice about even looking at a pretty co-ed again. For his sake, it was a good thing Vasti's family lived on another continent. If it had been my sister who'd been playing doctor with Dr. Cooper, jail would have been preferable to what I would have done to him. Parents and guardians do not take kindly to people messing around with their babies, even when their babies are legal adults.

"If any of this gets out, my career could be ruined."

I shrugged. "You're an Ashmore. Play the nepotism card. Your family is not going to fire you from your own school. If you're really worried about it, get one of your dad's political handlers to sweep the whole thing under the rug."

"My father is likely to disown me over this," he muttered.

I didn't have a response for that, so I changed the subject. "I take it you lawyered up."

"Of course. That's why I'm not rotting in a jail cell right now. I'm taking a personal day tomorrow, by the way."

"That's probably a good idea." I stood up. "I need to go. I'll see you soon."

Cooper got up and caught me by the arm. He whispered, "Please don't let this change your opinion of me. I couldn't bear it."

"I have to go," was all I could reply.

5

Ashmore College, nestled in the well-to-do town of Carmel, has frequently been named Indiana's most beautiful college campus, and with good reason. The original buildings were built of sturdy Indiana limestone around the turn of the century, all sporting a Collegiate Gothic style abounding with arches, buttresses, and parapets. The dorms as a rule were new construction or at least remodeled, but designed with classic style and details to fit in with the aesthetic plan of the campus.

Ashmore's front lawn, most days a peaceful, wide-open stretch of manicured grass, well-tended flowers, and majestic oak trees, was crawling with television reporters, stopping students to harass them and beg for interviews. To watch and document their interactions would have been an interesting psychological study—some students were thrilled to be on camera while others ran away, either too shy or too upset about Vasti's death to be able to talk about it.

As I pulled into my parking spot, I wondered if I should have taken the day off like Cooper did. I didn't want to be bothered by any more reporters, so I scrounged around in my car for some sort of disguise. I found a knit cap wedged under the passenger seat and stuffed my long brunette hair into it, then put on a pair of Rachel's oversized sunglasses. Ducking my head, I hurried into the science building through a side door.

I kept my disguise on until I reached my office. When I got there, I closed and locked the door (otherwise students and faculty alike would barge right in) and then flopped down into my chair. I was not in the mood for a barrage of questions. Having been curious about how much my face was going to be plastered across the evening news, I had flipped on the TV when I got home last night. Big mistake. There I was, making an idiot of myself on camera when the reporter caught me off guard. An interview with me was still in high demand, judging from the forty-three missed calls I had on my phone from numbers not in my contacts list.

Steeling myself for the inevitable difficulty of getting through my classes, I gathered my things and entered the classroom with my Criminalistics 1 students. Every one of them was either reading or discussing a copy of the *Ashmore Voice*, which had a huge picture on the front page of Vasti ambushing Cooper at the fundraiser protest. The headline read "Student Protestor Found Dead, Professor Questioned." I grimaced. I didn't expect it to take long for the *Voice's* opinionated staff to connect the dots to Cooper. Even if he wasn't charged with the murder, his reputation with the students was damaged beyond repair.

My students quieted down when I reached the front of the classroom, which was a first. I didn't remember seeing any of my current students protesting Saturday night. I generally taught freshmen and sophomores (being assigned beginner-level classes since I held only a Master's Degree), and the protestors had seemed to be mostly upperclassmen.

I took a deep breath to calm myself, then cleared my throat. "I know you've all heard about the tragic passing of one of our students, Vasti Marais. Those of you who knew her, I'm sorry for your loss. I'm sure you have questions, but I can't and won't answer them, so please don't ask. The one thing I can tell you is that I found her body. This is an open case being investigated by the Hamilton County Sheriff's Office. As future criminalists, you must understand that I cannot, under any circumstances, give away any details of what I saw. Not only would it interfere with the investigation, but it would also put my credibility as a former criminalist on the line." I had an idea. "You know, maybe today instead of starting our lesson on handwriting analysis, we should discuss confidentiality and how a criminalist should handle media inquiries..."

My lecture on confidentiality and media pressure went quite well. The students seemed interested, and they asked questions that got some good discussion going. I thought it also drove home the point that in real life, it is extremely difficult to be at the center of an event that you can't openly speak about with anyone except the other people involved in the case.

I decided to go with the same lecture in all of my classes. After having success again in my second class of the day, I had all but forgotten about my problems. After class, as I turned down the hallway to my office, I froze when I saw a man in a suit standing by my office door, his back to me. I couldn't believe that a reporter would have the balls to enter one of the classroom buildings to get to me. I considered running in the opposite direction, but it was lunchtime, I was hungry, and my lunch money was in my locked desk drawer. While I was contemplating my options, the man turned around. My mouth nearly dropped open when I realized who it was. Standing there, smiling his dazzling smile, was Rob Larson—and he was holding a White Castle bag and two bottles of beer.

Stunned that he'd tracked me down at work so soon after we'd met, I approached him. "Hi, Rob. It's good to see you."

"Hello, Ellie," he said, his deep voice ringing down the hallway. "I hope you're okay with a surprise visit. I brought lunch." He held up the bag and bottles.

I was flattered that he had remembered what I'd said at the party. "Absolutely."

"Would you like to eat outside? It's nice out today."

There was no way I was going outside with those vultures hanging around. I ducked into my office. "Would you mind if we ate here?"

"Not at all."

I sat down at my desk and gestured for him to take the seat across from me. "Thanks for lunch."

"I feel like I owe you one. After all, you did get assaulted on my watch. It was a blow to my ego as a security specialist," he said, a sheepish grin on his face.

Laughing, I said, "Oh, stop. I don't feel assaulted. No one expected the kid to pull a stunt like that."

"I know, but I still feel bad. Maybe I could get your dress dry cleaned for you?"

I hesitated. My dress was probably being cut apart and the soiled fabric tested as we spoke. However, that was information I couldn't share with anyone. I had even lied to my sister about it last night when she asked why my dress was suddenly "evidence."

"No need. It was beyond repair. It...went out with the garbage."

His face fell. "That's too bad. You looked gorgeous in it."

Rob Larson certainly knew the right thing to say to a girl.

I blushed. "Thanks. Um...so is keeping Mayor Cooper safe a difficult job? I mean, surely his life isn't at risk all the time."

Laughing, he said, "No, he's not one of my high-risk clients."

"Clients? You don't work for him exclusively?"

"I'm sure he and his family tell everyone I'm his personal round-the-clock bodyguard, but I'm not. I own a private security firm, RZL Security." He fished a business card out of his pocket and handed it to me.

"Your own firm. Impressive."

"Speaking of security, are you being harassed about the murder yesterday? I saw the news. It looked like there was a swarm of reporters camped out at your house." He gestured to the winter hat and enormous sunglasses sitting on my desk. "It's warm out today, and I doubt you were wearing that hat as a fashion statement."

Sighing, I said, "You got me. It's been a little crazy. That's why I didn't want to eat outside."

"I figured as much. If you ever feel like you need help, call me."

I was beginning to wonder if this lunch was a sales pitch in a handsome disguise. "Thanks. I'll keep that in mind."

"I've been meaning to ask you—are you and Dr. Cooper...?" He trailed off instead of finishing the sentence.

"We're work colleagues and friends. Nothing more."

"I can't say I'm sad to hear that, but he's going to need someone in his corner. His father is circling the wagons, and I'm afraid poor Dudley's going to get left out in the cold."

I frowned. Cooper wasn't kidding when he said his father would disown him over the Vasti scandal. "Cooper's dad is really going to turn his back on him? That's pretty harsh, don't you think?"

"Yes, I think it's horrible, but Mayor Cooper doesn't ask my opinion. I'm just the hired help."

We both laughed.

Rob got up and gave me an apologetic smile. "I hate to cut our lunch short, but I have to get back downtown."

I stood as well. "Right. And I have to get ready for my next class. Thanks again for lunch. It was nice to have another adult to talk to."

"You're welcome, Ellie." Stopping on the way out the door, he added, "I was thinking, since you won't let me get your dress cleaned, how about you let me take you to dinner?"

For the last thirty minutes, I'd been trying to figure out if this surprise lunch had been about apologizing or winning my business or seeing me again. His invitation to dinner finally clarified it for me.

"Yes, I'd love to."

Breaking into one of his mega-watt grins, he replied, "How about tomorrow night?"

"Tomorrow is good."

"It's a date."

When I got home later that evening, I had another surprise visitor. My stepdad's truck was parked in front of my house. Excited, I hurried in to see him.

"Hey, David!" I exclaimed, ignoring Trixie's welcome and heading straight for my stepdad. He was sitting on the floor with Rachel and three-year-old Nathan, eating pizza and building Lego houses. He got up to give me a big bear hug.

"Hello, Ellie. How are you holding up?" he asked.

David was as close to family as Rachel and I had. He was the best thing that had ever happened to us, and he loved us as if we were his own children. Our mother got clean because of him, but sadly it didn't last long. They had only been married two years when she fell back off the wagon. He tried desperately to get her help, but she wouldn't hear of it. One night during a drug-fueled rage, she drew a knife on him. She didn't end up hurting him, but it was the last straw. He called the police, assuming my mother would be arrested and he would be allowed to take care of Rachel and me. But since we had no blood relatives (my grandmother had passed away by then) and were minors, we went into the system and had to go live with a foster family for six months. David was heartbroken. My mother divorced him, so there was nothing he could do to help us. She got clean again, sort of, and regained custody of us. David did all he could to stay in our lives, sending us cards and gifts on holidays and calling us often. He even paid for part of my college tuition and let me live with him and his family during my summer breaks. He has been a wonderful grandfather to Nate.

"I've been better," I replied.

David let me go and gestured to the coffee table. "I brought pizza. Pizza makes everything better."

Laughing, I joined them on the floor, giving Nate a kiss on top of the head. "It does."

"I couldn't believe it when I opened up the morning paper and saw your name. Truth be told, I was relieved when you decided to quit the homicide business," he said, worry evident in his eyes.

"I know. And it's strange to be on the other side. Really though, except for the reporters hounding me, it's not such a big deal."

"You found a d-e-a-d b-o-d-y, Sis," Rachel said, spelling as we often did to keep Nate's little ears from hearing our adult words. "That's a big deal."

I shrugged, reaching for a slice of pizza. "It's not like I haven't seen one before."

David and Rachel both stared at me like I'd sprouted a second head.

"I'm not trying to make light of the situation. I'm just saying the sight of it didn't upset me. What's hard is to not be able to talk about it with anyone."

Taking my hand and giving it a squeeze, David said, "Well, if you do ever need anyone to talk to about anything, you know I'm just a phone call away."

"I know." I smiled. To take the heat off myself, I said, "Hey, David, did Rach tell you she's seeing a new guy?"

Rachel blushed. "It's nothing serious. We've been out for coffee and lunch a few times."

"Good for you," David said, giving her a pat on the shoulder.

The Lego tower Nate had been building went tumbling down, and he started to cry. David scooped him up and gave him a big hug, then helped him rebuild the tower. I could read the look on Rachel's face, because she was feeling the exact same thing I was. David was an extraordinary person, and when he was around, all was right with the world.

After a while, we said our good-byes, and I started getting ready for bed. It was only eight o'clock, and Rachel was just starting to wrestle Nate into bed, but I was exhausted. While I was changing clothes, my phone rang. It was Detective Baxter.

"Hello?" I said, thinking nothing good could come from a late-night call from the cops.

"Hi, Ellie, this is Nick." He added, "Nick Baxter."

Chuckling, I replied, "Yes, I think I remember you."

"Right. I have something I want to run by you. Would you be able to meet me for a drink tonight?"

I was tired, but intrigued. "Okay. Where?"

"O'Loughlin's Bar. Are you familiar with it?"

O'Loughlin's was the cop hangout in Noblesville. I was familiar with it, having had a particularly bad incident there one time with Jason Sterling. "Yes, but—"

"Great. Come on over. I'm already here."

He hung up before I could reply.

O'Loughlin's was an old bar in one of the old buildings on one of the old downtown streets of Noblesville. I hadn't been there in years, but the place hadn't changed a bit. Law enforcement personnel, from rookies to retirees, packed the house. The place was loud and animated, but you could feel an odd, somber undercurrent of depression radiating from men and women who had seen too much violence and hate. Detective Baxter waved at me from a booth near the back. I weaved through the sea of faces I recognized, nodding and smiling as I went.

When I sat down across from Baxter, he smiled. "Thanks for meeting me. I didn't realize how late it was until after I called. Hope I'm not keeping you up. You probably didn't sleep much last night, did you?"

"I'm good," I lied.

He waved a waitress over and ordered us two beers. Once she left, his face grew serious. "I bet you're wondering why I was so cryptic over the phone. If I had told you the real reason I asked to meet with you, I was afraid you'd say no."

I didn't like the sound of that. Shifting in my seat, I asked, "Why did you want to see me?"

He reached into the seat next to him and produced a manila envelope. He took out some gruesome crime scene photos and set them out in front of me. "I need your expertise. There was a robbery that went bad two weeks ago at a gas station up in Cicero."

Of course I couldn't pass up a look at an actual crime scene, so I perused the photos. "I heard about it on the news."

"It was a mess." He pointed to a man in one of the photos. "This is Ronnie Jenkins, my dead shooter. He and the store owner got into a gunfight. Jenkins took a bullet to the chest and a through and through to the neck. He died en route to the hospital. The store owner took one to the face. He's alive, but he can't remember a damn thing that happened and can barely speak. The one and only working surveillance camera positioned on the front door showed another man with a gun come into the store with Jenkins, so we think he had a partner. We've not been able to ID the guy so we can question him." Frustrated, Baxter ran a hand through his dark blonde hair. "Durant's assistant was sick that day, so he processed the scene alone, and personally, I've never seen someone eff anything up so bad. He couldn't even find the bullet that went through my dead guy's neck."

Nodding, I said, "I'm not surprised. He's an idiot."

"Yes. Which is why I've asked the Sheriff...if I can try to persuade you to consult on some of our tougher cases."

"Why would she think I'd want to do that?" She knew exactly why I quit.

He sighed. "I'm struggling here. The whole department is."

"So fire Durant."

"You know who his mother is, don't you?"

"No. I made it my business to stay out of Durant's business."

"His mommy is Judge Ferguson. She uses her maiden name."

I choked on my beer. "What? The Dragon Lady is his *mom*? Now I understand."

Judge Ferguson was a hard-ass, and it was like pulling teeth to try to get a warrant out of her. She would yell at you during a trial if she thought you were trying to pull any shenanigans in her courtroom. Firing her incompetent son would not be worth the wrath of the Dragon Lady.

"So you'll help me?"

I gave him an apologetic smile. "I can't. With my classes and the new research facility...my plate is full right now."

Baxter wasn't backing down. "You'd of course be paid for your time."

"It's not about that. I just...can't."

"How about a one-time shot tonight? Help me with this one case."

"I..." I began, unable to come up with a good excuse why not.

"You're already out. Come on. Please come to the scene with me."

I tensed. I didn't know if I could handle two crime scenes in two days. More than anything, I didn't want to be pulled back into the real world of criminalistics. I was perfectly happy in my ivory tower. But Baxter was giving me such a pleading look, complete with puppy dog eyes, it was hard to resist him and the opportunity to peruse just one more actual crime scene, minus the dead body this time.

"Fine," I relented. "But only tonight."

Already sliding out of the booth, he grinned. "I'll take what I can get. I'll drive."

6

It only took ten minutes to arrive at the rundown gas station in Cicero. Detective Baxter let us into the convenience store building and went to the back to turn on the lights.

When he returned, he said, "The owner is incapacitated, and the staff is unwilling to help run the place, so it's closed indefinitely. The good news is that our crime scene has been preserved."

I took in my surroundings. For the most part, it was a regular convenience store filled with snack foods and other items one would need on a road trip. The unmistakable difference was the giant pools of dried blood on the floor in front of and behind the cash register. The wall of cigarette packs behind the counter was splattered and smeared with blood, some of the packs crushed from the store owner crashing against them when he was shot. A freestanding wire basket of candy bars was overturned in front of the counter, its contents mixing unappetizingly with the blood pool.

Baxter handed me a pair of gloves and donned one himself. "Do you have a particular place you want to start?"

"I usually like to take in the whole scene first, but since it's already been processed, we can start by recreating the incident. You be the owner, and I'll be the robber. What was his name again?"

He got behind the counter. "Jenkins. He was standing two feet to the left of where you are."

I moved accordingly, making a gun out of my thumb, forefinger, and middle finger and leveling it at Baxter. "Here we go. This is a stick-up."

Baxter rolled his eyes. "You think he said, 'This is a stick-up'? This is the twenty-first century."

"Fine. Um... Dude, this is a stick-up...yo," I said, trying for a straight face.

Bursting out laughing, Baxter shook his head. "You're way more fun than Durant, too."

"Damn right I am. Now pull yourself together, Detective. Who do we think shot first?"

"I would say the store owner, because Jenkins took one square in the chest. I don't think anyone could have centered a shot so perfectly after getting popped in the face."

I nodded. "That sounds like a good theory. Okay, shoot me."

"Bang."

"I'm falling back, cracking off a shot that catches you in the face." The detective and I mimicked the motions as we described them.

"On my way down, is there any way I can get off a shot that goes through your neck?" he asked.

"What's the angle?" I asked.

He straightened up, pointing to the right side of his neck, near the middle. "It went through here." He then pointed to the left side of his neck, also near the middle. "And came out here."

"So it went straight through horizontally, basically right under his ears?"

"Yes."

I thought for a moment, getting back into my shooting position, facing directly at Baxter. "How could I take a bullet to the chest..." Trailing off, I pointed at my chest. "And be knocked back..." I looked behind me, my mind still trying to visualize how this could have happened. I turned my attention back to Baxter. "He would have fallen straight back, right? I don't think he would have been able to turn his body to the side in order for that bullet to go through the way it did."

"That's exactly what I thought. And to top it off, we never found a second shell casing from the Colt .380 the store owner was holding."

"Where was Jenkins's partner in crime during all this?"

Baxter smiled. "Where do you think?"

Realization dawning, I pointed to my right. "He was over there shooting Jenkins."

"Bingo. Jenkins was a known dealer, and word on the street is he had a falling out with the leader of one of the most dangerous drug gangs in Indy."

"So this was a hit, masquerading as a robbery," I surmised.

He came out from behind the counter. "That's what my gut says, but I have no evidence. That's why I need you." Looking around the store helplessly, he said, "Find my evidence."

I got back into my position one more time. "I get shot here." I touched the right side of my neck. "The bullet passes through and comes out here." I touched the left side of my neck. Swiveling my head to my left, I pointed in the direction I was looking. "That means the bullet is somewhere over there."

Baxter and I started moving from the spot that Jenkins dropped in the direction of our presumed trajectory of the bullet. In the middle of our imaginary line, there was a long shelving unit filled with canned and boxed goods, none of which seemed to be disturbed. We began pulling items off the shelves, inspecting them and the metal shelves behind them for bullet fragments. At the far end of the unit, I came across a dried brown substance on one of the can lids on a middle shelf. The metal shelving had tiny holes for air circulation, and when I looked underneath the shelf above, I found the same brown substance caked in the air holes. Calling Baxter over, I peered at the upper shelf, pushing the front two cans of chili aside. Hiding at the back of the shelf was a can of chili with a telltale bullet hole in one side, but no exit hole.

Elated, Baxter exclaimed, "That's it! We found it!" Getting out his camera, he snapped several photos. When he was finished, he reached into his camera bag and produced a paper sack. "Would you like to do the honors, since you're such a whiz at bagging and tagging?"

I shook my head. "No, a civilian handling evidence would cause all kinds of trouble during the trial. You do it. You don't even have to tell anyone I was here."

"Well, if you're a paid consultant, then you're an official part of the department."

"But I don't want to be a paid consultant."

He placed the can of chili in the sack, sealed it with red evidence tape, and scribbled on the evidence tag. "I happen to think we make a pretty good team. What do I have to do to convince you? At least let me buy you another drink."

"Fine. One more drink. And then we're done."

One more drink turned into one drink too many. I ended up laughing and snorting beer out my nose at Baxter's impersonation of Judge Ferguson.

"Stop, please stop. You're killing me," I choked out in between laughing fits.

"I'm just getting started. How about another round?" he asked, starting to slur his words.

"I think you've had enough, Detective Baxter."

"I think you should start calling me Nick, Ellie."

"Okay, *Nick*, I think you've had enough."

"I think you've had enough, too," interjected Jason Sterling, who had snuck up to our table when we weren't looking.

"Piss off, Sterling," I said, frowning.

Sterling ignored me and addressed his partner. "Now I know why you had to run off so suddenly tonight. Chasing a piece of tail, Nicky?"

"Hey!" Baxter yelled, his indignation fueled by too much alcohol. "Ellie is not a piece of tail. You should apologize to her, you dick."

Turning to me, Sterling sneered, "Ellie, I'm sorry...that the last time I saw you in here, you were taking a ride on the Sterling Express in the men's restroom. Forgive me if I assumed you came to this bar for another reason than to hook up."

Enraged, I lunged at Sterling, but Baxter snapped out of his drunken stupor in time to grab me before my fist made contact with Sterling's face.

"That was out of line, Sterling. Get the hell out of here," growled Baxter. Sterling smirked at us and swaggered off toward the bar.

I pulled away from Baxter and grabbed my purse. "I have to go."

He stepped in front of me. "Neither of us can drive."

"I can walk. It's not too far to my house."

"I'll walk you home."

"I'm a big girl. I can take care of myself." I turned to go, embarrassed and wishing for this night to be over.

Baxter followed me out of the bar and down the street. I didn't slow down, so he jogged to catch up with me. We walked in silence for a while. I had no idea what to say to him after Sterling's bombshell about our unfortunate men's room tryst.

"I'm sorry about what Sterling said. He's a jackass," said Baxter.

"No shit. He's never going to let me live it down. It was a stupid mistake. We were celebrating one night after we'd solved a big case. I didn't mean for it to happen..."

"You don't have to explain anything to me."

"I want to make it clear that the only reason it *ever* would have happened with Sterling was that I was falling down drunk. That, and I tend to have horrible taste in men."

He laughed. "Things like that happen to the best of us. So about you consulting for the department..."

"Look, Detective—"

"Nick," he corrected me.

"Nick. I don't want to be a part of that world anymore. I don't want to have to deal with the violence and the hurt that comes with it." I shook my head, trying to clear out the disturbing images that had popped in uninvited.

Baxter caught my arm and stopped me. "Did something happen? Usually people don't have such a strong repulsion toward the job unless it was something big."

"This is me," I said, ignoring him and nodding to the next house. His question was one I didn't want to answer. Walking backward toward my door, I said, "Thanks for walking me home. Goodbye, Nick."

He sighed. "Goodbye, Ellie."

"Listen up!" I shouted, in an attempt to get my Intro to Forensic Science class quieted down so I could explain our lab practicum for the day. "Each group has a paper sack containing an article of clothing. Your task is to collect the loose trace evidence on the clothing, use your microscopes to determine what materials you've found, document the different types of trace, and properly bag and tag your evidence."

One of my prissier female students removed a shirt from her bag and looked at it with disdain. Her group had received an old shirt of mine that I had rubbed all over my hairy Golden Retriever yesterday. Clouds of golden fur clung to the dark fabric.

She complained, "Um, Professor Matthews, like, what all kinds of trace are we going to find on this clothing? This is super gross."

I refrained from rolling my eyes at her. "Maddie, most of the time, forensic work *is* 'super gross.' If you're upset about a little hair, how are you going to be able to handle collecting blood, saliva, and semen samples at crime scenes? Most crimes aren't committed in someone's freshly cleaned living room. They occur in dark alleys, crack houses, seedy bars, and old abandoned buildings, just to name a few. Criminalistics isn't a field for those who are afraid to get dirty. You'll see, smell, touch, hear, and possibly even taste things you wish you hadn't. There will be bugs, vultures, rodents, bodily fluids, rot, mold, and unspeakably horrid odors. And that's on a good day."

Maddie stared back at me with wide, frightened eyes.

I continued, "Not only is there the gross-out factor, but there's also the emotional side. Humans do more heinous and awful things to each other than you can begin to imagine. And to do your job, you're going to have to be able to stare at the aftermath of these demented acts for hours on end and not let it get to you. When I worked for the Hamilton County Crime Lab, I saw things that still chill me to this day." I hesitated for a moment as an upsetting memory flashed through my head. Clearing my throat, I went on, "I don't want any of you to be blinded by how cool and exciting they make careers in forensics look on television. I want you to fully understand what you're getting yourselves into. Despite the opposition, the new outdoor forensic research facility will be a good test to find out if you have what it takes to make it in the field. And if forensics isn't for you, there's no shame in that. Better to decide now than after spending four years getting a degree you're unable to use."

I was fairly certain Maddie hadn't thoroughly thought her college major through. From the concerned looks I was getting from her fellow students, it was clear that she wasn't the only one. It wasn't a terrible idea to run the prospective forensics students through the new body farm during their initial campus visit. If they vomited or passed out, they'd go to the bottom of the list for acceptance into the program.

Getting back on track, I said, "But to answer the question you asked, Maddie, our lab today will concentrate on hair and fibers. Once you get the trace onto your tape, you should be able to easily distinguish the different types of hair under the microscope and what mammal they came from. Remember to look at the scale pattern of the hair shaft's cuticle. You don't have to worry about determining the origin or composition of the fibers. You'll only need to be able to describe them on the evidence tag. Now let's get lifting."

After class, I went in search of Cooper to see if he had made it in to work today. He wasn't in his office. Down the hall, I could hear shouting, and when I rounded the corner into the main concourse of the science building, I found him.

"You bastard! Vasti's blood is on your hands!" yelled Tristan Sellers, one of the protestors from the night of the fundraiser.

"That is absolutely untrue. Please, let's go and talk about this in private," Cooper pleaded, his voice wavering.

Several of the students were filming the exchange on their phones. Between social media and the *Ashmore Voice's* new video blog, or "vlog" as the kids called it, these videos would be shared and viewed by everyone on campus. Poor Cooper was going to be a viral sensation for the second time this week. By dinnertime, he would be convicted in the court of public opinion, guilty or not.

"No way, man. I'm not going anywhere with you! It wasn't enough that you used her and broke her heart, but now..." Tristan trailed off, sobbing.

He raised his hands in a gesture of despair and muttered almost to himself, "I almost had her out of her shell, and now...she'll never..."

"Tristan, I—" Cooper reached out to him.

Tristan shoved Cooper's hand away and ran, bumping into gawkers on his way out the door. The crowd dispersed, but not before some of them threw Cooper disgusted looks. Cooper strode my way, likely running for the sanctuary of his office. As he passed me, he grabbed me by the elbow and whisked me down the hall with him. Once we were inside his office, he slammed the door and hastily closed the blinds that covered the window facing the hallway. He collapsed on his chair and put his head down on his desk.

"What was that all about?" I asked.

He groaned. "I made the mistake of giving my condolences to Tristan."

"He seemed to know an awful lot about Vasti—and about your relationship with her. Did they have a connection besides being fellow protestors?"

His head still down on the desk, he answered, "They were dating."

I snorted, "Those two were dating? She's way too cool for him. I'm not seeing Vasti with a little hipster loser like Tristan."

"It's true."

"If it is, then that gives him some serious motive. The significant other is often the strongest suspect. Do you know if the police questioned him?"

"I don't know. And I don't want to talk about it."

"Okay, sorry."

We sat in silence for a while, neither one of us moving until Cooper suddenly reached into his desk, pulled out a bottle of Mylanta, and chugged it.

"Coop, you need to calm down," I said, my unease growing as I watched him begin to pace back and forth in his office.

He wiped a hand down his face and exploded, "I cannot calm down! The police are at my home as we speak, going through my possessions, trying to find something to tie me to the murder!"

My stomach clenched. I had never seen this much emotion out of Cooper, and rightfully so. If the police were searching his place (the guest house on the grounds of his parents' estate), they knew what they were looking for—most likely the murder weapon. They were confident of his guilt if they had enough on him to secure a warrant to enter his home. I didn't tell him that, though. Even though I was trying to keep an open mind, I was beginning to feel nervous around him.

After his outburst, he went back to pacing. I didn't have any encouraging words to say, so I kept my mouth shut. There was a knock at the door. Cooper jumped, a terrified look on his face. He stood frozen in his tracks.

When he didn't open the door, a voice called, "Dudley, it's Tyler. Open up."

Cooper's face crumpled into a disgusted frown. I could tell he was contemplating not answering, but Tyler wouldn't give up.

"I know you're in there, cousin. I can see you through a crack in the blinds."

Emitting a low growl, Cooper opened the door and ushered Tyler inside, quickly closing the door behind him. "It's not a good time, Tyler," Cooper warned.

"You can say that again," Tyler replied, his expression waffling between concern and glee. Something about his demeanor coupled with his slicked-back hair and beady eyes made him look like a caricature of the greasy political toady he was. He turned to me, purring, "Ellie. What a pleasant surprise."

Unsmiling, I waved my hand in greeting.

Cooper eyed Tyler. "What is it, Tyler? You've never come to my office before."

Grinning like a Cheshire cat, Tyler said, "I'm afraid I have to be the bearer of bad news, Dudders. Your mother sent me here. The police evidently didn't find what they were looking for at the guest house, and now they have a warrant to search your father's gun collection." He seemed to enjoy delivering bad news.

Dumbfounded, Cooper asked, "Why in the world would the police need to look through my father's guns...and what does it have to do with me?"

Growing serious, Tyler said, "They think they're going to find the rifle that was used to shoot that girl at your research park."

I gasped out loud, a cold chill sweeping through me. Not only did they have probable cause to search Cooper's home, but they also had the murder weapon narrowed down to a specific type of rifle. Recalling Tyler's one-sided pissing contest with Cooper at the fundraiser, I realized that Cooper would at least have to know his way around a firearm to take part in his family's annual big game hunting trip. That gave Cooper means *and* motive to kill Vasti. To top it off, Cooper had told me himself that he was "out for a drive" around the time when Vasti was killed, therefore also having the opportunity to have killed her. I felt an overwhelming urge to get out of this office, but I didn't want to make it obvious.

During my internal struggle, Cooper had started pacing yet again. He was muttering, "But I didn't kill her... There's no possible way they could find any evidence... Because I didn't kill her..."

Placing his hands on Cooper's shoulders, Tyler halted his pacing. "Listen, Dudley. Your dad is scrambling to do damage control, mostly for himself. If I were you, I would steer clear of him for a while. Your mother said for you to go to the family cottage on Lake Monroe until this blows over. Let your lawyer take care of it." Tyler handed him a set of keys.

If Cooper fled, it could seal his fate, no matter if he was truly guilty or not. A little circumstantial evidence and a suspect skipping town would give the DA the upper hand at a trial. Perception could make or break a jury's decision.

His face contorted with the pain of his own inner struggle, Cooper choked out, "I...I don't know..." He ran his hands through his hair. "Maybe...maybe some time away would clear my head."

Tyler patted him on the shoulder. "If the cops can't find you, they can't arrest you."

Unable to hold my tongue any longer, I exclaimed, "That's the worst advice I've ever heard! Cooper, you can't run. If you're innocent, the evidence will prove it."

His eyes desperate and close to tears, he cried, "You said 'if.' Don't you believe me, Ellie?"

Realizing my slip a little too late, I didn't know how to respond. I'd said 'if' because I was no longer convinced of Cooper's innocence.

He shook his head. "I need some air." Wrenching the door open, he stormed out and down the hall.

Tyler turned to me, smirking. "Ruining someone's day always makes me hungry. Why don't you join me for lunch, sweet thing?"

It took all of my self-control to keep from decking him. Instead, I stood and brushed past him on my way out the door. "Not a chance in hell."

"Your loss."

7

Hoping to find a better lunch date than sleazy Tyler, I stopped by my office to grab my purse and continued down the hall to my friend Samantha Jordan's office. Not finding her there, I turned back around and headed for the forensic anthropology lab. Sam was a true scientist—all of her free time went to research, and she was a total scatterbrain when it came to real life. I found her, or rather smelled her, boiling down a foot in a large pot in her lab.

"Tell me that's not your lunch," I joked, entering the room.

"Ha, ha. You're the third person who's said that," Samantha replied, not amused. Holding the skinless, dripping, severed foot over the pot with a large pair of tongs, she studied it like it was a thing of wonder.

"Speaking of lunch, would you like to venture off campus for something to eat?"

Returning the foot to the pot, she removed her gloves and replied, "Yes, I'm starv—"

"Dr. Jordan," snapped Dr. Gianna Alessi, stalking into the lab.

Gianna was a biology professor and the resident shit-stirrer of the department. She could have been a beautiful woman, but she always wore her hair in a severe chignon and had an angry frown on her face. She had no use for me, I assumed since I had no doctoral degree. I usually tried to steer clear of her.

Flinching, Samantha replied, "Yes?"

"Why are you taking Dr. Cooper's classes this afternoon? What the hell is going on with him? I was out in the hall when he burst into Dr. Graham's office, announced he would be out the rest of the day, and then ran." Dr. Thomas Graham was the head of the science department, our boss. Gianna was always busy tattling on the rest of us and sucking up to the poor man. She pretended she was his right hand woman, but she wielded no actual power.

Samantha shrugged. "I'm not sure what's going on with him. He raced in here a few minutes ago and asked me to cover his classes. My TA is capable of taking over my lab this afternoon, so I agreed."

Gianna turned her wrath onto me. "You're close to him, *Ms.* Matthews. Tell me what you know, right now."

What I knew was a mix of gossip and confidential information pertaining to a murder case, neither of which I would ever share with her. I answered simply, "No."

Narrowing her eyes at me, she said, "This is a departmental issue I need to be brought up to speed about. I'm sure you know *exactly* what's going on."

"Not really, and even if I did, I wouldn't tell you," I said. "You should cut Dr. Cooper some slack. He's beside himself about what happened out at the research facility. We all are."

She let out a nasty bark of laughter. "I told him that ridiculous facility would be nothing but trouble. It's morbid and disgusting, and I was against it from the beginning. But of course, he's an Ashmore, so he gets whatever he wants." She turned on her spiky heel and headed for the door. "Now maybe our esteemed board members will do what they should have done all along and pull their support," she added over her shoulder.

Once she was out of earshot, I said, "Am I the only one who hears the 'Wicked Witch of the West' music when she walks into a room?"

Samantha laughed. "No, I hear it too." Sobering, she asked, "So what *is* up with Dudley? Something is definitely wrong with him."

I sighed. "I shouldn't talk about it. I know too much."

"Ugh. For once in your life you finally have some gossip, and you won't share it."

I didn't mind telling Gianna to piss off, but it was much harder to have to keep things from my closest friend. "Sorry, Sam. It may not be the gossip you're craving, but I *can* tell you about my hot date tonight."

"Hot date?" she cried, grabbing her purse. "Let's go. I want to hear all about it."

We walked out the back entrance of the science building and across the street to the nearest off-campus café. Samantha insisted I give her Rob's vital information on the short walk over. After ordering our lunch and finding a table, she started the inquisition.

"So about this hunky bodyguard. You said you chatted him up at the fundraiser for the research facility when you were supposed to be begging rich people to hand over their money with Dudley. That's some pretty good multi-tasking," she said, popping a whole strawberry into her mouth.

I rolled my eyes. "Cooper was in charge of the begging, not me. Besides, Rob is handsome and charming and impossible to resist."

"Where is he taking you tonight?"

"I don't know. I'm meeting him at my office at six."

"Hmm. Maybe I'll happen to be hanging around right about then so I can see for myself how handsome he really is," she said, twisting a strand of her red hair around her finger. "Oh! I almost forgot. Speaking of handsome men, a little birdie told me you had drinks with some hot cop last night, and that you got home *really* late. By my count, that's two dates in three days."

I grimaced. My sister and Samantha had a bad habit of discussing my love life behind my back, more often than not embellishing it for their own amusement. "Now, that was *definitely* not a date. A detective I know had a case that didn't add up, so he asked me for my help. That's all. We happened to meet in a bar."

She clapped her hands together. "You got to consult on a real case? That's great! The most fun I've had in years was when I got to help out the department after they found that skeleton buried at that old farm in Sheridan."

"Yes, well, it's not the kind of fun I like to have anymore. He offered me a consulting gig, but I told him I didn't want to make it a recurring thing. I'm done with real-life forensics."

Sam gave me a sympathetic smile. "Bad memories, huh?"

"Yeah," I muttered, getting up from the table, my lunch for the most part untouched. Something wasn't sitting well with me about Cooper, but I couldn't put my finger on it. "I need to do some prep work for my lab this afternoon. See you later?"

"Yeah, later." She pointed to the uneaten muffin on my tray. "You gonna eat that?"

"Nope. Knock yourself out."

I wandered back to my office, mulling over the two conversations I'd heard Cooper having this morning. His discussion with Tyler was troubling. It bothered me that Cooper thought running away would even have been an option. More disturbing was the incident with Tristan, especially since he accused Cooper of killing Vasti in front of a couple dozen students.

There was something else Tristan had said that stuck in my head. He'd said Cooper used Vasti and broke her heart, which meant he knew about their affair. I wondered how many other students knew about it or had now figured it out from Tristan's rant. If Cooper were to be charged and tried for the murder, gossip like that could ruin his chances at acquittal, not to mention ruin his career. Tristan had also said something about almost having Vasti out of her shell. I would never have described her as someone who had a shell—she was more outgoing than practically anyone on campus. I didn't understand what he'd meant by that.

This tangled web was getting more and more dramatic by the day. I didn't envy the detectives on this case. There were too many extraneous issues clouding the facts. The evidence would have to speak for itself. Cooper was going to have one tough road ahead of him, and I decided I couldn't accompany him down it, given my unfortunate involvement with the situation. I had too much to lose to get sucked into the center of a murder investigation, especially since I had Rachel and Nate to think about. I hated to have to do it, but I felt it necessary to distance myself from him— both personally and professionally. The next time I saw him, I would have to break the news that I needed to step down as his assistant for his research facility.

I went through the motions of instructing the students in my Criminalistics 1 lab. My mind slipped in and out of focus, and my emotions were in an upheaval over making the decision to cut a friend and colleague out of my life. I forgot what I was saying several times, my notes were in disarray, and to top it off, I dropped a brand-new bottle of luminol, a chemical used to detect bloodstains, on the floor. The plastic cracked, and some of the liquid leaked out onto the floor, so I had to don protective gear, clean up the spill, and safely dispose of the broken container.

Once the chemicals were put away and my students were making notes about their lab findings, I slipped out the door and into the ladies' restroom. Splashing some cool water on my face, I willed myself to calm the hell down. I resolved to treat this case like I used to treat the cases I worked as a criminalist. I would simply shut down my personal feelings, mentally detaching myself from the people and the circumstances. Dudley Cooper was a suspect—a valid one in my opinion. Therefore, as a witness to the crime scene and the body of the deceased, I shouldn't be talking to him under any circumstances, for his own good as well as my own. Drawing a deep breath, I took a hard look at myself in the mirror. I could do this. I just had to find that magic switch I had inside that could turn off my emotions. It was in there, but it was rusty.

Feeling better, I returned to the lab and finished my instruction, focused and in control. After the students left, I reset the lab for my other Intro to Forensics class, relieved that all I had to do was duplicate the trace collection exercise from this morning's class session. I had three of those Intro classes in all, and some days it got tedious teaching the same lesson three times. However, today I was grateful to be able to sail through the class on autopilot.

Word had travelled fast about the incident between Tristan and Dr. Cooper. As students began filing into the room, every conversation I over-heard was on the same topic.

Once everyone was seated, I said, "I know you all have questions and that gossip is spreading like wildfire all over campus. Vasti Marais's murder is an active investigation, so discussing it in a classroom setting would be inappropriate. If you need counseling, please contact your Resident Assistant or your Residence Hall Director. They can point you in the right direction. If you have information you feel is pertinent to the case, please contact the Hamilton County Sheriff's Department. If you only want to spread gossip for the sake of entertainment, you need to re-evaluate your decision to pursue a career in forensics. There is no forensic job on the planet that doesn't require strict confidentiality."

From their frowning faces, I could tell my students were bummed that I had shut down their gossip session, at least for the next hour. There was some grumbling, but they settled down enough to concentrate on the lab.

I picked up one of the bags from the nearest table and repeated my instructions from this morning's lab. "Each group has a sack containing one article of clothing with hair and fibers on it. You are to collect the loose trace evidence with lift tape, use your microscopes to determine what you've found, document all the types of trace, and then correctly bag and tag the evidence. Let's get to work."

About halfway through the lab practicum, as I was helping a group having trouble focusing their microscope, the door opened. I glanced over and stopped short. It was Detective Baxter, a grim look marring his face. He beckoned me to him.

Anxiety washed over me again. I said to my class, "Um...keep doing what you're doing. I'll...be right back."

Once I got out into the hallway, I realized there was no chance this was a social call. Jayne was here. The Sheriff didn't come out unless it was a big deal.

She said, "Hi, Ellie. Sorry to bother you during class, but this is urgent. Is there somewhere we could go to talk privately?"

"Yes...my office," I replied, leading them down the hallway on my shaking legs. Once we were inside my office, I closed the door, apprehensive about what they had to say. Both of their faces were deadly serious.

Jayne began, "We need you, Ellie. I'd like to call this a friendly request, but..." She sighed. "I'm going to lay it out for you. There's been another death."

My breath caught in my throat. "Oh, no," I whispered. My stomach rolled as I wondered who it could be.

Baxter said, "It appears to be a suicide, but something feels off. I want you to work the scene with me."

They were both adamant about me helping them. Had it been anyone else, I would have said no, but I owed my career to Jayne Walsh. And after getting to know Baxter, I felt a pull to want to help him as well. He was one cop who would go the extra mile to make sure justice was served. I didn't relish the thought of going back to the life I left, though. The only bright side was that suicides, or apparent suicides, were not terribly grisly scenes if found within a short time. As crime scenes went, this one wouldn't be one of the worst I'd seen, but the thought of working any death scene still disturbed me.

"Jayne, you know what you're asking of me..." I said, my voice barely above a whisper.

She nodded. "I know. And if I thought Durant could handle it, I wouldn't be here. You know that."

"I know." I took a deep breath, trying to gain some focus. "I'll do it," I said finally. "But you have to tell me who the victim is first."

Baxter said, "It's Tristan Sellers."

My heart sank. "Poor kid. Are you sure it isn't a suicide? It would make sense. Vasti Marais was his girlfriend. He was an absolute wreck when I saw him earlier today."

"His day got worse from there."

Using every last ounce of will I had, I flipped that emotion switch.

After dismissing my current class and cancelling my last class of the day, I followed Jayne and Baxter across the street and down a block to an off-campus student apartment building. Emergency vehicles peppered the parking lot, lights flashing. The second floor balcony was cordoned off by police tape, as were the stairs. A sheriff's deputy stood guard at the bottom of the stairwell. An outer perimeter had been cordoned off as well, encompassing most of the parking lot. Gawkers and reporters were lined up at the border, hoping for a glimpse of the action.

Once we were allowed inside the perimeter area, Jayne took off toward a group of people clustered near the stairs, including Jason Sterling and the coroner, Dr. Berg. Baxter motioned for me to follow him to a Sheriff's Department SUV. Opening the back hatch, he produced a forensics field kit and handed it to me.

I took it in my shaking hands. "I'm also going to need a jumpsuit and a hat. And an elastic band for my hair, if you can find one." I wasn't dressed for the occasion, having worn a skirt and blouse to work today. At least I'd had a pair of sneakers in my office to trade out for my sandals.

He scrounged around in the back of the vehicle and produced two full-length navy jumpsuits and gave one to me. He removed the ball cap from his own head and placed it on mine. It had the Hamilton County Sheriff's Department insignia embroidered on it.

"Thanks. Give me one sec," I said, hopping in the back of the SUV and closing the hatch. Inside the cramped quarters, I shimmied out of my skirt and pulled on the jumpsuit, grateful for the privacy of the SUV's tinted windows.

When I emerged, Baxter was suited up and had found another hat for himself. He was armed with a box of disposable gloves, two respirator masks, two pairs of protective booties, and a camera. He fished in his pocket and handed me a well-used rubber band. "Sorry, this was the best I could do for your hair."

"It's fine. Thanks." I took it, removing my cap and twisting my hair into a messy bun at the nape of my neck. It was going to be hell to get the rubber band out later, but beggars couldn't be choosers.

"I'm going to work the scene with you, but you're in charge. Sterling is on the case, too, but I told him to steer clear of you while you work."

Putting the cap back on my head, I replied, "You don't have to protect me from Sterling."

Smiling, he said, "Oh, I wasn't protecting you—I was protecting Sterling."

"Very funny."

"Ready?" he asked, his face expectant but tinged with worry.

I nodded, afraid my voice might have warbled if I'd verbally responded to his question. After we signed ourselves in, a deputy held the tape up for us and ushered us into the secured area. Baxter shot photos of the stairs and walkway, and I followed behind him, looking for anything out of place. The stairs had a normal amount of dirt and debris for an outdoor stairway. We made our way toward an open door protected by another deputy I recognized from years ago. My heart pounded in my chest as I steeled myself to enter apartment twenty-eight.

Baxter greeted the officer and gestured to me. "This is Ellie Matthews. She's the consulting criminalist on this case."

Deputy Carlos Martinez scribbled some notes in his notebook and returned it to his pocket. He smiled at me. "Long time no see, Matthews."

"Hey, Martinez," I replied, relieved that he was the one securing the area where I'd be working. Martinez was a tough guy, and he would let no one in who didn't absolutely need to be there. I'd seen him turn away law enforcement officials who outranked him without even batting an eye.

After we put on our gloves, masks, and shoe covers, Baxter handed me the camera and took my field kit. "You said you like to take in the whole scene first. I'll be right behind you. Nothing has been moved or touched, besides the first responding officer checking the body for a pulse. Sterling and I have been just inside the front door. When we realized something seemed wrong about the scene, we left so as not to contaminate it. Dr. Berg is hanging back so we can get plenty of photos before he moves the DB." His use of the term "DB" referred to our dead body.

"Who called this in?"

"A friend of the vic's. She came over and found him, and she's been in hysterics ever since. She won't say much of anything besides 'he's dead.' We don't even know her name yet. The Sheriff is going to see if she can coax the girl into talking to us."

I stepped into the apartment. There were no lights on, but there was a decent amount of afternoon sunshine filtering in through the half-drawn window blinds. I began to take wide-angle photos of the apartment, trying not to focus my attention on the young man ten feet in front of me hanging by his neck from a pull-up exercise bar attached to the top of the door-frame. Baxter had been right—something about this crime scene was amiss. My eyes zeroed in on a metal folding chair that was upended several feet from the body. After taking some photos of the chair, I glanced at the body, trying to get a feel for the distance between the two. I took a few mid-range shots of the room, and when I zoomed in to take a closer shot of the body, I did a double take.

My disbelieving eyes still trained on the body swinging from a knotted jump rope, I called, "Nick...you said this was Tristan Sellers. Who ID'd the DB?" I turned around to get his answer.

Wrinkling his forehead, he said, "Well, technically no one, but this is Tristan Sellers's apartment, so..."

"I hope no one's tried to contact his parents yet. Because this isn't Tristan Sellers."

8

Baxter stood motionless, taking in my words. "That's not Tristan Sellers?"

Taking another look at the body to confirm, I replied, "No, it's Eli Vanover. He's the editor of the college newspaper."

"Damn it," said Baxter, clearly disgusted with himself.

"Don't beat yourself up. They look a lot alike. All hipsters look alike."

He didn't react to my joke. He shook his head. "I need to go talk to Sterling. Will you be okay by yourself?"

"As long as Martinez is outside, I'm fine."

When Baxter left, I approached the body for a closer look, careful not to step on anything in my path. Tristan did not keep a tidy apartment. It would take me hours to go through all the crap strewn around the place, trying to determine if the trail of stray candy wrappers on the floor had been dropped by the killer or if they were simply stray candy wrappers that didn't make it to the trash can. I dreaded the thought of shining a UV light around this place. By default, Tristan was going to be in a heap of trouble. Since this was his apartment and he was nowhere to be found, he would be the prime suspect. In order to find as much evidence as possible, however, I would have to keep an open mind, assuming that the killer was a nameless stranger.

I opened the field kit and retrieved a voice recorder. Turning it on, I rattled off the standard case information. I slipped the device in the breast pocket of my jumpsuit, leaving it on so I could record my findings instead of having to take the time to write out my case notes here at the scene. I got out a flashlight and shined it on Eli's hands.

"The victim has fresh wounds on his hands, and there is blood under his fingernails, one of which has been ripped off. The coroner will collect a sample during the autopsy." The blood could belong to the killer. I moved my flashlight up to Eli's neck. "The murder weapon seems to be a black jump rope, which has been wrapped around the victim's neck three times and tied to a doorway pull-up bar situated between the living room and a short hallway. The exercise bar is fastened to the top of the doorframe, roughly seven feet above the floor. The victim has a new wound on his left temple, evidenced by clotted blood around it. There are scratches on the victim's neck, as if he may have tried to claw the rope loose. It's possible the blood under his fingernails is his own." This was no suicide. I snapped several dozen photos of the body and the noose, and when I was finished I let Martinez know that the coroner could come in to retrieve the body.

I returned to snapping photos, and Baxter appeared at the door. "Sterling went out looking for Tristan Sellers. What can I do for you?"

"Dr. Berg will be here any second, so if you could help me decide on a path for the gurney, that would be great."

Disgusted, he looked around the messy room. "There's nowhere to walk in here without tripping over something."

"Right. We probably need to keep the direct path from the body to the door as untouched as possible."

There was a knock at the open door. It was Dr. Berg. "Ellie, I'm happy to see you again, but of course not under these circumstances. It's nice to have you back, though."

"Oh, I'm not back," I protested. "This is only a favor."

He jokingly punched Baxter on the arm. "She's on the hook, son. Now all you have to do is reel her in."

Baxter chuckled, and I threw him a glare. He sobered and began instructing the coroner on the path he and his assistant could take to get to the body. I took it as my chance to go outside and get some air. Once the assistant coroner came in with the gurney, it would be too crowded in the tiny apartment, so I went outside, happy to be able to remove my mask if only for a few moments.

I nearly ran into Dr. Berg's assistant, Kenny Strange, on my way out. He was wheeling the gurney toward the apartment.

"Hey, girl. Good to see you." Kenny was a favorite colleague of mine. He was always jovial and smiling, except if you called him by his last name, which would upset him.

"Hi, Kenny," I replied.

"How's that nephew of yours doing?" Kenny was a grandpa to three boys about Nate's age. We had always traded stories about our baby boys.

"He's great. Can you believe he's nearly three and a half now? It wouldn't surprise me if he started reading pretty soon. He's starting to recognize a few words when he sees them."

"No kidding? My daughter is trying to potty train little Max. It isn't going too well," he chuckled.

"Don't get me started on potty training. Nate is resisting."

"In here, Kenny," Dr. Berg called from inside the apartment.

"Glad to have you back," Kenny said to me with a wink, wheeling the gurney into the apartment before I could explain that this was a one-time gig.

Baxter emerged from the apartment and came over to stand next to me. We leaned on the balcony railing, squinting in the afternoon sun.

I asked him, "What tipped you off that it wasn't a suicide? Was it something specific or a gut reaction?"

"A little of both, but mostly the positioning of the chair. Our DB wasn't a tall guy. I figure if this were a suicide, he would have needed the chair to get close enough to tie the rope to the pull-up bar since it was probably just out of his reach. Once he was ready to do the deed, he would have either stepped or jumped off the chair. His flailing legs might have knocked it over but wouldn't have had the force to kick it several feet across the room."

"Good detecting, Detective."

"There was a fresh mark on his temple, as if he'd been hit. And I noticed the scratches at his neck. It looked like he was trying to get free of the noose. Granted, that can happen during a suicidal hanging if someone changes his mind during the act, but trying to get free is more common in homicidal and accidental strangulation."

"Are we ruling out autoerotic asphyxiation? One possibility is that some not-so-innocent fun went too far and his partner freaked out and bolted."

Blushing, Baxter replied, "Um...I'm going to say it probably wasn't that, because the vic was fully dressed and there was no...uh, paraphernalia around."

I found it humorous that a detective who dealt with sick and twisted crimes on a daily basis was shy to talk about unusual sex acts with me. Baxter was sensitive, especially for a cop. He threw up at first glance of a dead body, and he obviously couldn't talk openly about sex to a female colleague. His vulnerability was rather endearing. I didn't let my amusement show, though.

Dr. Berg and Kenny came out the door, guiding the gurney out of the apartment.

"We tried not to disturb too much of your crime scene," Dr. Berg said, shaking his head. "This is a damn shame. Too many young kids have been on my slab lately."

A pang of sadness shooting through my heart, I nodded. "I agree."

Baxter asked him, "Did you find a wallet on the vic?"

"No, we didn't," replied Dr. Berg.

"Cell phone?"

"No, sorry. Nothing in his pockets."

"Can we take another look at his face?" Baxter asked. He turned to me. "You're positive this isn't Sellers?"

Dr. Berg unzipped the body bag for us to be able to see the victim's face.

I took off my gloves. "Anybody got a phone?"

Baxter handed me his. I Googled the *Ashmore Voice*. On the staff tab of their website, there was a big picture of Eli with his name listed underneath. I put the phone next to the victim's face so everyone could compare. Eli's face was bloated and red from being hanged, but his features were recognizable.

Baxter grimaced. "You're right, our victim looks like Eli Vanover, not Tristan Sellers."

Dr. Berg said, "Since there's been some confusion, we'll do what we can to positively identify the body so there's no question. Maybe his finger-prints are in AFIS for some reason or he has a distinguishing tattoo. The last thing I want to do is to bring the wrong parents in to identify their deceased son." Despite the grisly things he had to deal with as a coroner, Dr. Berg was one of the kindest, most empathetic people I'd ever met. He continued, "I'm placing the time of death between noon and two PM today. As for how he died, he's got petechial hemorrhaging, so I think the prelimi-nary cause of death is asphyxiation. However, with his face and neck being engorged with blood, I would say his jugular veins being compressed by the ligature contributed to his death as well. I'll verify that once I do the autopsy. Moreover, I'm troubled by the abrasion here on his temple. I think there's something more going on than simply a suicide, and I can assure you I'll get to the bottom of it."

"I know you will," I replied. "By the way, Doc, I'm sure you'll see it, but we'll need a sample of the blood under the victim's nails."

"Of course." He smiled. "It's good to see the twinkle back in your eyes. Don't have too much fun in there."

As the two of them made their way to the stairs, I turned to Baxter and huffed, "Twinkle? There's no twinkle."

Grinning, he replied, "There's definitely a twinkle. Protest all you want, but you're enjoying this."

I put my respirator mask back on and glared up at him. "I am not."

But as a rush of adrenaline hit me when I re-entered the apartment, I had to wonder if they were right. I did feel more alive than I had in a long time. On the other hand, I had a calm, easy life now. It would be stupid of me to give that up to go back to the gore and violence I used to see every day.

Speaking of gore, my first order of business was to take a photo of the stain on the carpet resulting from the victim's body emptying itself upon death. While I was there, I studied the nubby, commercial carpet itself. It was no surprise to me that it wasn't in great shape. There were a few noticeable scars in it, much like a chair had been scraped across it, its legs snagging the carpet fibers as it went. I found Eli's broken fingernail, which I would have to mark, photograph, bag, and tag later. I also took a look at the doorframe, where I found scratches and blood smears at my eyelevel, which would have been consistent with the victim attempting to grab hold of something to try to pull himself up and take some pressure off his neck. Down at my knee level there were scuff marks on the doorframe as if he'd also tried to get a foothold. The scuff marks could have been from normal use of the pull-up bar, but the blood was fresh and from today. My gut said the scratches were from today as well, and if there were splinters found under Eli's fingernails, that would prove it. After snapping pictures of my findings in that area, I made a quick note to my voice recorder and found a clipboard and some paper for my rough sketch of the room.

Baxter, armed with a stack of evidence markers and a ruler, stood looking around the room, seeming overwhelmed. "How in the hell are we going to separate the garbage from the evidence? This kid was—is, I mean, a pig."

"I say we start with the path of entry and exit. Then we can section off the room into quadrants."

"You're the boss," he said.

"Let's go outside and enter the apartment, just as a random killer off the street would have," I said, heading for the door.

Baxter laughed. "A 'random killer off the street,' huh? Are there lots of those lurking around Carmel?"

"Look, if we assume the killer is Tristan and work the scene with that in mind, I can guarantee we're going to miss some evidence."

We stood outside the door, and the first thing I did was crouch down to be eyelevel with the doorknob. Fishing a magnifying glass out of one of the many pockets of my ugly jumpsuit, I studied the area around the lock.

"There are no fresh-looking scratches on this lock and no other signs of forced entry," I noted, checking the face of the door and the doorjamb. "No shoeprints and no damage to the door itself."

"The victim must have let the 'random killer off the street' into the apartment, then."

"Damn it, Baxter. Would you give that a rest? Maybe he knew the killer."

"You don't like to be teased, do you?" he asked.

"Not especially. I'll need to print this door later."

"Moving on, let's say the killer is inside the apartment now." He stepped inside and looked around. "Where did he, or she, go from here? Did the killer sit down with our DB and have a chat or go straight for the throat?"

"That was a terrible pun."

"Really? I thought it was clever." He grinned at me. "Do you see signs of a struggle? Or will we be able to tell with all of this mess?"

I walked slowly next to our supposed path of entry, getting out a flashlight and shining it on the floor as I went. The path was a minefield of dirty laundry, empty food wrappers, crumbs, pizza boxes, dirt, and wads of crumpled paper. If we didn't run into some kind of rodent, I'd be surprised.

"Hell if I know," I grumbled.

"What about the coffee table? It looks askew." He took out his own flashlight and shined it on the floor next to the coffee table. "See those indentations in the carpet? I think the table used to be a few inches to the left."

"You're right." I handed him the camera. "Shoot it." While he placed the evidence marker and took pictures, I began drawing my rough sketch of the room.

Shining my flashlight under the coffee table, I said, "Check it out. There's a busted bong under here. As a rule, aside from neglecting to clean them, college kids are careful with their bongs. They're breakable, and some of them aren't cheap. I would say it could have been broken during a struggle." I took an evidence marker from his stack and set it beside the broken glass, and he photographed what was left of the bong.

He gestured at several books scattered on the floor by the table. "I wonder if these were on the table and got knocked off or if they were on the floor to begin with."

I shrugged. "Beats me. Shoot it just in case."

Baxter glanced between the coffee table and the doorway where Eli was hanged. He switched on his flashlight and illuminated the floor in between. "There had to be a decent amount of struggle here. The clothes scattered in this area look more disturbed than the rest. Some of them are even ripped. I don't think you could get another person up on a chair and hang him without some kind of fight."

"Unless he was otherwise incapacitated," I pointed out.

"Like drugged?"

"Yes, or knocked out. Or even held at gunpoint."

Shooting me a dubious glance, he asked, "You mean a 'hang yourself or I'll shoot' kind of scenario?"

I wrinkled my nose. "It sounded better in my head."

He chuckled, bending down to place an evidence marker next to the clothes at his feet.

I thought I saw something sparkle amongst the clothes littering the floor, but lost sight of it. Wanting a better view, I asked, "Can I have the camera back? I think I saw something."

Baxter handed me the camera, and I took some mid-range photos showing the clothing, then zoomed in on each item individually. In the light of the flash, I saw that sparkle again, so after I took the last photo, I reviewed the close-ups on the screen of my camera. The photo of a pair of jeans caught my eye. Peeking out from under one of the legs was a small, blue rock. I switched on my flashlight and shined it on the floor, crouching down for a closer look.

"Did you see this?" I asked, pointing to my find.

Baxter crouched down next to me. "What is it?"

Placing another evidence marker and a ruler next to the rock, I lifted the jeans leg and took a couple of photos. Then I took out a small plastic pill bottle and some forceps. I carefully picked up the rock, which was about a half-inch long, holding it up for Baxter to see.

"This looks like the same type of decorative glass rock that's in the fire pit in my backyard," I said.

"Ooh, fancy," he said. His tone was light, but his eyes were sharply zeroed in on the rock and his face was serious.

"Not really. I got it at Walmart." I hesitated. "You look awfully interested in this rock, Detective. Care to share your thoughts?"

"No." He changed the subject. "Why would a rock from a fire pit be inside a college kid's apartment? I can't imagine Ashmore has open fire pits on campus."

I dropped the rock into the plastic container and labeled it. "No, they don't, but I'm sure there are other uses for this material. Unless we find a bag of it somewhere in here, someone brought it in, probably stuck in a shoe tread. Could have been the killer; could have been the victim. Do you see any more of it?"

Down on our hands and knees, we found four more similar glass rocks in the same area. We also found a few pieces of pea gravel, and since they were near the unusual blue glass, we decided to photograph and collect all the stones. As we were doing so, I couldn't help but wonder what about the glass rock had Baxter so interested.

He stood up and groaned. "This is taking forever. Do you want to divide up some tasks?"

Smiling, I said, "You don't work crime scenes much, do you?"

"Not if I can help it. I'd much rather be out catching the bad guys. It's more fun."

"I know it's tedious, but I want us to search for evidence together so we don't miss anything. Once we've determined what we're going to collect, then we can split up."

"You're very thorough. This is going to take all night, isn't it?"

"You betcha."

He said, "I had no idea you were such a slave driver. Maybe I shouldn't have been so quick to kick Durant to the curb."

"I'll be happy to turn the investigation over to Durant. Call him up," I countered.

Holding his hands up, he said, "Kidding. I'm only kidding." Looking down at his feet, he said, "Hey, this pizza box is crushed, like it's been stepped on. Is that a shoeprint on it, or am I seeing things?"

I squatted down and shined my flashlight on the mangled box. On the back of the box, there was a faint outline of what could have been a shoe. "Good eye. I can enhance it at the lab." I took photos, and Baxter collected the box to take with us.

I gestured to the folding chair. "Speaking of shoeprints, I think I see one on the side of that chair. It may be bulky, but I want to take the whole chair as evidence. I have a feeling it's going to be a gold mine."

Sizing up the chair, he said, "We're going to need a bigger bag than the ones in the kit. Be right back."

I placed another evidence marker next to the overturned folding chair and took a dozen shots of it. I then measured the distance from it to the doorframe, noting the eight feet of distance on my rough sketch. Baxter returned with a much bigger evidence bag for bagging the chair later.

We continued combing the area around the doorway for more evidence. We collected the fingernail I had spotted earlier. In the small hallway that led to a bathroom and a bedroom, we found two more of the blue glass stones. After photographing and searching the bedroom and bathroom and finding nothing amiss, we decided the crime scene was contained to the living room/kitchen combo area and the hallway.

Removing his gloves, Baxter asked, "Are you about ready for a break? I'm starving."

Just having realized the sun was on its way down, I said, "Yeah, I had no idea it was getting so late."

"I can have someone run out and get us some dinner."

I gasped. "Dinner!" My heart pounding, I asked, "What time is it?"

"Seven o'clock."

"Son of a bitch!" I had stood up Rob Larson.

9

"What's wrong?" Baxter asked.

Heading for the door, I said, "I need to make a call. I'll be back."

Stripping off my gloves, mask, and foot protectors as I went, I hurried down the stairs and out to the vehicle where I had stashed my purse. I rooted around and found my phone, groaning as I saw the twenty-three missed calls, five texts, and nineteen voice messages. Holy hell. As I scrolled through the missed call list, I noticed that the majority of the calls were from unknown numbers, which probably meant they were news reporters. I had six calls from Dr. Cooper, which I didn't intend to return, and one from Rob.

I listened to the message Rob had left. His deep voice said, "Hi, Ellie. I waited for nearly an hour at your office, but you never showed. I guess we'll have to try this again some other time. I hope everything's all right."

My heart sank. I was looking forward to this date, but the moment I got on the scene everything else went out of my head as I focused on the job. I hoped I hadn't screwed things up with Rob. The only thing I could do was call and beg for forgiveness. I called him back, nervous about whether or not he would even want to bother with me. His message sounded friendly enough, so maybe I had a chance.

"Hello?" he said.

"Hey, Rob, this is Ellie. I'm so sorry about our date."

"Are you okay? I was beginning to worry about you," he said.

"I was asked to consult on a police case. I was focusing on my work and not watching the time. I feel awful that you waited so long for me."

"It wasn't all bad. I got to meet your friend, Dr. Jordan. She's chatty."

I laughed. I was sure Sam had given him the third degree. "Sorry about that, too. Do you think we could try this again?"

"I could pick you up now if you'd like."

Sighing, I said, "No, I can't get away tonight. How about tomorrow?"

"It's a date. Same time, same place?"

"Yes. I promise I'll be there this time."

"No harm done. I'll see you tomorrow, Ellie."

Relieved, I hung up and sat down on the tailgate of the SUV. Now that I was out of the apartment and had a chance to take a breath, I realized how sore I was from crouching and being on my feet all afternoon. I had grown unaccustomed to the physical stress this job put on my body.

Baxter approached me. "What the hell happened? You darted out of there like a woman possessed."

"Sorry. I'd just remembered I stood up my date for dinner tonight."

"Oh." Something flashed in his eyes for a moment, but then was gone. "I had one of the deputies go out and grab us some burgers. Hope you're not a vegetarian."

"Not even close. While we're waiting, I'm going to go find a restroom."

Not thinking, I unzipped my jumpsuit and let it fall to the ground. Baxter's face reddened, and he moved to stand very close in front of me.

"What are you doing?" I asked.

"Creating a human shield. It seems that you're not wearing any pants."

"Oh, shit!" I yanked my jumpsuit back up and looked around. "Tell me no one saw me."

He turned and scanned the parking lot. The gawkers and newshounds had for the most part gotten bored and dispersed. It was mainly law enforcement officials, and they were all deep in discussion.

"Nope. I think you're good."

Good other than the fact that Baxter had seen me with my pants down. He was quite a gentleman about it, though. Sterling would have announced it to the entire town. I wondered how they got on as partners, being such complete opposites.

After a much-needed dinner break and a short conference with the Sheriff to relate our findings so far, Baxter and I re-entered the apartment, ready to get back to work. We were confident we had found all the evidence relating to the murder, but we still had to search every inch of the room for anything we might have missed.

Baxter helped me measure the room so I could have accurate dimensions for my sketch. After dividing up the room into four quadrants, we each took two of them, scavenging through the mess and collecting anything that struck us as out of place or interesting. We collected and separately bagged all the clothing we thought had been in the area of the struggle. Once that was picked up, we went over the carpet again. There were numerous hairs on the floor, but we collected only the ones in the struggle area. Both of our writing hands were cramping from filling out an obscene amount of evidence tags—one for each piece of evidence we collected—and logging each piece of evidence that needed further testing on a lab request form. Once we had everything up off the floor in the path from the body to the exit, Baxter vacuumed the area with our special sweeper.

He handed me the filter attachment that had collected the debris. "Does this kid even *own* a vacuum cleaner? Look at how much crap I picked up. This is disgusting."

After emptying the filter's contents into a bag, I sat back on my heels and removed and discarded my gloves. "I know. In the back of my mind, I keep thinking we're spinning our wheels. All of this trace could have been here since the beginning of the semester. Maybe even earlier than that, depending on when Tristan moved in here, and whether the super bothered to have the apartment cleaned between renters."

"Are we finally done with the collecting?"

I looked around the room. "Almost. How about our vic's cell phone? We didn't find one here during our search, and the Doc said there wasn't one in his pockets, so it's not on its way to the morgue with him."

"I thought college kids wouldn't go anywhere without their phones—even the morgue."

Rolling my eyes at his stupid joke, I said, "They don't go anywhere without their backpacks, either. Did we miss that, too?"

He shrugged. "I didn't see one."

"In that case, will you sweep the apartment one more time looking specifically for the victim's phone and backpack? And could you run the UV light over the place and swab for blood and any other bodily fluids you might find?"

He made a face and glanced around the room. "I'm afraid to run the UV light over this place. And what will you be doing while I'm doing the dirty work, Bossypants?"

Smiling, I said, "My specialty. Dusting for fingerprints."

Baxter grabbed the UV light, goggles, and a fistful of swabs out of the kit and started his task. I went behind him, armed with a brush, magnetic fingerprint powder, and print tape. To our surprise, the floor was devoid of any bodily fluids, but when he shined the light on the couch, he groaned.

"I don't even want to know what's happened on this couch," he said.

I counted several fluorescent stains. "It's a college boy's apartment. I think we both know what's happened on this couch. You have to swab it though, because it's part of the scene."

Grumbling, he set to work on the couch while I dusted for prints on the front door of the apartment. After I'd finished dusting, I noticed to my dismay that there were too many prints on the doorknob, door, and frame to count.

"This sucks," I said, starting to get tired and crabby.

Baxter had moved on to taking samples of the blood on the doorframe. "It can't be worse than cleaning up some other guy's jizz," he muttered.

I didn't know whether he meant for me to hear that or not, so I ignored his comment. "I enjoy fingerprinting, but I forgot how much I hate trying to grab prints off doors. There are so damn many on here."

"Have fun with that." Baxter boxed up his samples and disappeared into the hallway leading to the bedroom and bathroom.

I finally got all the latent prints I could off the door and dusted several other surfaces throughout the apartment. Baxter appeared in the living area empty-handed.

"The only thing I found that might be of interest in there is a laptop belonging to Tristan Sellers," he said.

"We probably can't take a computer without a separate warrant."

"Right. I doubt there's anything damning on there, unless he was Googling 'how to kill someone with a jump rope'."

I wrinkled my nose at him. "Too soon."

"Come on, I've been pretty good about the jokes today. If Sterling were working this scene with you instead of me, do you think he would have been such a gentleman?"

"If Sterling were working this scene with me, it would have turned into a double homicide, straight up."

He laughed. "You two need to kiss and make up."

"Did you have to say it like that? Now I have a very unwanted visual. Thanks," I grumbled. "Hey, instead of giving me a hard time, why don't you bag and tag the pull-up bar? I'm almost finished with the fingerprinting. After that, I think we're done here."

"Hallelujah. But you know we're far from finished. We have to do our pre-autopsy meeting with Dr. Berg, and then we have to go over everything with Sterling and the Sheriff."

"I know. I'll just be happy to get out of this nasty pit."

While he gathered up our evidence, I printed the doorframe where Eli had been hanging, again coming up with hundreds of prints, most of them partials like on the front door. It wasn't surprising, given that this doorway was in a high traffic area of the apartment, a place inhabitants would have to pass through multiple times a day to get from room to room.

We grabbed the bins of evidence and let the officer outside know we were leaving for the night. Martinez had been replaced, as it was well past midnight and his shift was over. Baxter and Sterling would be pulling double shifts tonight. I figured I'd be lucky to get home in time to shower and drive back to campus to teach my first class in the morning.

Baxter drove me over to the parking lot of the science building to get my car. I followed him straight to the Sheriff's station, where my old lab was, if you could call it a lab. There was much more sophisticated equipment in the criminalistics lab at Ashmore, which I intended to use as much as I could to analyze the evidence for this case. It would be better for the chain of custody to keep the evidence in-house once it got to the station, but some tests were going to need a little more technology than the station's lab could offer.

We checked our evidence in and went to change out of our coveralls. I remembered my skirt this time, waiting to remove my jumpsuit until I was safely inside the ladies' room. Splashing some water on my face, I steeled myself for the long night ahead of me. *Welcome back, Ellie.* Agreeing to work this case was not one of my better ideas.

Baxter had a cup of coffee waiting for me when I emerged. "I thought you could use this," he said.

Accepting it, I replied, "Thanks. I haven't been up this late in years. If I fall asleep, slap me."

"Surely it won't come to that," he said, chuckling. His laughter died quickly, and his face became serious. "Ellie, when you said you had a date tonight, it wasn't with Dudley Cooper, was it?"

"No. We were never more than friends and colleagues. Given the present circumstances, though, I think it's best if I sever all ties with him."

He seemed relieved. "Good. I think he could be dangerous, so I don't want you anywhere near him. We have enough evidence to charge him for Vasti Marais's murder. There's a warrant out for his arrest, but he's in the wind."

My heart sank. Dr. Cooper was officially wanted for murder. My mind was reeling from the thought of it, and what made it worse was that he ran. I remembered his conversation with his cousin Tyler this afternoon. I simply couldn't believe he ran. Only guilty people ran.

Baxter must have misinterpreted my silence, because his expression darkened. "Do you know where he is? Because if you do and you're not telling me, don't think I won't bring you up on obstruction of justice," he said, a sharp edge to his voice I hadn't heard before.

Shocked by what I was hearing, and especially by how fast Baxter turned on me when given the chance, I gasped. "Really? After what we've been through this evening, you think I'd purposely keep something from you? What the hell, Nick?"

"Do you know where he is or not?"

"No! The last time I saw him was before noon today. He had an altercation with Tristan Sellers in the middle of the science building, and then—"

"What kind of an altercation?" he demanded.

"Tristan was screaming at him about how Vasti's blood was on his hands."

"And you didn't think this was something you should have told me?"

Raising my voice to match his, I replied, "I was a little preoccupied with processing a *crime scene*! You don't have to be such a dick about it."

He ran his hands through his hair in frustration. "Fine. Just...go on."

"After that, Dr. Cooper told me the police were searching his place. Then his cousin Tyler Harris showed up and informed him that the police had moved on to searching Mayor Cooper's gun collection for the murder weapon that killed Vasti. Tyler gave him the keys to the family's lake house and suggested he go and stay there for a while. Dr. Cooper stormed out, and I haven't seen him since."

"And he hasn't tried to contact you?"

Remembering the messages on my phone, I said, "Actually, he has. He called me several times tonight, but my phone was in your vehicle, so I missed the calls."

"When were you planning on telling me this?" he cried. "You're a smart woman—you had to know we were looking for him."

"What crawled up your ass? It's not like you've kept me up to speed on your investigation of Vasti's murder. I'm not a mind reader."

He closed his eyes, and I could tell he was trying not to let his anger consume him. "I'm going to need to see your phone."

Fuming, I plucked it out of my purse and threw it at him. "Knock yourself out."

I stalked away from him and down the hallway, headed for the break room's vending machine. I fed my money into the machine and punched in the number for my choice of snack. Ripping off the wrapper, I took nearly half the Snickers bar in one bite, muttering curses as I chewed. Damn Baxter and his holier-than-thou attitude. Was it my job to inform the police every time I had a conversation with Dudley Cooper? Especially when they were intentionally keeping me out of the loop of their investigation? To be fair, it was none of my business, plus I was a witness, so they technically couldn't discuss the case with me. Regardless, Baxter didn't have to treat me like a criminal.

When I was halfway through my third candy bar, Sterling came sauntering into the break room. He took one look at the mess of candy wrappers on the table and smirked. "I heard you and Baxter had a little spat. Figured I'd find you here."

"The last thing I need right now is you, Sterling," I grumbled, my mouth full of Twix this time.

"Stress levels are running high enough around here without us having to deal with one of your hot-headed fits."

"Did you come in here to pick a fight with me?"

"No, I came in here to tell you it's time for us to go meet with Dr. Berg over at the morgue. Now clean up your shit and get your ass over there."

He turned to leave, and I flipped him off.

"I saw that, Matthews," he called on his way out the door.

10

Sterling and Baxter didn't offer to give me a ride over to the morgue, so I went by myself. I didn't want to be around them anyway. When I got inside, the two of them were suiting up to go into the room where the autopsy would be conducted. With no help from them, I found protective gear for myself and donned a surgical gown, mask, and gloves. I followed them to the table where Eli's body lay. Dr. Berg and the District Attorney, Wade McAlister, were already there waiting. This meeting was the initial conference to discuss the preliminary details of the case before the autopsy was preformed. The coroner, the prosecutor, the lead detectives, and the lead crime scene technician were required to be in attendance.

Dr. Berg greeted us with a solemn, "Good evening." To him, the morgue was a sacred place. Everyone knew better than to screw around or tell jokes in Dr. Berg's morgue.

DA McAlister, looking like he'd been dragged out of bed, threw us a glare. He was dressed in sweats and his normally slicked-back hair was tousled, making him seem almost approachable until he opened his mouth. "It's about time you three got here," he barked.

Grimacing, Dr. Berg said, "Let's begin. The autopsy for Elijah Vanover will be at ten o'clock tomorrow morning. Detectives, at least one of you will need to be in attendance. As I told you at the scene, I've determined the preliminary cause of death to be asphyxiation by strangulation. Notice the lacerations on his neck from the ligature and the blood underneath his fingernails, which I suspect is his own. Our victim was trying to get out of the noose he was in." He pointed to Eli's temple. "We spoke about this abrasion at the crime scene. I believe it was made by the side of a handgun."

Baxter said, "The scene did show some signs of a struggle."

Dr. Berg nodded, pointing to the middle of Eli's forehead. "See this contusion here? I think it's a muzzle imprint, as if someone had a gun pressed to the victim's head or jabbed at him with it. The force it took to make this muzzle imprint and the placement of it are inconsistent with a self-inflicted wound as is the abrasion on the temple. Between that and what the Sheriff told me about the scene, I'm fairly certain this will be classified as a homicide, pending autopsy."

I glanced at Baxter, who gave me a sheepish look. Back at the crime scene I had theorized that the victim could have been coerced at gunpoint into submitting to his killer. Baxter had made fun of my idea, but now it didn't seem so stupid.

Disbelief on his face, DA McAlister said, "This kid was hanged, and we're going with homicide based on a little pistol-whipping? How the hell am I going to sell that to a jury?" The DA often seemed more interested in how he could win a case than in justice actually being served.

Sterling grunted, "We'll get you your damn evidence, McAlister."

"Get me a suspect, too, if it's not too much trouble," the DA fired back.

Dr. Berg ignored both of them, continuing, "I've sent the jump rope, which I've determined to be the murder weapon, and the victim's clothes to the lab. I believe that Beck Durant is working on them as we speak."

Sterling turned to me and raised his eyebrows. "*Becky* is handling evidence? What the hell's the point of having you around if not to keep his bumbling paws off it?"

Glaring at Sterling, I replied, "I'm here to see that this case doesn't get screwed up, not to put anyone out of a job. Durant can handle most of the analysis. He's not totally incompetent."

"Could have fooled me."

Dr. Berg stepped in. "If you all are finished, get out of my morgue."

We all headed for the door to the changing room. Stripping off their gear and slamming it into the trash, Sterling and McAlister both stormed away. Baxter took his time. He was looking tired and drawn.

I stopped Baxter before he exited the room. "Hey, Nick, I wanted to say I'm sorry about before."

He shook his head. "No, I'm sorry. You're doing me a huge favor here, and I was a total ass to you."

"It's okay. My claws came out, too."

"It's already forgotten."

Sterling stuck his head through the door. "You ladies coming? We have work to do."

Not wanting to start another fight, I followed the detectives out to our cars. Even though I'd ingested three candy bars before we came over, I was still starving, as was the norm when I pulled an all-nighter. I stopped to grab a burger on my way back to the station.

Baxter was waiting for me when I walked through the front door. "I thought I should return your phone." Handing it back to me, he added, "Um...you didn't listen to the messages from Dudley Cooper yet, did you?"

"No. Honestly, I'm not interested in getting sucked back into that mess."

"He wants to meet with you."

"Well, that's not going to happen."

Baxter scratched his chin, his five o'clock shadow fast turning into scruff. "I hate to ask this of you, but...I think it *does* need to happen."

"Didn't you say you wanted me to stay away from him?"

"You wouldn't be alone with him..."

Finally I realized what Baxter was getting at. "You want to ambush him."

"Ambush is such a harsh word. I want to draw him out."

I rubbed my forehead. It would be a crappy thing for me to do to set him up like that. Regardless of whether he was a murderer or not, Dr. Cooper trusted me. "Ugh. That's really shady."

"So is he. He knew we were searching for the murder weapon at his and his parents' homes. He also knew that once we located it we'd come after him. He's nowhere to be found, so he obviously ran. The guy's guilty."

"I don't know. I'm still on the fence about that. From what I've heard, the evidence seems to point to him, but I can't believe he'd do such a thing."

"You know I can't talk about it with you since you're a witness, but let's just say after we tie up a few loose ends, the Vasti Marais case should be a slam dunk."

"Really?" It hurt to think that Dr. Cooper could have done such an awful thing, all the while insisting to me how innocent he was. That was true sociopathic behavior. I thought I knew him so well.

Baxter, noticing the inner struggle I was going through, put his hand on my shoulder. "I'm sorry. I know this must be difficult, but I wouldn't be asking if it wasn't important."

"Why don't you just find out where his family's lake house is and go pick him up there?"

He sighed. "We tried that. I reached out to Monroe County, and they had a unit go out there. No one was home. They're having someone sit on the place, but so far Cooper hasn't shown. It's a big pain in the ass, and it's looking like it's going to be a lot easier to get him to come to us."

"Which brings it back to me."

Smiling, he joked, "You're our only hope."

"This sucks."

"I know."

I blew out a disgruntled breath. "Fine. I'll do it." I looked at my watch. "It's nearly two AM. He'll think something's up if I call him in the middle of the night. Can I wait until morning?"

Relieved, he said, "That'll work. According to the messages he left on your phone, he's got a safe place to hide out and he's not going anywhere. He insists he's innocent and says he's going to wait it out."

I shook my head, wishing Dr. Cooper had taken my advice.

"You look like you need more coffee. Come on." Baxter led me down the hallway and poured us both a cup of coffee. "We have to go now and brief the Sheriff on our progress with the case so far. After that, do you want to talk to Tristan Sellers with me? We have him in holding."

"Sure. Sounds like fun."

He squinted at me. "You don't sound like you mean that."

"You are quite the detective, Detective."

Chuckling, he continued down the hall to the conference room. Sterling was already seated at the large table, perusing a file. He didn't look up when we came in. His bad behavior was typical Sterling. When he became focused on a case, everyone had to give him a wide berth. He got cranky, belligerent, and downright nasty sometimes. All that aside, he had the best case closure rate in the county, so he was doing something right. Baxter and I took seats opposite Sterling, and Jayne appeared within a few moments.

Tossing a notepad down onto the table, she said, "I know we're all tired, so let's get down to business. Sterling, you're up."

Sterling shuffled some papers around in his file, placing a handwritten, bulleted list on top. "The scene is secured, awaiting your approval for release, Sheriff. This evening, I apprehended the resident of the apartment, Tristan Sellers, and he's currently being held on suspicion. I interrogated him, but he is insisting he's innocent. The kid's a mess, going on and on about how our vic was his 'best bro.' "

"Did you find out why the victim was in that apartment in the first place?" she asked.

"He had a fight with his roommate, so he was crashing at Sellers's place for a while."

"Did you question the victim's roommate?"

"Yes, and he alibied out. He was at an orchestra rehearsal during the time of death window."

"Do you feel that Sellers is a valid suspect then, especially considering his involvement in the Vasti Marais case?" asked Jayne.

"Aside from being Vasti's boyfriend, how is he involved?" I asked.

Frowning, Jayne replied, "I hate discussing the other case's details with you since you're involved as well, but you probably need to know that Tristan Sellers was present when Vasti Marais was shot."

My jaw dropped. "Why didn't he call the police or an ambulance or something?"

Sterling said, "When I talked to him, he said he freaked out and ran. He swears he didn't see the shooter. Back to your question, Sheriff, I don't like Sellers as the killer for either murder. I don't see how he could have gotten his hands on the type of rifle that killed his girlfriend. His alibi during Eli Vanover's time of death is tight. He was in class except for a period of about ten minutes, which wouldn't have been enough time to run to his apartment and do the deed. Based on that and his demeanor while I questioned him, I think he's telling the truth, but I wanted to keep him around for Baxter to take a crack at him."

"If you believe Sellers had nothing to do with it, then who is your next best suspect?" Jayne asked.

Sterling hesitated, and Baxter jumped in. "What about the girl who called it in?"

"Amber Corelli? No," she replied. "Sterling and I talked to her afterward, and I don't think she has what it takes to pull something like this off. She was a basket case. The poor girl could barely speak. Sterling verified her alibi as well. She was in class during the entire time of death window." She looked from Sterling to Baxter. "Come on, guys. Give me a name."

Sterling had been brooding about something. He gave me a hard stare, then finally said, "Dudley Cooper."

"What?" I said, disgusted. "Just because another college kid is dead, you blame him? Do you have anything to support your wild theory?"

"No, but I hear you do."

"Me?"

Baxter murmured to me, "I think he's talking about the confrontation you heard between Sellers and Cooper earlier in the day."

I threw my hands in the air. "What does that have to do with anything? Eli wasn't a part of that."

Shrugging, Sterling said, "Maybe Cooper was angry over their confrontation and decided to continue the argument at Sellers's apartment. In his fit of rage, he didn't realize he had the wrong kid."

My eyebrows shot up. "He killed the wrong kid? Seriously? That has to be the most ridiculous theory ever."

"They do look a lot alike," Baxter muttered, undoubtedly remembering his earlier mistake.

Deep in thought, Jayne said, "It's not such a crazy theory. What if the killer, not necessarily Dudley Cooper, decided that Tristan Sellers is a loose end because he was a witness to the other murder?"

"Then why did he wait three days to finish the job? He could have shot Tristan at Carnival Cove," I pointed out. I still wasn't done with Sterling and his stupid theory. "And by the way, Sterling, Dr. Cooper would have been able to tell Eli and Tristan apart. Besides, he wasn't mad at Tristan, he was only trying to give him his condolences about Vasti, and Tristan went nuts. He was trying to calm Tristan down, not start something. He didn't want to have the conversation in front of the whole science department. He tried to get Tristan to talk about it in private, but Tristan ran off," I said.

"Exactly. Cooper went to Sellers's apartment to finish the conversation and silence the kid once and for all. He just got the wrong kid," replied Sterling, a smug look on his face.

I was about to fire a smart remark back at Sterling, but Baxter put a hand on my arm. "When was the last time there was a murder at Ashmore College?"

I said impatiently, "Never? I don't know."

"Close. In over a hundred years, there have only been two murders on campus. One in 1918, when a professor came back from the war and found out a fellow professor had been having an affair with his wife. He shot the guy on the front lawn in broad daylight. The other was in the sixties when some hippie got high on LSD, thought his roommate was a bear, and beat him to death with a baseball bat."

"Thanks for the history lesson, but I don't see your point," I said.

Baxter explained, "We've got two deaths within one week. Vasti Marais was Tristan Sellers's girlfriend and Eli Vanover was staying at his place. It's likely the deaths are connected."

"The MO changed, though. Vasti was shot, and Eli was hung. Normally don't killers stick with what works?" I asked.

Sterling said, "Serial killers, yes, but that doesn't hold true if one murder was committed to cover up another. The intention and reasoning are different for the second murder so the method can be, also."

"It's possible that I have something besides Tristan Sellers to link the two crime scenes, but it's a long shot and it won't hold up in court," said Baxter.

"Look, until you people get me some actual evidence, we're dead in the water. And I need to make some kind of statement soon to the press," Jayne said.

"We're going to pick Dudley Cooper up this morning, as soon as we can set up a time for him to meet Ellie," said Baxter. "I don't want his name mentioned in the media before then for fear that we'll scare him off."

"Agreed." She narrowed her eyes at Baxter. "Don't forget, Detective, that Ellie is a civilian. Don't go putting her in harm's way."

"I would never do that," he said.

Sterling jumped in, changing the subject. "Dr. Berg said he thought a handgun might have been used, possibly to intimidate the victim." He turned to Baxter and me. "Did you find one at the scene?"

"No," I replied. "There were no weapons of any kind, aside from the jump rope, of course. And before we get going on a different topic here, I want to point out that Eli Vanover was the editor of the campus newspaper. He wasn't exactly well-liked around the place. Maybe whoever killed him had the right person and had a vendetta. His stories were always pissing someone off. He's just started this new video blog, and he's been going around campus recording people's conversations and catching them in... compromising positions and posting it for the world to see."

Jayne nodded. "That's a valid theory. Has he done a harsh exposé lately that would make someone come after him, or has he caught something on video that might get someone into trouble?"

I sighed. "Yes...Dr. Cooper, actually. I haven't looked at Eli's vlog lately, but Monday's paper had a big headline about Vasti's death and him being questioned about it."

Sterling guffawed. "There you go proving my point again about Cooper being the killer. Maybe he didn't get the wrong kid. Maybe he thought Eli Vanover had done some digging and knew too much, so he axed him."

Jayne said, "I'm afraid this puts even more suspicion on Dudley Cooper, but it also opens up a lot of other possibilities. We need copies of that news-paper going back at least two weeks. Go through them and come up with a list of people who might have a reason to want to get back at Eli Vanover. Question the rest of the newspaper staff as well. And I also want one of you to view every video on that blog." She stood, flipping her notebook shut. "It seems that you three have some work to do. Get to it."

As I got up to leave, Jayne pulled me aside. "Ellie, thank you again for coming on board. The case is a difficult one, and we need all the help we can get."

"You're welcome. I'm a little rusty about some things, but I think I have a handle on it."

"Good. I hate to ask, but I'm going to need you here every free moment."

"I figured that," I replied.

"Your teaching job comes first, and I respect that, but you're going to have to eat, sleep, and breathe this case otherwise."

"I know, and it's not a problem. I can run some tests at my lab between classes, and once I'm done each day, I'll head over here."

"Sounds like a plan." She hesitated. "About using you as bait to draw out Dudley Cooper—I'm not happy with the idea. Is there another way?"

Even though she didn't have any children of her own, Jayne had always been better at mothering me than my own mother ever had. Smiling, I said, "I appreciate your concern, but Baxter assured me I wouldn't be alone with Dr. Cooper. And besides, I don't think he would hurt me."

"When cornered, people will do things you never imagined." She squeezed my arm. "Be careful, okay?"

"I will."

11

Baxter caught up with me in the hallway. "Are you ready to go scare some information out of that little hipster kid?"

Rolling my eyes, I replied, "I don't know about that. I have to be inspired to rip someone a new asshole, and I doubt that Tristan killed his 'best bro.' Maybe you could play bad cop and I could play good cop. I do have a decent relationship with Tristan. I could try to convince him to open up to me."

He grinned. "I was hoping to get to see you play bad cop."

We headed downstairs to the interrogation rooms, where Baxter had already made arrangements for Tristan to be brought. The kid looked rough. He was pale and haggard—a boy who had just lost his best friend and his girlfriend.

When Tristan saw me, he brightened. "Professor Matthews? Hey, did the school send you over here to bail me out or something?"

I sat down across from him and gave him a sympathetic smile. "No, Tristan. I'm sorry. I'm consulting on the case."

Seeming to deflate right before my eyes, he said, "Oh."

"I'm so sorry for the loss of your girlfriend and your friend."

He nodded, too overcome with emotion to say anything.

I said, "I know you've already spoken with Detective Sterling."

He nodded again and frowned. Poor kid. I wouldn't have wanted to be interrogated by Sterling, especially with the mood he was in today.

Gesturing to Baxter, I said, "This is Detective Baxter. He's also working this case." I leaned forward and whispered, "He's a lot nicer than Sterling."

My comment got a ghost of a smile out of Tristan.

"We have a few questions for you if that's okay, Tristan."

"Okay," he whispered.

"Detective Baxter, did you want to start?" I asked.

Baxter approached the table and took a seat next to me. He put the case file in front of him and got out a legal pad to take notes.

He asked Tristan, "You said Eli Vanover was staying at your place?"

"Yeah."

"And why was that?"

Tristan didn't look too interested in talking to Baxter. He wiped a tear from his eyes and shrugged. "He needed some space."

"Was that because of the fight between him and his roommate?"

"Yeah."

"When was the fight?"

"Monday."

"What did they fight about?"

He shrugged again, casting a wary glance at me. "I told this to the other cop..."

Baxter was starting to fidget. I could tell he was getting frustrated.

I said to Tristan, "I know you gave Detective Sterling your statement. But we really want to catch whoever did this to Eli. I'm sure you want to bring his killer to justice as well. I know some of these questions are redundant, and you probably don't appreciate being treated like a criminal, but even the smallest bit of information you can give us might be all we need to figure out who did this. We owe it to Eli."

Tristan ran his hands through his hair. "What do you want to know?"

"Do you know what the fight was about?" I asked.

"All Eli said was that his roommate was being a dick over some story for the campus paper," he said.

Baxter and I shared an uneasy glance. Baxter asked, "Do you know what the story was about, Tristan?"

He shook his head. "No, I don't know any specific details, but Eli was all hyped up about it. Whatever the story was, it was epic."

"Does Eli's roommate work for the newspaper, too?" I asked.

"Yeah, Tad is the managing editor, just a step under Eli, and he and Eli butt heads over stuff all the time. Those two bros really shouldn't live together." He stopped, as if what he said had suddenly sunk in. His shoulders slumped. "I guess that won't be a problem anymore."

"You're doing a great job here, Tristan. We only have a few more things to go over. Do you need a drink or something? Maybe a snack?" I asked, hoping to steer his mind away from his emotional distress.

"Could I get a Red Bull or something? I feel like I'm in a daze."

"Sure. Anything else?"

"Some Skittles would be awesome."

I nodded to Baxter. Normally, I wouldn't be left alone with a suspect, but my gut said Sterling was right—Tristan wasn't to blame for Eli's death. Baxter hurried out of the room to fill Tristan's snack order.

"Had Eli and Tad ever had such a big fight over a story before?" I asked.

Tristan shook his head. "I don't think so. Evidently Eli had something on someone that would ruin their rep. He said heads were going to roll on campus over it. Tad tried to block him from breaking the story for some reason. Eli was bitching about Tad losing his balls all of a sudden."

"It doesn't seem like anything ever stopped them in the past from running stories that tarnished people's reputations." Like the headline story about Vasti and Dr. Cooper, which along with campus gossip had already ruined him, regardless of the warrant out for his arrest.

"I know, right? Like why was this story different? Whatever the reason, Eli said Tad was hell-bent on not running it."

"Did you get this specific with Detective Sterling?"

He cast his eyes down. "No, he yelled a lot, and I got nervous. I don't think I answered his questions very well." Fighting back tears, he continued, "He mainly grilled me about whether or not I killed Eli—not so much about the fight."

I grimaced. Sterling needed to dial it down. He came on way too strong with Tristan and may have missed some key information. He had also questioned Eli's roommate and right-hand man at the newspaper, Tad Ogelsby, but all that seemed to have come of it was learning Tad had been in orchestra rehearsal when his roommate was murdered and therefore couldn't have been the killer. I wondered if Sterling had questioned him further and got to the bottom of why the fight occurred. Something told me we needed to find out more about this news story.

Tristan put his head down on the table. He said, "I'm so exhausted. I haven't slept for days, especially after seeing Vasti get shot..."

I knew I wasn't supposed to be talking to him about Vasti's murder, but he brought it up, so I urged him to continue. "That must have been so hard on you, Tristan. I hate that you had to go through it."

He lifted his head and a tear slid down his cheek. His voice was rough. "I didn't know what to do. She was dead, and I snapped. I should have called the police, but I didn't. There was no point. She was already dead."

I put my hand over his and asked gently, "Did you see who shot her?" Sterling said he had asked him that, but it didn't hurt to ask again.

"No," he whispered. "I heard the shots and saw her fall. I was several yards away, and by the time I got over to her, she was gone. The shots sounded like they'd come from far away, and I didn't see anyone anywhere. I went back to my place and...self-medicated."

Baxter returned, so I abandoned my line of questioning about Vasti's murder. He placed a can of Red Bull and a package of Skittles in front of Tristan. Tristan ripped open the Skittles bag and poured half of them into his mouth, chasing them with a big gulp of soda. The poor kid probably thought he was never going to get to eat again. Baxter was watching him with disgust.

"We'll give you a minute to finish eating," I said, getting up and motioning for Baxter to follow me into the hallway. Once we were out of Tristan's earshot, I said, "We need to talk to Tad Ogelsby."

"The roommate? I thought he alibied out," Baxter replied.

"He did, but I think he may know something else. Tristan said Tad was adamant about not running whatever big story Eli had. I think we should find out more about it. If the story is as dramatic as Tristan made it out to be and it got run or even leaked, we may find someone with sufficient motive to kill. He said the story could ruin whoever it was about. It could be

anything from cheating to hazing to drug abuse to inappropriate relationships between students and faculty."

"Speaking of inappropriate relationships between students and faculty,
were you aware that your friend Dr. Cooper and Vasti Marais had a sordid
past?"

I frowned at him. "Yes, I know, but I wasn't aware of it until a few days
ago. What does that have to do with the Eli Vanover case?"

"Nothing. I just want to make sure that you're not going to feel sorry for
Cooper when we nail his ass to the wall."

"Don't worry about me. I can deal with disappointment like it's my job,"
I muttered.

He opened his mouth to reply but stopped, seeming to be at a loss for
words.

I used his silence as an opportunity to change the subject. "What do
you have that connects the two crime scenes?"

Baxter shook his head. "It may be nothing. Besides, I don't want you
anywhere near the Marais murder evidence. I don't even want you to think
about it."

"If the crimes are connected, I'm going to be involved whether you like
it or not."

"Let me take some time to research it first."

"Fine," I replied, miffed at not being kept in the loop. "Do you want to
ask Tristan any more questions?"

"Just a few."

"Do you need me? Because I'd love to get cracking on the folding chair."

"No, I'm good. I'll catch up with you later."

I headed for the forensics lab, looking forward to processing the chair
we found at the crime scene. My excitement was extinguished when Beck
Durant greeted me.

"Hello, Ellie," he sneered. "Are you gunning for my job? It was kind of
shitty of you to swoop in and yank this case out from under me."

I sighed. Staying up all night had already given me a headache, and
Durant wasn't helping. "Look, Beck, I didn't swoop in. This case is complex,
and the Sheriff wanted someone with a lot of experience."

"Experience? I have as many years under my belt at this job as you do."

"But I've continued my work in Criminalistics since I left here. I've been using my skills every day."

"Oh right, by sitting on the sidelines, *teaching*." He said the word as if it left a bad taste in his mouth.

"I'm not here to argue. I'm here to work." I said, shutting down his catty taunting.

Beck turned his back on me in a huff. His assistant, who had been watching our exchange with wide eyes, went back to examining the clothing on the table in front of her.

After finding a lab coat to wear, I went across the hall to evidence and requested to check out the chair to take to the lab. The evidence clerk got it for me, and I took it back to the lab and placed it on a workspace under a bench magnifier. After putting on gloves and removing the chair from the bag, I took a few additional photographs of it while it was illuminated by the magnifier's light. By giving the chair a quick once-over with the magnifier, I saw that in addition to the partial shoeprint I'd noticed at the scene, I could get several dozen fingerprints from this piece of evidence. I loved lifting fingerprints from metal objects. Besides glass, metal was one of the easiest surfaces to process.

Before I got out the fingerprint powder, I wanted to get any touch DNA I could off the chair. Noticing several fingerprints too smudged or too incomplete to be useful, I found a good source of possible epithelial cells, skin cells left behind when a person touches an object. Taking out a swab, I applied a drop of distilled water to the tip and rubbed it over one of the prints. I repeated the process for each smudged print I found, being careful not to disturb any of the usable prints. I set my samples aside to send to the Indiana State Police lab for testing.

Since I was in the lab, I used regular fingerprint powder to dust for prints. Magnetic powder was less messy and much simpler to work with at a scene, but you couldn't beat good old-fashioned black fingerprint powder for getting the best results. I brushed the powder onto the surface of the chair, paying special attention to the top of the chair back. I had seen the highest concentration of prints there, as people normally used the rolled frame as a handle of sorts when moving a folding chair. Once the powder was applied, I changed my gloves and took another look at the chair under the magnifier. I counted about twenty viable full and partial prints. Taking out some fingerprinting tape, I lifted them from the chair and labeled each one. Between the prints from the apartment and the chair, I was going to have one tedious and lengthy session in my future with the AFIS computer to examine and mark the individual features of each print and enter my findings into the system.

Fingerprint identification is not as simple as on television where prints are scanned and magically matched by the computer in mere seconds. Real fingerprint matching is done by a human plotting all of the features of a fingerprint—core, ridge endings, bifurcations, deltas, et cetera—and inputting that information into AFIS, which can take anywhere from two to ten minutes per print, depending on the quality of it. The results are not absolute. Instead of one positive match, AFIS provides a list of possible matches, which then have to be compared (by a human) to the original print to be verified. If you know what you're doing, it isn't a difficult process, just a time-consuming one. Maybe I could convince Beck or his assistant to do the work for me while I taught my classes later this morning.

I turned my attention to the shoe impression on the side of the chair's seat. I was fairly certain that this shoeprint belonged to the killer because the chair frame was bent where the shoe had made contact with it. In my opinion, the chair would have been damaged when the killer kicked it out from under Eli's feet. I pondered which method would be best to capture the shoeprint. The print looked dusty, so I could lift it straight from the chair using a large section of lifting tape, rather than getting more technical with an electrostatic lifting device. Lifting single shoeprints made me more nervous than collecting a handful of fingerprints because I only had one shot to get the single impression. Before I disturbed the print, I took a swab and got a sample of the dusty residue left by the shoe, being sure to take my sample near the edge to eliminate as little of the print as possible. The sample would have to be sent to another lab because we didn't have the staff or the technology to determine unknown substances here, if it was even deemed relevant enough to be processed at all.

I smoothed the lifting material onto the side of the chair over the shoe impression, and then I used a fingerprint roller to eliminate any air pockets that might have formed. After taking a deep breath, I pulled the tape up and studied the impression under the bench magnifier. From the rugged pattern of the tread, it seemed to be some sort of work boot. It wasn't a great impression, and having come from the side of the chair, it was only about a two-inch by four-inch section of the shoe. The only saving grace was that there was part of a word on the sole of the shoe: STICK. I couldn't recall any brand of shoes with "stick" in the name, so I would have to do some research.

I then remembered that we had found another possible shoeprint at the scene on a busted pizza box. Returning the chair to its bag and resealing it, I checked it back into evidence and took the pizza box. On my way back to the lab, I bumped into Baxter.

"Hey, working hard?" he asked, his eyes red and bloodshot.

"Yes. I'm going to compare the partial shoe impression I found on the chair to the mystery impression on this pizza box." I took a closer look at his eyes. "What have you been doing—crying or hitting the sauce?"

"Very funny. I've been watching the videos on your dumbass campus newspaper blog." He shook his head. "I hate to say this, but that editor guy was asking for it. He's got videos of a lot of kids doing a lot of stupid shit they should be ashamed of. I've got a list of potential suspects a mile long now. The guy must walk around perpetually taking videos. There are dozens of them on that blog, and he's only been at it a few weeks."

"I told you Dr. Cooper isn't the only person with motive."

"Right, but the last video Vanover ever uploaded was of the fight between Cooper and Sellers."

"Ooh. That looks bad. I don't remember seeing Eli there during the fight, but there were plenty of students recording it on their phones. Maybe he had a street team or something."

He rubbed his eyes. "Hell if I know. What I do know is that when I was in college, I didn't do idiotic stuff like these kids are doing."

"Or, back in the olden days before everyone had a smartphone, your every move wasn't being recorded," I pointed out.

"I'm not that old."

"You're older than I am."

"Not by much."

I laughed. "I need to get back to work."

"Want to grab some breakfast after you're done?"

"Is it almost that time?" I asked, yawning.

"It's five AM already. By the time we get to a stopping point here and grab something to eat, it should be time for you to call your buddy Cooper and set up our meeting."

"You mean ambush."

"You say potato…" he joked.

"The man is not going to last a day in jail," I murmured, worry forming a knot in my stomach.

Dr. Cooper was used to his easy, privileged life. Murderer or not, he was not going to fare well with the other inmates. He was weak, and it showed. He was also quite handsome, and for some reason hardened criminals seemed to delight in rearranging nice faces.

"Then he shouldn't have killed someone."

Ready to end the conversation about Dr. Cooper's impending incarceration, I nodded, pushing past Baxter and making my way into the lab. My mind knew the evidence against Dr. Cooper had to have been strong, otherwise they never would have been able to get a warrant issued for his arrest. However, my heart couldn't accept the fact that he was a killer.

Beck was nowhere in sight, so I assumed he was taking one of his lengthy "smoke" breaks. I wasn't convinced that he even smoked—he just liked breaks. His assistant was missing as well. Maybe both of them had given up and gone home. Nevertheless, I was happy for the quiet.

I removed the pizza box from its evidence bag and set it on the table in front of me. Once again, I took extra photos from all angles of the alleged shoeprint, now slightly more visible to the naked eye in the good lighting of the lab. I went to the storage cabinet full of chemical reagents and perused the stock. If I sprayed the incorrect reagent on the print, it could become unrecoverable. I was waffling back and forth between using Bromophenol Blue and potassium thiocyanate. The proper chemical to be used would depend on the compounds making up the dust or dirt I was trying to enhance. For example, Bromophenol Blue worked better for soil containing carbonate while potassium thiocyanate worked better for soil with traces of iron. I needed a chemist, and I didn't have time to wait for weeks to send my sample to the usual lab.

Not caring that it was only a little after five in the morning, I called my fellow Ashmore professor, Rich Porter.

He answered, griping, "Why would you call me at this ungodly early hour of the morning?"

"Good morning to you, too, Rich," I said. "I need your chemistry expertise."

"Can't it wait?"

"Not really. I need to know how much of a substance you need in order to mass spectrometerize it."

He snorted. "*Spectrometerize* is not even a word. Are you trying to ask how much of a sample I need to run a gas chromatography mass spectrometry analysis, Professor?"

"Yes," I replied, knowing I hadn't used the proper term. I was exhausted and not overly worried about correct word choice.

"Just a dab will do."

"That's not a very scientific measurement, *Professor*."

He ignored my jab. "You know, you forgot to ask me pretty please if I would agree to run your little test for you. How do you know I won't say no?"

"Because it's for the Sheriff's office."

"Are you back in the saddle again?"

"You could say that."

"In that case, I'll do it. I've done testing for them in the past." He changed the subject. "Hey, speaking of the long arm of the law, did you hear that the *Voice's* editor is dead and that foul play is suspected?"

"Um...yeah." The less I could tell Rich, the better. Even though he was a brilliant professor in his fifties, he gossiped like a thirteen-year-old girl.

"All of campus is buzzing about it. I could barely teach my night class yesterday with my students so amped up. The other big story is that Dr. Dudley Dipshit is AWOL. He left campus yesterday after a fight with a student and no one's seen or heard from him since."

"Yeah," I said, trying not to let on what I knew. "Gianna was running around telling everyone."

"I'm not surprised. She's a bitch on wheels."

"So I'll get those samples to you first thing, okay?"

"Samples? Like more than one?" he asked.

"Only two. Thanks a bunch." I hung up before he could protest.

I swabbed an area of the shoeprint, trying to disturb as little of the outline as possible. I also measured the length of the impression as best I could, so we would at least have a general idea of the size foot we were looking for. The dust pattern was between twelve and thirteen inches long. Quickly consulting a shoe sizing database online and doing some simple math, I surmised that the wearer's shoe size had to be roughly a twelve or thirteen. I noted that in the file. Once I was able to enhance the impression and get a true measurement, I could more accurately pinpoint the shoe size. After returning the pizza box to the evidence bag, I gathered my chair swab and my pizza box swab and placed them in a container to take to Rich. I checked the pizza box back into evidence, created a chain of custody sheet for both swabs, and checked the swabs into evidence for safekeeping until I was ready to transport them to Rich.

When I found Baxter, he was sitting at his desk, eyes glued to his computer screen.

"Are you at a stopping place?" I asked.

He looked up, his eyes even redder than before. "I thought you'd never ask."

12

"You're telling me you had to chase down and cuff a naked guy your first day on the job?" I asked, trying not to snort coffee out my nose between laughs. "That's too ridiculous to be true."

Baxter and I were sitting across from each other in a booth at Mabel's Coffeeshop, having breakfast. It wasn't far from O'Loughlin's Bar, and the place was equally as old and rundown, but they served the best omelets in town. We were guzzling coffee like it was water, and our waitress had given up on trying to keep our mugs topped off. She brought a full carafe to our table for us to serve ourselves so she could be free to flirt with a guy sitting at the counter.

Baxter pretended to be offended, but he couldn't help smiling. "It's the honest truth. Cops don't lie."

I stared at him. "I'd like to meet a cop who doesn't lie."

"You're so cynical. You're too young to be that jaded."

He was right. "If you only knew."

"Come on. So you had a bad childhood and you suck at dating. Is being you really that bad?"

"Wow. Are you going to call me fat and ugly, too?" I demanded.

He held his hands up as if to shield himself from my wrath. "That came out wrong. I only meant you seem to have your shit together now, so your life can't be too terrible."

"It's good right now. I couldn't have said that a few years ago."

"What happened?" he pressed.

I didn't want to talk about it, especially over breakfast and after I'd been awake for twenty-four hours. Come to think of it, I'd only had five hours of sleep the night before because Baxter kept me out late, so I was running purely on caffeine. Granted, he was, too. But I wasn't asking him to delve into his unpleasant past.

"Let's just say that there are some skeletons I'd rather keep in the closet at this time."

His face softened. "Sorry. I'll leave you alone." Shoveling a forkful of eggs into his mouth, he continued, "Hey, I forgot to tell you—the bullet we recovered from that can of chili at the convenience store was from a nine mil."

I gasped. "Really? That proves your theory about multiple shooters. The store owner had a Colt .380, right?"

"Right. My dead shooter, Jenkins, also had a nine mil, but the striations on his bullet we pulled out of the store owner didn't match the ones on the chili bullet. Durant was able to find some blood on the chili bullet, so we're waiting on DNA confirmation that it belongs to Jenkins. Even better, the firearms examiner ran the bullet through IBIS, and as luck would have it, the bullet matched another bullet from a murder six months ago. When I finally catch this guy, he's going to fry."

"Good for you, Detective," I said, proud of his persistence.

"I couldn't have done it without your help. And speaking of your help, do you think it's time to give your boy Cooper a call?"

Sighing, I said, "I was hoping you'd forget about that."

"Nope, sorry."

Reluctant to put this plan in motion, I took out my phone and dialed Dr. Cooper's number. I got out of my seat and scooted into the booth next to Baxter, placing the phone between our ears to allow him to hear the other end of the conversation.

Dr. Cooper answered after one ring. "Ellie! Thank you for calling me.

I...I don't know who else I can trust." He sounded shaky and worried. I would have been, too, in his situation.

I gave Baxter a reproachful frown and said into the phone, "What's going on? Where are you?"

He hesitated. "I hate to tell you over the phone in case someone is listening in."

Again, I looked pointedly at Baxter. "Right. So you said something about needing to talk with me?"

"Yes, Ellie, I need to talk to someone. Please say you'll meet with me," he pleaded.

"I will. Can we do it this morning?" I cringed. Being the one responsible for setting up this ambush made me feel dirty.

Baxter gave me an encouraging smile.

Dr. Cooper said, "Yes, can I come to your house?"

"No," I replied, my tone sharper than I'd intended. There would be no ambushing going on at my house, especially with my sister and nephew there. "I mean, Rachel and Nate are still sleeping. How about somewhere else?"

"I'm afraid people might be...looking for me. We need someplace out of the way where there aren't a lot of people."

Baxter was shaking his head and mouthing, "No."

I asked, "Can you come to Noblesville to meet me?"

"Sure."

"How about...the donut shop on Tenth Street? It's called Cup of Sugar."

"Won't it be crowded?"

"No. It's never crowded. I think they're not doing so well lately."

Cup of Sugar had been around forever, but their business had been in a slow decline in the last couple of years. It could have been because the owners regularly had fistfights in the shop and the Noblesville police were forever having to go and break it up. Being on the cops' shit list did substantial damage to a donut shop's profits.

"Can I meet you there in thirty minutes?" he asked.

I raised my eyebrows at Baxter. He nodded in agreement.

"I'll be there." I ended the call and added to Baxter, "Along with a dozen of my closest cop friends."

Now that the call was over, I began to scoot out of Baxter's seat, but he caught my arm. "You know you're doing the right thing here," he said, his expression serious.

"I know, but I wish it didn't make me feel like such a backstabbing bitch."

With one phone call from Baxter, a fleet of unmarked law enforcement vehicles converged on the area around Cup of Sugar. He and I headed straight over after I spoke with Dr. Cooper so Baxter could clear the donut shop and be in place well before our meeting time. The owners were bickering as usual, and with one lone customer in the shop, it took only a few minutes to get everyone out and undercover cops stationed in their places. I was wearing a wire, so if Dr. Cooper said anything incriminating, it would be on tape. I felt ill. Baxter, who had donned an apron reading CUP OF SUGAR, was supposed to have already been in position behind the counter, but he stayed with me in the tiny eating area, a gesture for which I was grateful.

Pacing the floor, I said, "I haven't been this nervous since...well, probably since my sister went into labor."

"How long ago was that?" he asked.

"Three and a half years ago."

"Wow. You live a quiet life, then."

"If by 'quiet' you mean 'boring,' that's where you're wrong. Living with a three-year-old boy is anything but boring."

"I can see where that would be true," he said. "Your sister looks awfully young to have a kid, though."

I nodded. "Yeah, she started early. Rachel's only twenty-one, but she's a great mom. Sometimes I think she's more mature than I am. And Nate is one fantastic kid." I got out my phone and showed him a picture I had taken earlier in the week of Nate and Trixie snuggled up together on the couch. "These two are best buddies."

"You seem to be a very doting aunt," he said, smiling.

Eyeing him, I said, "And *you* seem to be trying to distract me from the situation at hand."

"Is it working?"

A wave of nausea hit me when I settled back into reality. "No," I groaned. "I feel like I'm going to puke."

"As luck would have it, I happen to have a lot of experience with puking on the job." He took off his ball cap and held it under my chin. "Why do you think I always wear a hat out in the field?"

Laughing, I pushed the hat away. "Because it's standard procedure to cover nearly every inch of yourself so as not to add your own DNA to a crime scene."

He put his hat back on. "Nope. It's so I always have a vomit catcher." Putting a finger to his earpiece, he said, "Roger that." He looked at me. "Cooper's coming down the street now."

I sucked in a breath. This was it. My heart pounded, and my mind began racing. "What if he has a gun...or...or a knife or something?"

Baxter put his hands on my shoulders. "I'll only be a few feet away from you, right behind the counter. I promise I won't let anything happen to you."

"I'm not worried that he'll hurt me. I'm more worried about him doing something stupid like brandishing a weapon. That could start a gunfight. What if he shoots you? What if you or some other cop has to end him right in front of me? That's one thing I don't think I could handle witnessing. Oh, and what if I get caught in the crossfire?" I demanded breathlessly.

"You don't even know that he has a gun," he pointed out.

"You don't know that he *doesn't*!"

His face softened, and he steered me to a table, settling me into a chair facing the counter. "You sit here. You'll be able to see me the whole time. Nothing bad is going to happen. We're going to take him as soon as all the exits are secure. This should be over in a minute or two. Do you trust me?"

"Yes."

"Then you have nothing to worry about." He punched me on the arm. "It's nice to see that you're not always a total badass. I was starting to think you didn't have any girly feelings."

"What is that supposed to mean?"

Baxter's expression became serious. "He's at the door. Game face," he ordered, hurrying to his position behind the counter.

I closed my eyes and took a deep breath, willing myself to calm the hell down. When I heard the door scrape open, my stomach lurched again. I took another breath and looked behind me. Dr. Cooper was standing in the doorway, "disguised" in a baseball cap, sunglasses, a ratty T-shirt, and ripped jeans. Actually, he looked nothing like himself. I couldn't imagine those clothes belonged to him.

He strode over to the table and took the seat across from me. Taking my clammy, shaking hands, he said, "Ellie, thank you so much for meeting me. I think I'm in a lot of trouble here. Mother said the police took a rifle from Father's gun collection as evidence and that they're watching our house. Gianna called to tell me that they're also inquiring at school as to my whereabouts. I'm scared." Taking a fearful glance around the room, he whispered, "And I think I'm being set up."

"Set up?"

The wheels in my head started turning. For my money, someone else trying to pin Vasti's murder on Dr. Cooper was a lot more plausible than him being a killer. I needed to get this information out of him before Baxter's team swooped in and arrested him because he would likely clam up in interrogation on the advice of his lawyer. I had to buy some time so I could talk to him. Getting out of my chair, I threw my arms around him and gave him a long hug. While I was doing so, I held up five fingers and mouthed to Baxter, "Give me five minutes."

Baxter shook his head and mouthed, "No."

"Five minutes," I pleaded silently. Out loud to Dr. Cooper, I asked, "Who would want to set you up for murder?" I raised my eyebrows and gave Baxter a meaningful look.

Grimacing, Baxter nodded his head. He went through a door behind the counter, I assumed to call off the dogs so I could have my five minutes. I released my hold on Dr. Cooper and sat down in my chair. Baxter appeared back at his post, his expression stony. It was clear that he didn't appreciate me changing the game plan.

Slumping in his seat, Dr. Cooper took off his sunglasses. "I hate to say this, but I think it could be Tyler. I can't believe my own cousin would do such a thing, but..."

"But what? Why do you think it's Tyler? I mean, sure, he's a snake, but why would he want to do something like this to you?" My voice wavered as I spoke. I hoped he didn't notice.

He sighed. "I think it has something to do with my father. Mother says he may have to pull out of the election over this. After last night's news report of the police searching my parents' home, the party is putting pressure on him to withdraw from the race. Democratic candidates have enough trouble getting elected in this red state without the stigma of a murder investigation. I think Father's opponent is trying to ruin our good name, and even worse, he's using my own cousin to do his dirty work. Evidently Tyler's loyalties lie with his employer instead of with his family."

I could see the logic in that. Flicking my eyes at Baxter, I could tell he was considering it as well. To Dr. Cooper, I replied, "It makes sense, but why not just honey trap your dad or even lie about an affair or something? That's an easy one, and no one would have had to die. Besides, after any bombshell is dropped, it doesn't matter if it's true or not. The damage is already done."

Shaking his head, he said, "All politicians cheat on their wives. It's not news. And it's not grounds for pulling out of a race if you have an otherwise positive image." He looked at me quizzically. "You don't look well, and you don't seem quite like yourself. Is something wrong, Ellie?"

He was on to me. Panic began to bubble up inside me again. I locked eyes with Baxter. I heard him utter, "Go, now."

Dr. Cooper's eyes grew wide. He turned to look behind him, but before he could even get up from his chair, all hell broke loose. Baxter vaulted over the counter, grabbed Dr. Cooper, and slammed him to the ground as uniformed deputies, led by Jason Sterling, began pouring into the tiny coffeeshop from the front and back doors. I pressed myself up against the wall. I couldn't bring myself to look at Dr. Cooper as Sterling read him his Miranda rights and escorted him out of the building.

After the last of the deputies filed out of the cramped eating area, I slid down the wall into a sitting position on the floor. I was mentally, emotionally, and physically drained. Baxter had hung back. He came over and sat down beside me.

Giving me a nudge, he said, "You did great, except maybe for the part where you went off book and decided to make the entire Hamilton County Sheriff's Department wait while you had a chat with a murderer."

Rolling my eyes, I replied, "Really? So you didn't want some admissible, candid information straight from the horse's mouth?"

He scoffed, "Not if it was him trying to pin the murder on some random killer off the street. I've got evidence on Cooper. I don't need to waste my time chasing down everyone with a grudge against the former mayor."

"Not everyone. Just Tyler Harris. He's a piece of work. Trust me—I've met the guy. And would you put it past any politician to make his campaign manager monkey go out and try to pin a murder on his opponent's son?"

"That's a stretch. Unless some kind of evidence drops into my lap, I'm going with Cooper. I'm sorry he's your friend. But you know as well as I do, the evidence speaks for itself." He got up and pulled me up with him. "Now go to work like nothing happened. I'll see you this afternoon."

13

I was a walking zombie. Barely managing to stay awake as I drove home, I stepped through my front door and was immediately peppered with kisses by an excited little boy and his excited big dog.

"Auntie Ellie, you've been gone *forever*! I missed you!" Nate cried, clinging to my neck.

"I'm sorry, sweetie. I had to work all night. I missed you, too," I said, feeling a glimmer of happiness in my otherwise shitty day. I wanted nothing more than to cuddle up with my nephew and sleep for the next three days, but I wasn't going to allow myself to even sit down for fear of falling asleep and never waking up.

He pulled back from me. "You smell funny."

Yet another thing I didn't miss from my criminalist days—coming home smelling like a crime scene. "I'm sure I do. So, now Auntie Ellie needs to go take a shower and then head back to work again."

"What about breakfast? Mommy says everyone has to eat breakfast," he said.

I smiled. "Can you pack me breakfast to go?"

His eyes lit up. "Yeah, I can!"

As Nate zoomed into the kitchen, Rachel came out and said, "Hey, Sis. You look rough."

Frowning at her, I said, "Thanks."

"Seriously though, are you okay? I thought you said you'd never work another case after..."

"I know. Like I said when we talked last night, this is a one-time thing. Jayne asked me to do her a favor. Unfortunately, it's going to take up a lot of my time for the foreseeable future."

She smiled. "Just don't overdo it. You get grouchy if you don't get your rest."

"Understatement of the year," I said as I stumbled to the bathroom.

A hot shower made me feel somewhat human again, as did looking through Nate's bag of "breakfast" he made for me—a few loose gummy bears and a still-frozen waffle. However, I drove halfway to Carmel before remembering I'd left the swabs of the unknown soil substance back at the station. After speeding all the way back to Noblesville and then to campus, I had to sprint from my car to the science building so I wouldn't be late for my first class. There was no way I was going to make it through the day without a nap. I had my date with Rob tonight, and I didn't want to be so tired that I wasn't good company.

I could tell from the confused looks on my students' faces that I wasn't making a damn bit of sense in class. I couldn't remember what I'd said, but I knew it couldn't have been coherent. Finally, someone spoke up.

A girl in the front row asked, "Professor Matthews, are you okay? You look, like, hung over or something."

I forced a smile. "Thanks for your concern, and I apologize if I'm not making sense. I had a...an unforeseen...family issue occur yesterday, and I wasn't able to get any sleep last night. I'm fine, but I'm exhausted." It wasn't exactly a lie because I thought of Jayne as family, and because of her request, I'd had no sleep. Normally, when the word "family" was thrown into a vague comment like that, people normally didn't press the issue.

But today wasn't a normal day. Another student raised his hand and asked, "Does it have anything to do with Dr. Cooper being arrested for killing Vasti? It's all over the news."

I closed my eyes. The official news was out. When a high-profile crime was committed, the Sheriff's Department always got pressure from county officials and town mayors to rush to catch the suspect so they could assure citizens that the streets were safe again. I was sure the second Dr. Cooper was arrested, Jayne was expected to call a press conference to announce that the alleged killer had been caught. I hadn't had time to watch any television this morning, not that I'd wanted to. This breaking news story would pre-empt local programming for a big chunk of the day.

My heart aching, I managed to say, "Only the police know the particulars of that...incident. For us to try to discuss it would mean we're doing nothing but gossiping, and that is the least productive and most damaging thing we could do. Don't forget that a suspect isn't guilty just because he's been arrested. Guilt is decided at trial by a judge and jury. Not on this campus."

A rumble went through the class, and since we only had fifteen minutes left, I ended my lesson early. There was no way I could field another question like that.

After dismissing my students, I went off in search of Rich Porter. I found him in his chemistry lab, frowning at a beaker filled with a bubbling green liquid, his graying hair sticking up in his signature spiky, mad-scientist style. Infamous for his hobby of experimenting with dangerous chemical reactions, most of the time the man had no eyebrows.

"Hey, Rich," I said. "I brought you those samples we talked about earlier."

He glanced up at me. "You mean when you woke me up out of my beauty sleep?"

"Right. Sorry about that."

"You look like you didn't get much beauty sleep, yourself."

"Is it that bad?" I asked, hurrying to the mirror over his handwashing sink. "Ooh," I groaned as I took in the dark circles under my eyes, my pale complexion, and my red, glassy eyes. My hair even looked strange because I was too out of it this morning to style it properly. I was a fright.

"So what am I analyzing for you, exactly?" he asked.

"It's some kind of soil or dust I got off two shoeprints. I need you to determine if it's the same substance on both swabs. I also need to know what it's composed of so I can decide which chemical reagent to put on one of the prints to get it to show up better. Dirt isn't all the same, you know."

"I do know," he said, accepting the container of swabs from me.

"I need you to sign this chain of custody form. Anything happens to these swabs while they're in your possession, and I'll have you thrown in the pokey," I joked.

He gave me a withering look. "I'd like to see you try." After signing the form with a flourish, he said, "So I guess you're not going to tell me what case you're working on."

"You guess right."

Rich shook his head. "The only thing I don't like about working with law enforcement is that I can't brag about working with law enforcement. I'm sure there's a great story behind these swabs, but I'll never know what it is."

"Trust me—the less you know, the better." I wished I didn't know so much about what had happened in the last week. Even more so, I wished I hadn't seen the things I'd seen.

"Hey, did you hear? They arrested Dudley this morning for Vasti Marais's murder. Holy shit. I couldn't believe it when I saw it on the news. You think you know a person..."

I shrugged. "I heard some students talking about it."

"Wait a minute," he said, eyeing me. "You're working with the Sheriff's office on a case. You already knew, didn't you?"

"For the record, I'm not working on that particular case. Look, I'm sorry I can't tell you more. I appreciate you running the tests for me. Can you give me a shout when you're done?" Not wanting to have to dodge any more questions, I made for the door.

"Will do. And get some sleep. You look like hell," he called after me.

I had nearly an hour until my next class, so I headed to my office to do just that. Closing my blinds and locking my door so I wouldn't be disturbed, I lay down behind my desk and fell asleep the moment my head hit the hard floor. After what seemed like only a few seconds, an incessant pounding on my door jolted me awake. So much for not being disturbed.

"I know you're in there, Matthews! I can see your feet!" yelled a bitchy voice. Gianna.

I must not have closed the blinds as well as I'd thought. I sat up too fast, my head throbbing from my much-needed rest being yanked away from me.

"Open the door!" she shouted, rattling the doorknob.

I stumbled over to the door and wrenched it open. "What do you want?"

She looked me up and down with an evil smirk. "Just as I thought. Sleeping off a bender, are we? I have it on good authority that you came to work hung over this morning." She gave me a condescending smile. "From the look in your eyes, you still might even be drunk."

Every ounce of my being wanted to slug her in the face. I settled for some verbal abuse. "Piss off, Gianna. I'm not hung over, and you can go to hell." I tried to slam the door in her face, but she was too fast.

Planting a manicured hand on the door to keep it open, she continued, "Oh, well, maybe your eyes are red because you've been crying over your dear sweet Dudley getting arrested for murder. Ha! I knew that cheating bastard would get what was coming to him."

My brain was foggy, but I was able to latch onto the one interesting thing she said. "Cheating bastard? Wait. Did you two go out?" I asked, wrinkling my nose in disgust.

Gianna laughed, her expression turning haughty. "You didn't know you were getting my sloppy seconds, did you? Your boyfriend and I had a quiet fling last semester."

Way too tired for this, I sighed. "Damn, woman. Get your facts straight. He's not my boyfriend, and he never was. A man and a woman can be friends without it turning sexual."

"Not with Dudley it can't. And don't try to tell me *you* of all people got the job as Head of Operations for his new research facility without giving him a little something in return."

"You're delusional. Maybe you should go over to the psych department and have your head examined."

Glaring at me, she spat, "Just wait until he cheats on you with a student. Then we'll see how you feel about it."

Realization dawned on me. "Whoa. He cheated on you with Vasti Marais, didn't he?"

Her face reddened. Plucking a tiny wisp of lint off her lab coat in order to avert her eyes from me, she said, "The little hussy. Karma kicked *both* their asses."

I needed to call Baxter. Gianna was guilty of something—that was for sure. "Okay, Crazy. You have five seconds to get out of my office before *I* kick *your* ass."

Startled, she took a step back. I slammed the door and locked it. Grabbing my phone, I dialed Baxter's number.

When he answered, I blurted, "I think I know who may have killed Vasti Marais."

"Me too. I just got done interrogating him," he replied.

"Nick, come on. Hear me out."

"Shoot." I could hear the smile in his voice.

"That was inappropriate."

"I thought it was right on target."

Groaning, I continued, "As I was saying, one of my fellow professors just came into my office, and she was acting completely insane. She told me that she'd been in a relationship with Dr. Cooper last semester and that he had cheated on her with Vasti Marais. She said that karma had kicked both their asses."

After a pause, Baxter asked, "That's it?"

"The woman is unstable, and I think she's hiding something!"

"You don't sound like yourself. Maybe you should try to take a nap."

"I'm *fine*."

"Clearly. You know you're not working the Marais murder case, right?"

I huffed, "Yes, but—"

"So you know I can't discuss it with you."

"Oh, I see what's going on here. You can't discuss the case with me, but it's okay for me to be the bait so you can catch your suspect."

Sighing, he said, "Ellie, come on. You know the rules."

"Yes, but I also know that you're someone who goes above and beyond to make sure that justice gets served."

After a long pause, he grumbled, "What's her name?"

"Gianna Alessi. You'll find her in the science building."

"Okay, I'll speak with her. I have to head over to Ashmore this afternoon to talk to the newspaper staff, anyway."

"Thanks, Nick."

"Don't thank me yet. I was planning on having you help me interview them since you may know some of them. You got Tristan Sellers to talk to you. I figure you may be able to get them to open up as well."

"I'd be happy to help you, except that I have about a thousand fingerprints to examine and upload into AFIS. I don't have enough time in the day to do both."

"You're not getting out of it that easily. I'll get someone else to do the grunt work so you'll have time to do the important stuff."

I breathed a sigh of relief. I was dreading that task, especially with how tired I was. Staring at a computer screen for hours was sure to have me falling asleep on the job. "In that case, I'm all yours. My last class gets over at two."

"I'll be waiting for you at your office."

No sooner than I had hung up with Baxter, Samantha started beating on my office door. "Hey, Ellie! Open up!" I opened the door for her, and she swooped in, squealing, "I don't know where to start! Oh, wait. I *do* know where to start—with that hottie you stood up last night. What could have possessed you to blow him off? You're lucky I didn't snag him for myself!"

Mustering a smile, I said, "It's nice to hear you approve of Rob, but I had a good reason..." I took a breath. "The Sheriff asked me to consult on a case, and time got away from me."

"I heard you cancelled your last class yesterday. I was going to ask you why, but you were nowhere to be found. Is it a big case?" Her eyes bulged out. "Is it Eli Vanover's *murder* case?"

I nodded, hoping she would take the hint and not ask me a thousand questions.

She wrinkled her nose. "You can't talk about it, can you?"

"No, sorry."

Samantha sighed dramatically. "Oh, well. Can we talk about the fact that Dudley got *arrested* this morning?"

"You can. I probably shouldn't."

She scoffed, "You're no fun. You need to quit this police nonsense so I have someone to talk to again."

"You could talk to Gianna. She seems to have a definite opinion about Dr. Cooper's arrest."

"*Dr.* Cooper? Are we being formal now?"

"I thought it best to distance myself from him."

Nodding, she said, "It's probably for the best, given your situation. What does our darling Gianna have to say about the matter?"

"Well, evidently she was seeing him last semester."

She shrugged. "Old news."

My eyebrows shot up. "She said they were keeping it a secret. How did you know?"

"Rich told me."

I frowned. "Oh. Why didn't anyone tell me?"

"You're tight with Dudley. I figured you already knew. What else did she say?"

"She said he cheated on her with...a student." I didn't want to be the one to bring up Vasti's name.

"Shocker," she said, sarcasm dripping from her voice. "Dudley nailing a student? Also old news."

It was as if I didn't know Dr. Cooper at all. "Oh. I've got nothing, then." I glanced at the clock and hopped out of my seat. "Sorry, I have a class in five minutes."

Giving me an apologetic smile, she said, "Sweetie, you'd better find a mirror first. You look like you've been hit by a truck."

"Maybe I should put a bag over my head and put everyone out of their misery."

She came over and gave me a crushing hug. "I know this has to be hard on you. I'm here for you, so if you want to get together and...*not* talk about anything, just say the word."

I laughed. "Thanks, Sam."

After she left, I splashed some water on my face and downed a soft drink, then began my next Criminalistics 1 class. "Okay, guys, we're going to be talking about handwriting analysis today. It's not used as much nowadays as it was in the past because most of the corresponding we do is type-written, mainly through email and texting. We don't write letters anymore, but we do often jot down notes, which can be useful clues in solving crimes. For that reason, we as criminalists need to keep handwriting analysis in our skill set. If you'll turn your attention to the board, you'll find several handwriting samples." I gestured to the dry erase board behind me.

"The sample on the left is my handwriting. Of the three samples on the right, two are forgeries and one was written by me. Decide which of the three matches our original sample, and then we'll discuss how you came to your conclusion."

I moved to the side of the room so the students would have an unobstructed view of the board. As they were studying the handwriting samples, I was studying them. Many of them seemed on edge, and some were nervously flicking their eyes back and forth between me and the board. Sooner or later, someone was going to ask a question I didn't want to answer, most likely about Dr. Cooper. Hoping my lesson would hold their attention enough to keep the questions at bay for a while, I went back to stand in front of them.

"All right. Raise your hand if you think Sample Number One matches my sample." Several hands went up. "Raise your hand if you think Sample Number Two matches my sample." The majority of the class raised their hands. "Raise your hand if you think Sample Number Three matches my sample." Two students raised their hands. "Most of you were right. Sample Two is my handwriting. Sample One belongs to Dr. Jordan, and Sample Three belongs to Professor Porter. Now we'll discuss what helped you distinguish the similarities between my two writing samples and discount the other samples. Anyone care to share their thoughts?"

Not a single hand went up.

I sighed. "You don't want to talk about handwriting, do you?"

They shook their heads and shifted uncomfortably in their seats.

I walked around to the front of my desk and leaned against it, trying for a casual demeanor. "What do you want to talk about?"

Every student in the room raised his or her hand.

At some point we had to address the elephant in the room, and I couldn't put it off forever. "Please keep in mind that I'm not allowed to speak about Vasti Marais's murder and I will not tolerate gossip about anything that has happened in the past week."

A few of them lowered their hands. I called on a young man in the front row who I thought would be likely to have a valid question.

He asked, "With Dr. Cooper being arrested, will plans for the research facility go forward?"

I hadn't given any thought to that. "That would be a decision Dr. Cooper would have to make, but I'm thinking with everything going on at present, plans are on hold."

A girl blurted out, "Should we be afraid? Do you think there will be more murders?" Several other students began nodding, their expressions frightened.

I hesitated. I didn't want to cause a panic, but there was no way of knowing if the killer would strike again if we had no clue who the killer was. "Um...there's no reason to believe that you're in danger. I think you guys should go about your lives and not be scared all the time, because that's no way to live. However, you also shouldn't take any unnecessary risks, either. Always go places in groups and stay alert to your surroundings, especially at night. Lock your doors and carry a can of pepper spray. Basically do what you should be doing anyway to keep yourself safe on campus."

I called on another student I could count on to have a decent question.

"Will Dr. Cooper ever be allowed to come back to teach? He's one of my favorite professors," he said.

With the backlash Dr. Cooper had been enduring lately both from the protests against the body farm and the accusations in the *Ashmore Voice*, I hadn't considered the students who were still on his side. They had to be devastated by the news of his arrest.

"Well, you all know that an arrest neither proves guilt nor equals a conviction. He could be exonerated and everything could go back to the way it was." Except that he'd never trust me again after the stunt I pulled on him this morning.

A few of the students frowned. One girl said, "Vasti and Eli are still dead, so *nothing* can go back to the way it was."

I felt like I was in danger of being led into a trap. "I meant back to the way it was with Dr. Cooper's job, nothing more. Please don't read anything into my answers."

With tears in her eyes, another student said, "How can you be so dispassionate about everything that's gone on? You found Vasti's body, and one of your fellow professors did it. How are you not a basket case right now?" Several of her friends murmured in agreement.

I'd had enough. "Let's get something straight—all of you," I snapped. "Until Dr. Cooper is tried and convicted in a court of law, *he is innocent*. Get that through your heads. As criminalists, you can *never* lay blame. It's not your job, and if you show any bias whatsoever, your evidence could be deemed inadmissible. You can have a mountain of rock-solid evidence against someone, or you can even watch someone commit a crime right in front of you, and they're still innocent until *proven* guilty. That's the law. If you can't deal with that part of the job—then get the hell out of forensics."

My students' eyes widened in shock, but I wasn't done.

"As for my supposed reaction to the events of this week—you don't know me. You've only dealt with me during class, where I have to put everything aside so I can do my job. When you're an adult, that's what you do. A little free advice—toughen the hell up. If you can't control your emotions, you'll never keep a job of any kind in forensics. And these four years of your life will have been a total waste."

The room was silent, and everyone's hands were down.

I walked around to the other side of the desk and opened my teacher's manual. "Our Q and A session is over. We're going to continue our discussion on handwriting analysis. Anyone who feels too emotional to participate—you know where the door is."

After the cathartic reprimand I delivered to my unsuspecting class and the full hour's worth of sleep I got during my lunch break, I was feeling well enough that I taught my third class of the day with no issues. My students actually listened to and participated in my handwriting analysis lesson and didn't ask any off-topic questions. I had to wonder if word had got around not to mess with me today. When I was finished, I headed for my office, and Baxter was there as promised.

"You look like I feel," he said, chuckling.

Dropping a stack of books and papers on my desk, I narrowed my eyes at him. "I wish people would quit telling me how shitty I look today." I was going to have to do a major makeover on myself so I didn't look like a complete troll for my date tonight.

He sobered. "I'm sorry. I work with guys all day. I forget you're a girl."

"Baxter..." I sighed. "I can't even..." I shook my head. "Just shut up."

"Right. So I talked to Dr. Alessi a few minutes ago. You were right—something is off with her, but I don't know that it has anything to do with the case. I think she's just crazy." He smiled. "She has some serious hate for you, though."

I still felt like she was hiding something, so I wasn't ready to cross her off my list yet. "Tell me something I don't know."

"Tad Ogelsby, Eli Vanover's roommate, has disappeared."

14

My jaw dropped. "What? Is he...?"

"Dead? I don't think so. I think he bolted. According to his RA, Ogelsby left late last night with a couple of bags. He has a vehicle registered on campus, which seems to be gone as well. It's not in any of the campus parking lots."

"That makes him look kind of guilty, don't you think?"

Baxter nodded. "That's why we're going to his dorm room to have a look around." He gestured to the big silver case and a black camera bag at his feet. "I brought everything you need."

I scrunched up my face. "Nick, I'm too tired to work another scene," I complained. "I'm sure to miss something important."

"I brought it just in case. Unless there's some sign of struggle, which I doubt, you may not even need it. I'm hoping to find some clue as to where he went, because we've tried all of his and his parents' contact numbers and received no response. I'm assuming his folks are hiding him. I want to know why." He picked up the case from the floor and shouldered the bulky camera bag. "Ready to go? I'll even carry your stuff for you."

"What a gentleman."

We headed outside into the afternoon sunlight. It had become muggy today—part of one last heat wave before it started cooling off for fall. Tad's dorm, Harris Hall (named after Tyler's family), was all the way across campus, so we had to hoof it a few blocks.

I felt Baxter staring at me, so I asked, "What?"

"I've been putting off telling you this...because I'm not sure how you're going to take it," he replied, seeming tense.

"I don't know how my day could get much worse. Out with it."

"Dudley Cooper wants to see you."

I blew out a breath.

"I told him no. It would cause all kinds of trouble if your name ended up on his visitor log."

Nodding, I said quietly, "I know." Regardless of what was proper, I felt like I'd abandoned Dr. Cooper and even turned on him when he needed me the most. Hating the fact that he was stuck in jail thanks to me, I changed the subject. "I forgot to ask—what about the murder weapon? Did Beck find any evidence on the jump rope?"

Baxter shook his head. "Only some partial fingerprints belonging to Vanover and Sellers, and they were smudged. If the killer touched it, he was wearing gloves."

"That's not helpful. How about Eli's clothes? Was there any cross-transfer on them?"

"There were some black cotton fibers, but you know you can't determine the source of cotton. It's too common. There was some blood, but it could be Vanover's or more of what was under his fingernails. So there was evidence, but it's likely a duplication of what we already had."

"Again, useless."

Smiling, he said, "Don't get discouraged. Solving cases wouldn't be nearly as fun if everything fell right into place."

We arrived at Harris Hall, happy to be out of the heat and humidity. After Baxter flashed his badge and his search warrant at the front desk, the dorm director showed us to Tad and Eli's room and let us in.

Baxter closed the door behind us and let out a low whistle. "Someone sure was in a hurry to get the hell out of town."

One side of the room looked like a bomb had gone off. Drawers were open, clothes were strewn everywhere, and there was a half-packed duffel bag on the bed. The other side of the room was neat enough for a boy's dorm room, probably because most of the items from the desk and dresser were missing. Eli had moved his essentials to Tristan's apartment but had left some things, intending to return to his dorm once the air had cleared between him and Tad.

I got the same overwhelmed feeling I'd had at Tristan's pigsty of an apartment. The aroma of the room didn't help, either. It smelled like dirty gym socks and moldy pizza. "Where do we even start? I don't think we're going to find anything in this mess."

Baxter got out the camera and handed it to me. "Has anyone ever told you that you're kind of grouchy when you're tired?"

I frowned at him and took the camera. As I always did, I started snapping wide-angle shots of the entire room, slowly making my way around and taking mid-range shots as well. There was nothing that seemed out of place or unusual to me, so I didn't mark anything as evidence or bother with close-ups. Baxter already had his gloves on and was pawing through Tad's drawers. I stopped taking photos of the room, thinking this search was a waste of time. However, since I was here, I decided to check Tad's shoe size for comparison purposes to the prints we'd found at the crime scene. He had an alibi for the time of Eli's murder, but in light of him skipping town, I felt it best to gather a little extra information. I made a note that he wore a size eleven.

I said, "If this kid packed a couple of bags and drove away in a panic, I'm thinking he didn't leave a detailed itinerary of his trip."

"I'm aware of that, and I'm not looking for an itinerary. I have a feeling that we're missing something about this kid."

Not wanting to discount one of Baxter's hunches, I got to work looking through Tad's desk. It was filled with normal desk stuff—pens, pencils, paper, highlighters, sticky notes, et cetera. There was a printer on the desk, but no laptop, which wasn't surprising. I also found several photos of Tad cozied up to a girl—Maddie from one of my Intro to Forensics classes.

Holding one of them up for Baxter to see, I said, "Looks like Tad may have a girlfriend. She's in one of my classes. Maddie Haynes."

Baxter made a note. "I'll have a chat with her. Surely the guy told his girlfriend where he was headed."

"His books seem to be missing. Maybe he went on a study retreat," I mused.

"I don't think it would be smart to skip class for a study retreat. Wouldn't that be counter-productive?"

"Probably."

"Hey, I found his secret stash," Baxter said, holding up a box he had retrieved from under the bed. "He's got all kinds of fun stuff—Adderall, vodka, condoms, porn, weed."

I snapped a picture of the contents of the box. "I thought boys used the Internet for porn these days."

He shrugged. "Not always."

I couldn't resist. "Where do you get *your* porn, Detective?"

Baxter ignored my comment, other than turning bright red. Holding up the bag of weed, he said, "The good news is I've got him on constructive possession. I'll reel him in with that and then make him talk."

"If you can find him."

"Oh, I'll find him," he replied.

"Since we're in here, do we have clearance to go through Eli's stuff?"

"Yes, we do."

I began snapping photos of Eli's side of the room. His cell, backpack, laptop, and books were nowhere to be found, which meant someone had to have them. Even though he'd been living at Tristan Sellers's apartment, those personal items were mysteriously missing from there as well, which made me wonder if something on his laptop could be the key to finding out who his killer was. It stood to reason that he wrote some of his news articles on it rather than trekking all the way over to the *Ashmore Voice* office every time he wanted to do some work. He may even have been downloading his vlog videos onto his laptop as well. We needed to see what was on it, but if the killer had it, we were screwed.

Baxter finished with Tad's side of the room and started going through Eli's desk. I went through his closet, which seemed to be about a quarter empty. His drawers were a mess, but there was nothing except clothes, socks, and underwear in them. I looked under his bed, but there were only a few stray socks and one shoe under there.

Frowning, I stood up. "Either this kid is a virginal teetotaler, or something's missing. I didn't find any contraband of any kind. Every college kid I've ever known has had something to hide from the RA."

"He probably took it with him to Sellers's apartment."

"We didn't find any of that kind of stuff there."

"Right, but we didn't go through every inch of the apartment, either. We were only focused on the crime scene, not on delving into someone's personal life. Besides, I don't think Vanover's contraband collection is going to give us any clues about his murder."

"True...but if he was into something shady or was hiding something, like information that could ruin someone's life, it might be in his stash." I had an idea. "Hang on." Taking out my phone, I called my sister.

"Hello?" she answered, sounding frazzled. I could hear Nate yelling in the background.

"Hey, Rach. What's going on with Nate?" I asked.

She growled. "He's throwing a tantrum because he doesn't want to take a nap. I have an exam tomorrow and need some d-a-m-n peace and quiet, so this has to happen. Can I call you back?"

I sighed. Normally when Rachel needed peace and quiet, I would take Nate and go to the park or nap with him so he would stay in bed. I was only twenty-four hours into this ordeal, and everything in my life was already suffering—my teaching job, my family, my dating life, and my overall health. These extra hours I was working had me stretched too thin.

"Let me talk to him," I said.

"I'll try anything."

My nephew came on the phone, sniffling and hiccupping. "Hello? Auntie Ellie?"

"Hi, sweet boy. I hear you don't want to take a nap for Mommy."

"Mommy yelled at me," he grumbled. I could imagine him giving Rachel the stink eye as we spoke, arms crossed and lower lip jutted out.

"I think I heard you yelling at Mommy, too. Were you yelling, buddy?"

He paused, and then said in a small voice, "Yes. A little."

"I'll tell you what—if you tell Mommy you're sorry and take a good nap for her, I'll bring you one of my special candies from school. You can have it tomorrow morning for breakfast."

Gasping, he said, "Really? Okay, Auntie Ellie!"

Rachel came back on. "I don't know what you said, but he's on his way to his room right now. Thanks. Hey, I heard Dr. Cooper was arrested this morning. Are you doing okay with all that?" I could hear the concern in her voice.

"Not really. I'm trying not to think about it."

"You know I'm here if you need me."

Even though she was ten years younger than I was, she was a wonderful sister and a great friend. Until the next couple of days were over, I didn't even have the time to sit down and talk to someone about my feelings. Plus, if I started thinking about Dr. Cooper rotting in a jail cell (thanks to me), I wouldn't be able to concentrate on what I needed to get done.

"Actually, I do need you. I need some gossip."

"You called me for gossip? Now I know there's something wrong with you."

I replied, "Ha, ha. I need to know the dirt on Eli Vanover. What was he into? Anything shady?" Rachel had worked at the *Ashmore Voice* for a semester her freshman year and hated it. She knew Eli from back then, and she didn't care for him.

"You mean besides filming people when they're not looking?" she snapped.

I winced. "I take it you got caught with your pants down?" That last statement earned me a questioning eyebrow from Baxter.

"No, nothing like that. I was bitching about Dr. Halloran ripping my last research paper to shreds. Eli caught it, and Dr. Halloran saw it online. He was none too pleased."

"Oh, well. It's not like he can do anything to you for expressing your opinion. Halloran's a dick, anyway. Everyone thinks so. If he bothers you again, make fun of his comb-over. It makes him cry."

She laughed. "And that is why I love you. You always give such grown-up advice."

"I try. So, is there any more dirt on Eli? Was he into drugs? Prostitutes? Gerbils? Anything I can use?" I got another look from Baxter.

"The gerbil thing wouldn't surprise me," she mused. "I do know that he was always trying to push Adderall on the staff at the *Voice* so they'd get their articles done faster. He always had a ton of it in his desk. He tried to get me to take it once, but I grossed him out by explaining how it would get into my breast milk and hurt Nate. He never offered it to me again. That's all I know, other than the fact that he was a total asshole."

"Maybe they shouldn't let you give the eulogy at his funeral."

"Yeah, probably not."

"I'll let you get to studying. I don't know when I'll be home tonight. Don't wait up."

"Ooh, is your sexy rent-a-cop going to keep you out late?" Lovely as she was, my sister never passed up a chance to needle me about my love life.

"I told you—he owns his own security firm. He's not a rent-a-cop. Well, maybe he kind of is, but not in a lame way," I said defensively. "I meant I might be working late."

"Do you think your rent-a-cop will try to show you his taser tonight? Or maybe he'll try to cuff you. Wait, they don't let rent-a-cops have cuffs, do they?"

I'd had enough. "I hope Nate wakes up and ruins your study time."

"Wow. Bitchy much?"

"Love you, too." I hung up, turning around to find Baxter trying to keep a straight face as he dug through an overflowing trash can.

"Tell me that wasn't your idea of detective work."

"It's a hell of a lot better than sifting through someone's underwear drawer. I was talking to my sister. She knew Eli, and she gave me something we might be able to use."

"If you start talking about gerbils, I'm out."

"Ha, ha. He was the *Ashmore Voice's* main supplier of Adderall. According to Rachel, he kept it in his desk at the paper."

He shrugged. "If he was getting the meds from a street dealer instead of a friend with a script, that could be a decent explanation for his murder. We'll go through his desk when we go to the newspaper office. I think we're pretty well done here."

"Good," I said, stripping off my gloves. "Going through a boy's dorm room is no better than sifting through a dumpster."

"I thought crime scene investigators loved dumpster diving."

"Is that why you detectives always try to push it off on us?"

He grinned, gathering up our gear. We left the room exactly as we had found it and headed over to the *Voice* office. It was in the Ashmore Student Center, where the dining halls, student life offices, bookstore, and campus radio station were housed. It was a newer building, mostly glass and steel, with fewer Gothic touches than most on campus.

The *Voice* office was about the size of two classrooms, crammed with desks and short cubicles. Private offices lined one wall. Several students were hunched over computers, typing away. Other than the clacking of keys and the occasional chair creaking, the room was silent.

Baxter walked up to the nearest desk and showed his badge to the kid sitting there. "I'm Detective Baxter with the Hamilton County Sheriff's Office, and this is Ms. Matthews. We need to ask everyone on staff a few questions."

The boy's eyes widened. He cleared his throat. "Questions? Is it...is it about Eli?"

"Yes. We'd like to use one of your offices for privacy as we speak to each one of you individually."

"I'll get Al. He's the one in charge at the moment." The kid hurried off and disappeared into one of the offices.

Baxter leaned toward me and murmured, "Is there a weird vibe in here, or is it just me?"

"There is. But honestly, the whole campus is giving off the same vibe." I sighed. "These poor kids don't know what to think. There have been two murders of two well-known students within a week, and one of their professors has been arrested for one of them. Everyone is sad, scared, confused, and even kind of...excited, for lack of a better word. Living on campus is like living at Disneyland—it's like they're in this weird bubble where everything is perfect and safe and politically correct. They don't know how to process real-world situations."

"That's an astute observation, Dr. Freud."

"Shut up."

The boy Baxter had spoken to came out of the office trailed by another boy I recognized from one of my classes a couple of years ago. I couldn't remember his name, but I did remember that he'd dropped out of the criminal justice program and changed his major to communications. It seemed that communications was a good fit for kids who didn't know what the hell they wanted to be if they ever grew up.

He approached us. "Hey, Professor Matthews." He stuck out his hand to Baxter. "I'm Albert Nishimura. My friends call me Al. I'm sort of in charge since Tad bailed and Eli...um...you know. You guys need to talk to the staff?"

"Yes," Baxter replied. "Can we use one of your offices?"

"Sure thing, brah. Who do you want to start with?"

Baxter flicked his eyes my way when Al called him "brah" but otherwise didn't react. He replied, "Why don't we start with you?"

"No probs," Al said, showing us into his office. After we sat down, Al smiled at me. "Yo, Professor, did you ever get the blood off that dress of yours?"

I hesitated, taken aback by the question. Then I thought back to that night. I vaguely remembered Al being one of the onlookers during the blood incident. "Um, no. It was pretty much a total loss."

He chuckled. "I'm sorry about the dress, but that had to have been the funniest freakin' thing I've ever seen when you slammed that bucket down on Justin's head and started smacking it."

A slow smile spread over Baxter's face. "I think I need to hear more of this story."

15

Al was full-on laughing now. "Oh, you should have been there, brah. It was epic. There she was, smokin' hot in that pink dress. Then my dipshit friend Justin runs up and dumps this whole bucket of pig's blood all over her. He thinks she's just some random fancy lady from the party, but then he realizes who it is and how screwed he is." He gestured to me. "Steam is pouring out her ears, and she grabs Justin by the collar and starts ripping him a new asshole. The rest of us are like freaking out, because the Prof here is usually pretty chill."

Covering his grin with his hand, Baxter replied, "Yeah, she doesn't get worked up often, but when she does, watch out."

I glared at both of them, but it didn't stop them from going right on with their conversation.

"I know, right? So then, she takes the bucket from Justin and shoves it down onto his head. He starts crying like a little bitch, and then..." Al had to stop here because he couldn't stop giggling. "And then she starts slapping the side of the bucket, which only makes him cry harder. It was freakin' hilarious. After that, we all bailed. I think she called us little bitches or some shit like that as we were running away."

Baxter was trying to hold his laughter in so hard he was shaking. I kicked his shin under the desk, and he lost it. He started cracking up, and it took him a good minute to get it out of his system. Needless to say, I was not amused.

Wiping the tears from his eyes, Baxter said, "That was a great story." He turned to me. "Your version was not nearly so interesting."

"I hate you so much right now," I said to Baxter under my breath, which only caused him to smile bigger. I said to Al, "We'd like to know if Eli was mixed up in anything dangerous. Was he still supplying Adderall to the *Voice* staff?"

Al's eyes widened, and he shifted in his chair. "Whoa. That's...um..."

Baxter said, "I'm not a narco cop. I'm only trying to find out who murdered Eli Vanover. If he was dealing, that's something I need to know."

Grimacing, Al said, "Yeah, Eli is, I mean was, our hookup for Adderall. Sometimes...sometimes he had other stuff, too."

"What kind of other stuff?"

"Weed and Molly."

It was one thing to befriend a college kid with a legitimate Adderall prescription and convince him to pass on the drugs to you, but dealing marijuana and MDMA landed Eli in a whole new category. If he was selling street drugs, he had to have an external source, and that meant he was consorting with some people who were way out of his league.

"Who's supplying him?" Baxter asked.

Al shook his head. "He never said. The only thing I know is that he always had a full stock on Fridays."

"Is it in his desk?" I asked.

"He usually had some in there, yeah."

Baxter said, "We'll need to go through his desk before we leave. One more thing. Eli was known for his inflammatory articles and his invasive videos. Did anyone ever get pissed off over one of them and threaten him?"

Al snickered. "Only all the time, brah. He got hate mail out the ass, and people were always stopping him on campus and bitching him out."

"Did any of them ever get physical?"

"Yeah, he's had a couple of black eyes over the years."

"How about recently?"

"Eli and Tad went at it over a story earlier this week. It got pretty intense around here."

"What was the story about?"

"Hell if I know. Eli didn't want it leaking out before he had a chance to break it. Tad was the only other one who knew anything about it."

"Tad left campus. Do you know where he might have gone?" Baxter asked.

Shrugging, Al said, "No. Sorry, brah. Tad and I aren't so tight."

"Thanks for your time, Al."

"Yes, thank you, Al," I said. "Can we look through Eli's office now?"

"Knock yourself out, Professor. It's two doors down."

Baxter and I found Eli's office and went inside, closing the door after us. He went around behind the desk and started opening drawers. The bottom right drawer was locked, a sure sign there was something interesting in it.

"Damn," he said, jiggling the handle. He began rifling through the other drawers again, looking for a key. Finding none, he slammed the top drawer shut in frustration.

I didn't want to do this, mainly so Baxter wouldn't have more ammunition to make fun of me, but in the interest of time, I caved. "Are there two paper clips in the drawer?"

He wrinkled his forehead. "Yeah," he answered, producing two paper clips from the top drawer and handing them to me.

Without a word, I unbent one end of each paperclip and fashioned two crude lock picking devices—one rake and one tension tool. Shooing Baxter away from the desk, I said, "You never saw me do this," and got to work on the lock. I inserted the tension tool into the lock, turning it slightly to the right. Once that was in place, I inserted the rake tool and began scraping it against the lock's pins. After several scrapes, the pins all bounced around and reached the shear line. Then I used the tension tool to slowly turn the lock. I pulled the drawer open and stepped back for Baxter to have a look.

He kept his eyes on me for a long moment, causing me to start fidgeting under his gaze. "Where in the hell did you learn how to do that?"

I blushed. "In high school, um...my friends and I would steal tests from teachers' desks and sell them. It was my job to pick the locks."

His mouth twitched. "And now *you're* a teacher."

"The irony is not lost on me."

"Just when I think I have you all figured out, you throw me a curve ball."

"Things I've seen and done would curl your hair. I really should have been put in juvie," I admitted.

Shaking his head, he took out the camera and shot a couple photos of the drawer. He then began taking items out, including several packs of cigarettes, a silver flask, and two Altoids tins. He opened the tins and, no surprise, they were filled with small orange pills instead of mints.

"There's Eli's Adderall, right where your sister said it would be," said Baxter, setting the tins down on the desk to take photos.

I looked over his shoulder into the drawer. "What, no 'weed and Molly' like Al said?"

"Not in here."

"Anything else incriminating?"

"Nothing."

"How about this computer?" I asked, pointing to the computer on the desk. "Can we take it to the nerds in Cyber and have them paw through it? Maybe they'll find a shocking article or video Eli hadn't released yet. I want to know what that fight was about."

Baxter studied the back of the tower. "This is property of Ashmore College. I'll need a separate warrant for it. Go give Tad's office a once-over while I make the call."

I went next door to Tad Ogelsby's office and began looking around. Unlike his dorm room, his office was neat enough. I took photos of a few notes on his desk, but again, nothing jumped out at me as a lead on where he'd gone. Tad's desk drawers were all unlocked, but they only held a benign mix of office supplies and snacks.

Baxter stuck his head in and said, "We've got more staff to talk to. Let's do it in Vanover's office. Being in there might get them off-balance and make them blurt something out."

"That's twisted, Detective. I didn't think you had it in you," I said, impressed. Baxter was such a straight shooter. I was surprised he would use psychological tactics.

We interviewed student after student, but they all said the same thing: Eli and Tad had a fight over a story, but no one else knew what it was about. They also all corroborated that Eli was the resident drug dealer, and that he dealt in more than just "study enhancers."

I drummed my fingers against the desk, annoyed that the last staff member was taking his dear sweet time coming to Eli's office.

"What's your problem? You in a hurry or something?" Baxter asked.

It was nearly four, which meant my date was in two hours. I had to finish up here, meet Rich to get the results from my swabs, and drive back to Noblesville to meet with the coroner for a post-autopsy briefing. After I finished all that, I had a mountain of work ahead of me in the lab. I really didn't have time for a date, but it was the only thing I actually *wanted* to do this evening. There was no way to get my running around done in time to meet Rob at my office at six o'clock.

"You know that date I missed last night?" I said to Baxter.

"Yeah."

"Well, we rescheduled for tonight, and I'm running out of hours in the day."

He shrugged. "So call it off."

"That's the thing—I don't want to call it off."

I decided against phoning Rob and having to verbally explain my problem in such an agitated state. I shot him a text instead, asking nicely if we could change our meeting place to Noblesville and push the time an hour later.

"Is this the date with the rent-a-cop?" he asked.

I gave him a dangerous glare.

Holding his hands up, he said, "Just making conversation. Don't kill me."

The last staff member walked in. It was the nervous kid we had talked to when we first arrived.

"Have a seat, Trent," said Baxter, checking the kid's name off his list.

Trent sat down slowly, not taking his eyes off Baxter and me.

"How long have you worked for the *Voice*?" Baxter asked.

"I'm...um...just starting my second year," replied Trent.

"And how well do you know Eli Vanover?"

He looked a little embarrassed. "Pretty well. He kind of thought of me as his unofficial assistant. He said he'd groom me for the editor's job if I, uh...took care of his busy work."

Baxter sat up straighter in his chair. "What kind of things did you do for him?"

"Oh, you know...running out for coffee or picking up dinner, answering his emails, filling out forms, taking his calls, um...writing his research papers... Things that assistants do."

"Trent," I said gently, "Eli shouldn't have asked you to write his research papers for him. That's not the work of an assistant—it's cheating. You didn't have to do that for him."

His shoulders slumped. "But I thought it would help free him up to do important things, like writing hard-hitting articles and exposing the truth." Eli had done a number on this kid.

"Do you know if there was a story he was working on or had published recently that would have made someone angry enough to kill him?" asked Baxter.

Trent flicked his eyes down. "There was one, but he wasn't ready to run it yet. He had a video of a conversation, but he said he needed to do a little investigative journalism to round out the story. He said he felt like he was sitting on the biggest news the *Ashmore Voice* had ever reported."

"Bigger than a professor being arrested for the murder of a student?" asked Baxter in disbelief. "Does this news have to do with the Vasti Marais murder?"

"He wouldn't say."

"Where is the video?" asked Baxter.

Trent blew out a nervous breath. "I don't know, but I do know he was keeping it safe. I think he had it stored on a flash drive because he didn't want someone hacking his phone or computer and scooping him."

"Had that happened before?"

"The hacking? Yeah, it happened once last semester when he pissed off a few of the computer science majors. They hacked the crap out of his laptop and posted his personal notes and article ideas all over the school website. They got in big trouble, but he also caught a lot of hell about inventing stories that weren't true. That's when he got paranoid and started saving everything to a flash drive."

"Where did he keep the flash drive?" I asked.

He shrugged. "I don't know that, either. Sorry." Wiping sweat from his brow, he asked, "Can I go now?"

I didn't like how squirrely this kid was being, and from the expression on Baxter's face, neither did he.

"We're almost finished," Baxter said, getting up to go over and stand in front of Trent. "We know that Eli was dealing."

Trent squirmed in his chair, but didn't say a word.

Baxter crossed his arms and stared the kid down. "I need to know where he was getting his drugs. Who's his supplier?"

Trent shrank back in his chair. "I...I don't..."

Leaning down and placing a hand on each arm of Trent's chair, Baxter growled, "You know something. You can either tell me here or down at the station after I book you for obstruction of justice."

Trent was either about to cry or mess his pants. "I can't..."

I was impressed by Baxter's bad cop routine. He had this kid ready to crack. In one swift motion, he tipped Trent's chair back and caught him just before he hit the floor. Trent was stuck in the chair, flailing from the sudden loss of balance.

Wild-eyed, he wailed, "Okay...okay...I...I...had to drive Eli to their... exchange every Thursday night. He didn't have a car so...he needed me to take him. I know what his supplier looks like, but I don't know his name. Please don't throw me in jail! And don't tell my *parents*!" He dissolved into broken sobs.

Baxter returned Trent and his chair to an upright position. I could have sworn I saw a smile playing at his lips. "Where do they usually make the exchange?" he demanded.

"Behind the...behind that crappy strip mall at Ninety-Sixth and College," he sniffled.

"What time?"

"Nine-thirty."

Baxter got in his face. "I'm going to let you go—for now. But if I hear that you've left town or if you're not keeping your nose clean, I'll find you. I'll throw you in jail, and then I'll tell your parents everything. Do you get me?"

"Y-y-yes."

"Good. Now get out of here."

Trent scrambled out of his seat and ran for the door. He was out of the office in a flash, probably heading to his dorm room to change his underwear.

Smiling at Baxter, I said, "You're such a goodie two-shoes, I never thought I'd see you pull off the bad cop routine."

"Are you kidding me? I'm a total badass. You just haven't had the chance to witness it until now," he said, puffing out his chest. "A bad cop needs his good cop, though. You weren't much help."

"You had this. I was enjoying the show. And don't forget, I'm not a cop." I checked my watch. "I have to go. I need to pick up some lab results back in the science building before I meet with Dr. Berg."

"Catch you later. After I'm done here, I'm going back over to Tristan Sellers's apartment to see if I can find Eli's stash. Now that the autopsy's over, we need to release the scene, so this is our last chance to look around."

"Good luck finding it. I'm betting it's in his backpack, along with his cell phone, laptop, and flash drive with the incriminating video."

"The way this investigation is going, I wouldn't doubt it." He grinned at me. "Have fun on your date."

16

I found Rich in his chemistry lab again, staring at the same beaker with the same bubbling green liquid he was staring at this morning.

"Have some info for me?" I asked.

"I do," he said, going to a different table to gather a file folder and the container I had given him. "The samples themselves are pretty well destroyed from the test, but here's what's left of what you gave me. Instead of doing a GC-MS analysis, I went old school and looked at it under a microscope first. I thought it might be some sort of rock dust instead of soil, so I did an acid test."

"I don't care what you did with it. I just want to know what it is."

"You're not being very grateful."

I rolled my eyes at him.

"Your mystery substance is calcium carbonate."

"Translation, please?"

"Limestone," he replied. "Limestone dust, to be more precise."

I thought for a moment. "Who would have limestone dust on his shoes?"

Rich shrugged. "A quarry or rock yard worker. A landscaper. Or anyone who has recently set foot on a gravel road, parking lot, or driveway in Indiana."

I groaned. "So it could be anyone."

"Pretty much."

"Well, at least you've answered my question as to what reagent to use. I'm going with Bromophenol Blue. Thanks."

"Excellent choice. Now do I get a free speeding ticket or something out of this little favor?"

Laughing, I said, "I'm afraid not. All I can offer you is the satisfaction of knowing you did your part for the greater good."

"That's a shitty reimbursement."

I picked up the folder and the container and headed for the door. "Take it up with the Sheriff."

Hurrying to my office, I made sure to bring home one of my "special candies" I'd promised my nephew. I had an addiction to the truffles from a local chocolatier in Zionsville and always kept a box of them in my desk. I didn't dare keep them at home for fear of eating an entire box in one sitting. Stopping by my lab, I grabbed a bottle of Bromophenol Blue solution, having noticed the bottle at the crime lab looked rather old. I pointed my car toward Noblesville.

It was nearing rush hour, so traffic was horrible. I was late getting to the morgue, and Dr. Berg and DA McAlister were already conferring by the time I got suited up.

"Sorry, traffic was crazy," I said, joining them next to Eli's body.

McAlister glared at me, but Dr. Berg smiled. He said, "No problem. We didn't start without you. I performed the autopsy this morning with Detective Sterling in attendance, who was later joined by Detective Baxter. The official cause of death is asphyxiation by strangulation, and I'm classifying it as a homicide."

"You're one hundred percent certain it wasn't a suicide?" asked DA McAlister, squinting down at Eli's body as if it might suddenly start speaking to him.

"Yes. The victim's hyoid bone has been broken. I believe that he was manually strangled before he was strung up. Ultimately, he died from the hanging. I assume the killer realized the boy was near death and then felt the need to cover it up."

A chill crept up my spine. Manual strangulation was an up-close, intimate kind of assault. This murder was personal. I didn't know how this information would affect the investigation, but it was disconcerting nonetheless.

The DA nodded. "That broken hyoid will make homicide a hell of a lot easier to sell."

Dr. Berg grimaced slightly but continued. "We spoke about the blood underneath the victim's fingernails. I also found a significant amount of dead skin, which could belong to his attacker if the two were in a struggle. I've sent samples to the lab for them to run DNA."

I nodded, already having heard about the blood from Baxter.

McAlister seemed happy to have some hard evidence. "Finally some good news. If we can get a positive DNA match, my case is as good as won."

"Yes, I hope so. I've put a rush on the test, but you know how that goes."

McAlister sneered, "You wouldn't think it would take weeks to do one simple test."

DNA testing was anything but simple, but I understood what he meant. Apprehending suspects could be done in a much more timely fashion if our labs weren't understaffed, underfunded, and overworked.

Dr. Berg continued, "I also found wood splinters and fragments of white paint under his fingernails, which is consistent with evidence you found at the scene, correct?"

"Yes," I replied. "It seemed as though he scratched the doorframe where he was hanging to try to get a handhold."

He nodded. "I swabbed the area around the muzzle imprint on his forehead and the abrasion on his temple, and they tested positive for gunshot residue. He was held at gunpoint and assaulted before he was hanged. Poor kid."

Poor kid, my ass. He was a drug dealer and all-around scumbag. His bad behavior finally caught up to him. Granted, maybe what he'd done didn't warrant a brutal murder, but he seemed to have done something that pissed off the wrong person.

Dr. Berg said, "Not that this is particularly pertinent to the case, but I found evidence of drug abuse. There is a significant amount of irritation in the mucous membranes of his nasal cavity." He looked at me. "You don't seem surprised by this, Ellie."

I shrugged. "He was a drug dealer. Not a shock that he was his own customer as well. He wasn't the upstanding student he would have liked everyone to believe, and he may have been into more kinds of trouble than anyone realized."

"I see," said Dr. Berg.

The DA turned to me. "What, do we think this is a drug-related hit now? You guys are all over the place with your theories on who killed this kid. First it was his teacher and now it's his supplier? Make up your damn minds and get me a suspect!"

"Calm down, Wade," Dr. Berg warned.

Still grumbling, McAlister said, "I don't have time for this shit. I'm late for dinner with my wife." He stalked out of the morgue.

I heaved out a heavy sigh.

Dr. Berg smiled. "Can you go home and get some rest now?"

"No, I have a date." I yawned. "I hope I can stay awake."

Dr. Berg shook his head, chuckling.

When I got to the lab, the lights were off and no one was in there, which meant Beck and his assistant had gone home for the day. That was perfect for me, but not cool of them to leave at their regular time considering we were working a murder investigation. They had pulled a double the day before, but so had the rest of us, and we were still hard at work. Then again, they had pulled a double earlier in the week, too, because of the Marais case. They were undoubtedly exhausted and deserved some time to decompress.

The first thing I did was sit down and get out my case notes for the Vanover murder. I jotted down the information I had received from Rich about the substance on the footprints being limestone dust. I flipped through my notes from the scene and read the section about the out-of-place items we had found on the apartment floor—blue glass rock and pea gravel. The only place in the apartment where we found those two kinds of stones was in the area where the struggle and murder had occurred. If any of the apartment's inhabitants or frequent visitors had tracked those rocks in on his or her shoes, we would have found them all around the apartment instead of concentrated in the struggle area. The victim was barefoot when he was found, so I surmised the rocks had to have come from the killer's shoes.

I Googled "limestone, blue glass rock, pea gravel, Indianapolis." I got back thousands of hits, most of them pointing me to landscape suppliers in the area. I then searched for "landscape rock, Indianapolis," which got me a map with dozens of local businesses fitting that description. When I perused the list, a name jumped out at me: Powell Stone Supply. Morris Powell was the name of George Cooper's opponent in the senatorial race. After a bit of searching, I found that Morris Powell did indeed own Powell Stone Supply and that Powell Stone Supply sold pea gravel and several kinds of crushed limestone rock. And right on their homepage, Powell Stone Supply featured a new-to-the-market landscaping material, "landscape glass," a soft-edged recycled glass product gaining popularity across the country.

Something about this information didn't settle well with me. In fact, it raised more questions than it answered. After printing out my findings, I headed off to find Baxter to run my thoughts past him. He was at his desk, eating a cheeseburger while reading emails.

When I sat down in the chair next to him, he looked up and said, "I thought you were supposed to be on your date with the rent-a-cop."

"Soon."

"Don't forget to fix your face."

Frowning, I changed the subject. "Did you find anything interesting at Tristan's apartment?"

Shaking his head, he said, "I struck out."

"Well, maybe I can give you some good news. I found out what was on our killer's shoes. Limestone dust, like from crushed limestone."

His brow furrowed. "You mean what they use on every rock road, parking lot, and driveway in a thousand-mile radius?"

"Yes, but considering we also found pea gravel and blue landscape glass at the scene, I think I've drawn a possible conclusion. The killer had recently been at a landscape rock supply yard."

"Is there any way Sellers, Vanover, or another student could have picked up those rocks on campus or on the grounds of the apartment?"

"Ashmore uses mulch in all of the flowerbeds on campus. I don't know if it's for looks or so the kids won't have rocks to throw at each other. And those apartments are crappy. They don't have any landscaping."

Baxter thought about it for a moment, pursing his lips. "Okay, I could go with the idea that the killer brought it with him, possibly from a supply yard. You seem to know something more, though."

"Well, I did some digging, and I found out that Morris Powell, George Cooper's opponent for the US Senate seat, owns a landscape supply business on the north side of Indy. It seems to be the only place in this area that sells landscape glass in bulk."

He sat up in his seat. "Powell owns a rock yard?" I could tell from his face that this information piqued his interest, but he quickly sank back into his chair and feigned disinterest. "Why would Powell have had anything to do with Eli Vanover's death?"

"You said yourself that Vasti's and Eli's deaths are related, although I think if landscape rock were to be found at a scene, it would have been at Vasti's, not Eli's. You heard Dr. Cooper swear up and down that his cousin Tyler, Powell's campaign manager, is trying to set him up for Vasti's murder in order to ruin his father's chance at winning the election."

"It's a possibility, but don't know that I can see Powell as the link between the two murders."

"But you have to admit this is awfully coincidental."

He shrugged. "Not really. You said anyone could get that blue glass from a fire pit bought at Walmart, right?"

"Yes, but—"

"Some random killer off the street could have picked up the fire pit glass and the pea gravel in his own flowerbed, walked across his rock driveway, and headed straight for Sellers's apartment. And by the way, it's not your job to draw conclusions on the Vasti Marais case."

"Damn it, Baxter, it was a good observation."

I got up and stalked away, heading for the restroom to fix my makeup and hair. I didn't know why Baxter was shutting me down all of a sudden, except that my involvement in the Marais case could do something to jeopardize their investigation. I was only trying to help, and since neither Baxter nor Sterling seemed to want my help, screw them. It made my head hurt to think about Vasti's case anyway.

17

I had inadvertently left myself little time to primp. I did what I could to my hair, and it looked better, but not great. On the positive side, my makeup job turned out to be a success, so I no longer looked like I had been punched in both eyes. At seven o'clock I went outside, and Rob was there waiting. When he saw me, he got out of his SUV to meet me and took my hand.

Smiling down at me, he said, "Hello, Ellie. I was worried this date was never going to happen."

"I'm sorry. Since yesterday, things have been nuts. Thank you for being so understanding."

He led me to his vehicle and helped me into the passenger seat. "No problem at all. I hope you don't mind, but after you said you wouldn't have much time tonight, I took the liberty of picking up dinner for us. I thought we could go to Morse Park and have a picnic."

I was floored by his thoughtfulness. "That's perfect. Thank you."

He got into the driver's seat. "I hope you like Maggiano's."

"I love it." I thought I'd smelled garlic when I got into his vehicle, and that explained it.

We made small talk on the short drive to Morse Park. It was north of Noblesville, situated on Morse Reservoir, a decent-sized (for central Indiana) body of water. Once we got there, he drove to the end of one of the roads and parked. He got a blanket and our dinner out of the back of his vehicle and led me to a secluded spot in the woods, right on the water. The sun had just begun to dip down below the tree line, creating a blaze of orange and bright pink streaks across the sky. The temperature had dropped, finally, and there was a nice breeze cooling the air.

"It's beautiful here. I've never come to this part of the park before. I've only ever hung out at the beach," I said.

He smiled, gazing out across the smooth reservoir as he spread the blanket out over the grass. "This was my favorite spot growing up. My dad used to bring my four brothers and me here all the time. My mother needed some quiet time to herself every once in a while with five boys running around the house. We spent nearly every Saturday afternoon here, exploring every inch of this place."

"Five boys? Your mother must be a saint."

"She is. My dad passed away when I was a senior in high school, so she had to raise my younger brothers on her own."

I frowned. "I'm sorry to hear that."

"I shouldn't complain. I had a great childhood with some fantastic memories." He handed me a container of food. "What about you? Did you grow up here?"

I certainly did not have a great childhood, and my memories were more like nightmares. Maybe it was for the best to steer the conversation away from that topic. "In this area, yes. We moved around a lot." I changed the subject away from me. "So...five boys in the house? I get tired sometimes with only one."

He wrinkled his forehead as he poured me a glass of wine. "You have a son?"

"No, I have a nephew. He and my sister live with me." As my sister was quick to find out when she started dating again after having Nate, some men were turned off by children. I hoped Rob wasn't one of those kinds of men.

"That's not a bad deal you have there. You can be the fun aunt and pass him back to his mom for the hard stuff. I have several nieces and nephews, so I've become a pro at the pass-off."

I was happy to hear he at least didn't run screaming when children were mentioned. "That works most of the time. Nate's a pretty good kid, and he's only three so there's not a lot of hard stuff yet. Besides, having them around is a lot more fun than living alone."

"You sound like me. I'm always taking in my brothers when they need a place to stay. My middle brother's girlfriend kicks him out of the house at least once a month." He shrugged. "I made a promise to my dad that I'd look out for them."

Rob Larson was looking like an excellent prospect, but considering my track record of poor choices in men, I was wary. "You take in stray brothers, you own your own business, and you're very understanding when it comes to being stood up on a date. Nobody's that nice." There had to be something wrong with him.

Rob flashed his signature smile at me and took my hand. "I really am that nice. I even call my mom once a day."

A mama's boy. It wasn't the worst thing a man could be, but it wasn't necessarily attractive, either. "Once a day, huh?"

"Why—don't you?"

Removing my hand from his and taking a swig of my wine, I replied, "I've spoken to my mother a grand total of one time since I was eighteen years old."

After I said that, I winced, berating myself for taking skeletons out of my closet for no good reason. Normally I didn't talk about my mother at all, but between my exhaustion, the wine, and the fact that I felt at home with this man, I shared more than I intended.

"Don't you think it's about time you get in touch with her?"

"Well, that would be impossible. She's been dead for years."

Rob's face fell, and he placed a hand on my knee. "Oh, I'm sorry. I had no idea."

"It's fine. Anytime we talked, it ended up in a fight, so it was more peaceful to ignore each other. But after I removed my sister from my mother's toxic household and moved her in with me, we never spoke again. My mother never forgave me for taking my sister away from her." I wished I could just stop talking, but Rob was a kind man and a good listener, plus his smile could melt a glacier. Taking a calming breath, I said, "But this isn't a first date conversation, is it? I'm sorry. I haven't slept in thirty-six hours, so I'm not myself. Tell me about your day."

He seemed a bit taken aback, but he got the hint and moved on. "Big day at work. I had to spend the day pushing reporters back from Mayor Cooper's house." He cast a worried look at me. "I don't know if this is a better subject for you, though."

"What, about Dr. Cooper being arrested? I'm not happy about it, but there's nothing I can do." Other than try to convince Baxter to look at a few more suspects, even though he seemed to think the case was closed.

Furrowing his brow, Rob asked, "Do you think he's innocent?"

"Yes, I do. Even if they have evidence on him, it doesn't make sense to me that he would do such a thing. I'm with the man every day. He's no sociopath."

"I heard on the news that he and the girl had an affair. People do crazy things when love is involved. I see a lot of that in my profession. Many of my clients retain my services for help with stalkers, who are often their former lovers." He hesitated. "I've seen...quite a few women coming and going from Dr. Cooper's place. He's not the altar boy you might think him to be."

I shook my head. "I'm well aware of his reputation, and it doesn't concern me. The problem I have is that it takes a certain kind of mindset to be capable of ending someone's life. That's the piece of the puzzle missing for me."

"I've heard he's a person of interest in yesterday's murder as well."

Rolling my eyes, I said, "He had no reason to—" Abruptly, I stopped myself. I couldn't believe how easy it was to spill my guts to this guy. "Sorry, I can't talk about that case."

He raised his eyebrows, his eyes registering shock. "*That's* the case you were consulting on yesterday?"

I slapped my forehead in frustration. "I've said too much. I need to quit talking."

Grinning, he said, "I have an idea."

He stroked my cheek and drew my face close to his, kissing me tentatively at first, then much more deeply. I kissed him back, wrapping my arms around his neck and pulling myself closer to him. I wanted nothing more than to forget about the horrible week I'd had, and being intimate with Rob was creating a euphoria that succeeded in pushing everything else out of my head. I wanted more. I needed it. I snaked one hand up his shirt and ran my fingers over the taut muscles of his back. With my other hand, I began tugging at his belt.

He broke our kiss. His eyes seemed worried. "Ellie, wait. I don't want you to think I brought you out here because I expect something from you. Far from it."

I put my hands on his chest and pushed him down onto the blanket. I threw one leg over him and straddled him, my skirt hitching up around my hips. "I thought we said we weren't going to talk."

Rob smiled. "Yes, but—"

I cut him off by pressing my lips against his. The euphoria was back, and it didn't take long until we were one, our bodies moving in sync.

Afterward, he lay on top of me for a moment, breathing but not speaking. He then rolled over beside me. "That was unexpected...but great. I've never...uh...done that here."

I had, but I wasn't going to admit it to him.

He continued, "I hope you don't think I was too forward."

I sighed. I usually attracted assholes, not nice guys, and Rob really *was* a nice guy, going so far as to apologize for me wantonly throwing myself at him. "No, I don't think that. If anything, it was me." I looked away.

He touched my cheek, turning my face back toward his. "I didn't mean I'm sorry it happened." Leaning down, he kissed me, leaving me breathless and unable to reply. He added, "In fact, I'd like to do it again sometime. Soon."

"Me, too," I said quietly, a lump in my throat. To make sure he wouldn't want to retract his last statement, I thought it best to end our date on a good note, rather than running my mouth again. Glancing at my watch, I said, "I don't want to leave, but I think I should probably be getting back."

"I understand. Duty calls."

Rob and I got up and packed everything back into his vehicle. He held my hand the entire drive back to the station. When I made a move to get out, he stopped me and kissed me again.

"I'll call you tomorrow," he said. "Don't work too hard."

I smiled. "Thanks again for dinner. I needed to get away for a while."

Still on cloud nine, I hopped down from Rob's SUV. The moment I reached the door to the Sheriff's station, I got accosted by Jason Sterling.

"Hey, Matthews. Out on a hot date?" he asked, holding the door open for me. His eyes flicked to the top of my head, and he reached up and plucked a piece of grass out of my hair. Smirking, he said, "Looks like you had yourself a roll in the hay. I thought you preferred the men's room."

"Go to hell," I said, pushing past him.

He followed me down the hall, chuckling. "Baxter said you went out with a mall cop. How was that? Did you do it on his Segway, or what?"

I couldn't punch him, especially in the middle of the Sheriff's station. I settled for ducking into the women's restroom and slugging the tampon dispenser, which turned out to be an idiotic mistake that only served to hurt my hand. Taking my time to ensure that Sterling would get bored and leave, I searched my hair for any more telltale plant material and fixed my makeup. My thirty-six hour day was almost over. I only had a couple more hours of work to do, and then I was going home for a much-needed sleep.

Opening the door a crack and finding no one in the hallway, I slipped out the door and headed for the lab. It was well past eight, and I figured the only work I should attempt in my exhausted state was examining and entering fingerprints into AFIS. Beck and his assistant had taken care of quite a few of the fingerprints I gathered, but there were still many to do. I sat down at the AFIS computer and got to work.

"Ellie... Ellie!"

I jumped, nearly falling out of my chair. I looked up at who was yelling my name.

Baxter stood over me. "You okay?"

Not really. I was so groggy and disoriented I couldn't see straight. "Did I fall asleep?"

He smiled. "I'm afraid so. You were drooling all over the desk."

Too sleepy to be embarrassed, I wiped my mouth and gave the desk a swipe with the arm of my lab coat. "Did you come in here to tell me again that my reasoning is stupid and my opinion is unwanted?"

Baxter rolled his eyes. "No, I came to tell you that your reasoning wasn't actually as stupid as I originally thought."

His comment snapped me awake. "How so?"

"You know the blue glass and pea gravel we found at the apartment? Well...not that I'm supposed to be sharing this, but we found those two kinds of rock plus some crushed limestone where Vasti Marais's shooter was standing. They were in the grass near the spent casings and...other evidence. That's the link between the crime scenes I'd mentioned. I'm starting to think your Tyler Harris idea isn't so far-fetched after all."

"Really?"

Nodding, he said, "I reached out to him tonight. I made him believe I was getting his statement about the protestors at the gala, but what I wanted to find out was what time he left the party. He said he left about thirty minutes after the blood-throwing incident and then headed down-town to Powell's campaign office. Trouble is, there are traffic cams in the city, unlike around here, and they show that *no one* came or went from that office anytime that evening."

My mouth dropped open. "He has no alibi for the time Vasti Marais was killed, *and* he lied about it."

"Exactly."

"As a family member, it would have been easy for him to gain access to the Cooper house and Mayor Cooper's rifle."

"Also correct."

"That night, I remember him bragging about his kill during the family's big game hunting trip. He has to be a decent shot if he dropped a moose. Would you say that shows he had means and opportunity?"

"I think it would be safe to assume he did. As for motive, I'd say campaign tactics could be a plausible possibility. However, aside from a gut feeling, the rantings of a murder suspect, and a handful of rocks, we have nothing to connect him to the scene."

"And nothing to connect him to Eli Vanover."

"That, too." He furrowed his brow. "What about your shoeprint?"

I flipped through the file on my desk and found the measurements I had taken earlier. "From my preliminary analysis, I'd say this print is at least a men's size twelve, maybe thirteen. Tyler Harris is a little man, so I doubt he has feet that big."

Baxter rubbed his eyes. "These two cases just keep getting better and better. I think we should call it a night, don't you? I know I can't think straight."

"Sounds good to me." I locked the case file in the desk drawer, removed my lab coat, and followed Baxter out the door.

I must have seemed out of it, because Baxter took my arm and gave me a good shake. "Don't fall asleep at the wheel. Do I need to follow you home?"

Chuckling, I said, "No, it's not far. I can make it."

"See that you do. I don't want to be called out to another scene anytime soon."

18

I slept like the dead for eleven glorious hours, but it wasn't enough. It would take me a few days to make up for the lost night of sleep, but I was clearer-headed than I'd been yesterday. Needing a Nate fix, I tiptoed into his room while he was sleeping. I loved getting to wake him up in the morning. He always wanted to be carried to the living room and held for a while as he woke up. This morning was no different. He opened one sleepy eye and gave me a lopsided smile, making my heart swell. He held up his little arms to me, and I picked him up out of bed, breathing in his warm, clean scent. We went out to the living room and lay down in the recliner together.

Yawning, he asked, "Auntie Ellie, did you bring me one of your special candies?" The kid's mind was like a steel trap. He remembered everything.

"Yes, I did. And you can have it with your breakfast, just like I promised, if you were good for your mommy last night. Were you?"

He nodded.

I smiled. "Good boy."

"Where were you?"

"I had to work, buddy."

Frowning, he said, "Did that man make you work again instead of coming home to play with me?"

"What man?"

"The one who took you to the Cinderella ball when you looked like Sleepin' Judy."

Nate always mispronounced "Sleeping Beauty," but it was so adorable, neither Rachel nor I had ever corrected him. When he had seen that I was wearing a pink gown to the gala, he equated me with the corresponding pink princess. The kid knew his princess movies—a casualty of being raised by two women.

I sighed, thinking about that night and how things had changed since then. An image of Dr. Cooper locked up in a cell popped into my head. I couldn't imagine how awful it must have been for him to spend last night in jail.

"No. Sheriff Jayne asked me to work with her."

"Oh, okay. I like Sheriff Jayne." He looked up at me with expectant eyes. "Will you be home tonight?"

I hated to disappoint him, but I had to tell him the truth. "Probably not, baby. Auntie Ellie is helping Sheriff Jayne catch a bad guy, and it takes a lot of time."

"Are you a police now?"

"No, I'm the science nerd who helps the police."

"How?"

"Well, you know how sometimes Auntie Ellie knows you've been in the cookie jar without asking?"

He stuck out his lower lip. "Yes."

"Well, I know because you leave sticky fingerprints and cookie crumbs all over the cookie jar and the kitchen counter. It's like when Scooby-Doo and the gang find clues to solve their mysteries. The sticky fingerprints and cookie crumbs are my clues. For the mystery Sheriff Jayne is trying to solve, we also have fingerprints that are our clues, and we have special rocks and footprints, too."

Bored by my kid-friendly forensics lesson, he said, "Can I have my chocolate now?"

I did a much better job with my first class of the day. Granted, I only passed out a test and told them to get to work, but at least no one accused me of being hung over. Rob texted me and asked about having dinner or coffee this evening, but I declined. If I had even a smidge of free time, I should make an attempt to see my nephew, especially since he'd asked so forlornly this morning. Not to be deterred, Rob asked about lunch the next day, and I did want to see him, so I accepted.

As my class was getting over, I received a call from Baxter. "Hey," he said. "I need you this afternoon. Can you get someone to cover your classes?"

"Seriously? If I skip out on more classes, I'm going to get fired," I replied.

"I've already had the Sheriff speak to your department head. He's fine with it."

"You're thorough, I'll give you that. What are we doing, anyway?"

"Talking to Tyler Harris. The firearms examiner found a partial print of his on one of the spent cartridge casings we found at the Marais murder scene."

"What?" I exclaimed.

"Interesting twist, huh? His prints are in the system from when he obtained a gun permit. With the evidence we have, we'll be able to collect his DNA, and then we can run it against the foreign blood found under Eli Vanover's nails."

"Why do you need me?"

"You know the guy. Maybe you can get him to talk."

I was tired of hearing that. I wished I didn't have a personal connection with so many of our possible suspects. "You know Tyler's going to lawyer up. We won't get a word out of him."

"Maybe," he replied. "But it's worth a shot. Can you be here by one o'clock?"

"See you then."

I didn't like the idea of skipping class again, but if Jayne had spoken to Dr. Graham and he agreed, I guessed it would be okay. I found Samantha and talked her into letting me steal her teaching assistant for the afternoon. I tracked down Samantha's TA and gave him instructions on what to do with my afternoon classes. Once I'd cleared my afternoon schedule, I grabbed lunch and headed to the Sheriff's station.

Plopping down in a chair next to Baxter's desk, I asked, "What's up with the suit?" The sharp gray suit he was wearing was a big departure from his usual business casual attire.

He smoothed his tie. "I had to look pretty for court."

The food I'd inhaled on the drive over started churning in my stomach. "Dr. Cooper's arraignment?" I had forgotten about that.

He nodded.

"Did it go well?" I asked.

"Yes, for me. Not so much for him. Judge denied bail."

"Ouch."

He shrugged. "You do the crime; you do the time."

Not wishing to dwell on Dr. Cooper doing time, I changed the subject. "How did you get Tyler Harris to come in voluntarily to give you a DNA sample?"

"I told him I needed his signature on his statement from yesterday and left out the part about the DNA. That way, I figure he'll leave his lawyer at home."

"Sneaky." I glanced at my watch and stood up. "Since we've got some time before he gets here, I'm going to go work my magic on a pizza box."

I checked out the pizza box with the phantom shoeprint on it and took it to the lab. After placing it on my work surface, I grabbed the bottle of Bromophenol Blue I had brought from my lab at school. I sprayed a fine mist of the reagent onto the surface of the white cardboard box and waited for a few moments. The shoeprint started to appear blue, but it was still faint. I put it under a strong light and snapped several photos. The last step would be to apply some steam to enhance the Bromophenol Blue solution I had sprayed on the box.

I got out the handheld steamer and allowed it to heat up while I worried over the potential outcome of my work. This part made me nervous, because too much steam could ruin the whole thing. Also, if the steamer happened to leak and splash any water droplets onto my shoeprint, it would distort the image.

Once the steamer was ready, I made one pass with it over the shoeprint.

The steam seemed to make the blue stand out, so I waited thirty seconds and made another pass. It helped a little more, so I chanced one more pass with the steamer. The shoeprint came to life, and I could even read the words from the bottom of the sole: TIMBERLAND and GRIPSTICK.

I rifled through my file to find my notes and photos from the shoeprint on the side of the folding chair. The word I had thought was "stick" was in fact "Gripstick," and the shoe treads from the chair were a visual match to the treads from the pizza box. Hallelujah.

I took dozens of shots of my shoeprint, with the scale and without, and with various types of lighting. Now that the print was clear and visible, I measured it again, coming up with a length of twelve and a half inches, which by my calculation meant the shoe's size was either a twelve or twelve and a half, but I was no expert. For the shoeprint to be used as evidence in a trial, I needed someone at the state lab to determine the exact model and size of the shoe, and if necessary, even the individual wear pattern. I emailed my pictures of the prints to the experts and set the box aside to dry before repackaging it and returning it to evidence. I also emailed a photo of the shoeprint and a brief explanation of my findings to Baxter and Sterling.

Beck's assistant came into the lab, seeming surprised that I was there. She was a pretty woman—tall, blonde, and a little younger than I was—but chose to hide her features beneath big glasses, a messy ponytail, and an oversized lab coat. I didn't blame her. Being one of a very few women in the Sheriff's station, it was sometimes better to be thought of as "one of the guys."

She said, "Um...hi. I don't think we've officially met. I'm Amanda Carmack."

"I guess we haven't. I'm Ellie Matthews." I got up to shake her hand.

"I've heard a lot about you."

She acted a little standoffish, but who knew what Beck Durant or anyone else had told her about me. I knew nothing about her, but I had taken a look at some of her work with the fingerprints on my case. I thought she seemed thorough and knowledgeable.

I smiled, hoping to put her at ease. "Well, don't believe everything you hear. Beck and I never really saw eye-to-eye on much of anything. I thought he should work harder, and he didn't agree. And I'm known to have screaming matches with Sterling. He doesn't seem to care for me much either."

Smiling, she said, "Beck doesn't see eye-to-eye with anyone. We should get along just fine." She came over to stand beside me. "Nice shoeprint. Did you use Bromophenol Blue?"

"Yes, the print was barely noticeable at the scene, but Baxter picked it up. I was happy he did, because it turned out to be a great print, and it's a visual match to the print on the side of the chair we think was pushed out from under the victim."

Amanda frowned. "That scene sounded awful. Honestly, I was happy not to have had to work that case. One young person in a week is too much for me."

Nodding, I said, "I know. This job can be rough." I hesitated. "I know Beck isn't too good with conversation, so if you need someone to talk to sometime, you're always welcome to call me."

"Thanks. I may take you up on that," she said, smiling. "I'm still working on examining fingerprints and entering them into AFIS. Is there any other evidence that's a higher priority?"

"Probably not. We still have the trace we picked up in the vacuum, but as dirty as that apartment was, I don't think we're going to find anything telling in it. There's also some clothing that was on the floor in the area of the struggle, but it presents a similar problem. I've got a broken fingernail, but Dr. Berg already got scrapings from the nine other fingernails on the victim, so it's hardly worth worrying about. The fingerprints are our best lead."

"I'll get right on them, then."

Baxter came into the lab. "Hey, Tyler Harris is here. You ready?"

Shrugging out of my lab coat, I grumbled, "I'm never ready to see him. He gives me the creeps. I always feel like I need a shower after talking to him."

He chuckled all the way down to the conference room. Instead of putting Tyler in a typical interrogation room, Baxter was smart and had him in a more comfortable, civilized space. Tyler wouldn't know what hit him.

"Thanks again for coming in, Mr. Harris," Baxter said, placing a document in front of Tyler. "I know you're a busy man and your time is important, so we'll try to keep this short."

Tyler puffed out his tiny chest, beaming at the fake compliment. "Yes, time is money to a guy like me." He turned to me and purred, "What a nice surprise, Ellie. You can't stay away from me, can you, darling?"

Choking back the urge to vomit, I flicked my eyes at Baxter. He was biting his lip, trying not to laugh. I said to Tyler, "On a normal day I can. But when you lie to an officer of the law, you suddenly become quite interesting to me."

"What?" he said, his voice going up an octave. Clearing his throat, he continued in a condescending tone, "Why are you even here? I thought you were just a teacher now."

"I'm consulting on a related case."

Baxter said, "Before we get into that, Mr. Harris, I want to make sure you're happy with the statement you originally gave me. You see, we checked the traffic cam footage from in front of Morris Powell's campaign headquarters, and you didn't go there after you left the fundraiser at your parents' house. Care to tell us where you really were?"

Squirming in his seat, Tyler crossed his legs. "I was there. Maybe you had the wrong camera."

Baxter produced a photograph of a downtown street and pointed to one of the buildings. "Is this Powell's office?"

After hesitating, Tyler replied, "Yes."

"No one went in or out of this building during the timeframe you said you were there. Why did you lie to me?"

"Detective, I work *with* the government, not against it." He smiled, but his eyes seemed frightened.

Baxter stared him down. After a minute or so, Tyler started fidgeting. Baxter kept staring until Tyler offered the first word.

"What about...what about the back entrance? Did you check that?" Tyler's hand trembled as he tried to place it nonchalantly on his knee.

Shaking his head, Baxter said, "Cut the crap. There is no back entrance. If you sign this statement as it stands now and it's used in a trial, you can be prosecuted for perjury."

"I think I may need to call my lawyer..."

I jumped in, my tone firm. "No, Tyler, what you need to do is be a man and tell the truth. Where did you go after you left the party?"

"Why does it matter so much?" he cried.

Baxter walked over and stood beside him, arms crossed. "Because if you can't give us an alibi, we might have to make you a person of interest in a murder." He could be intimidating when he wanted to be.

"Murder?" Tyler gasped. "Who?"

"Vasti Marais," Baxter said.

Tyler's jaw dropped open. "My cousin killed her! Why would you think I had anything to do with it?"

"We found your fingerprint on a discarded cartridge casing at the scene of the murder," said Baxter.

"What? How?" Tyler sputtered.

"I think you should be telling us how your fingerprint got on that casing."

"I can't imagine how... Wait. I use my uncle's rifles when our family goes hunting together. I'm sure my fingerprints are all over the rifles and gear we brought with us the last time—which would include extra ammunition we brought but didn't use."

"When was your last trip?" Baxter asked.

"About a month ago."

"Have you used any of your uncle's firearms since then? Or have you ever given your uncle's firearms to anyone else to use?"

"No, the only time I ever touch them is when we go on our hunting trips. Uncle George always brings the guns and ammunition for everyone." He shook his head. "I have no reason to want that girl dead. Besides the fingerprint, why would you even consider me?"

I said, "Several reasons. According to you, you're a fantastic shot with a rifle. As a family member, it wouldn't be difficult for you to gain access to your uncle's guns. You and your cousin don't seem to get along too well. You were the one who told him to run, which made him look guilty. And as an added bonus, the backlash from this whole thing is hurting George Cooper's chances of winning the Senate seat, if he can even continue with his campaign at all." I smirked at him. "Tyler, can you tell me who might profit from that?"

As realization dawned on him, his eyes grew wide. "Oh, no. I see where you're going with this, and I didn't do it. I swear. I *promise!*"

"We're going to need more than the promise of someone who works in politics," said Baxter. He leaned down to eye level with Tyler. "Where were you? Tell us, or we tell the media you're a person of interest. I can't imagine your boss will be too pleased."

Tyler looked like he was going to be sick. "I can't tell you... It will ruin me."

I joked, "What, were you at a pro-abortion rally or an ACLU meeting? Even for a Republican, that would be better than committing murder."

Hanging his head, Tyler admitted, "I was...with my...girlfriend."

"See? That wasn't so hard." Baxter slid a notepad and a pen toward him. "Now if you'll give us her name and contact information, we'll verify your alibi."

Tyler jotted down the information and sank back in his chair. He ran his fingers through his hair and sighed. "Can I go now?"

"Not yet. What's your shoe size, Tyler?" I asked, looking down at his feet. They couldn't have been bigger than a ten.

"Nine, why?"

"Just checking." Tyler's tiny feet couldn't have made the print on the chair or the pizza box from the crime scene. "And while we're at it, will you agree to giving a DNA sample? We want to be able to rule you out—since you swear you're innocent."

He wiped a hand down his face. "Whatever."

I got out a swab and took the sample from inside his cheek. "Out of curiosity, do you know Eli Vanover?"

"Who?" Tyler asked, perplexed.

Baxter had a thoughtful look in his eye. "Let's talk about your boss for a moment, Tyler. How far would he go to win this election?"

"Morris is a great guy. If you're trying to imply that he would kill someone to get ahead, you're completely off base. He's a decorated Gulf War veteran, he's on the board of several charities, and he coaches his daughter's soccer team. The man is a saint, not a murderer." He frowned. "If you want to talk dirty politics, try my uncle."

"Are you saying you think Mayor Cooper would stoop to something like murder?" I asked. "Why would he kill a person with his own firearm if he planned to pin it on someone else?"

"He's not the sharpest tool in the shed." Tyler shook his head. "You're obviously not aware of how little use he has for his son, are you?"

"I'm starting to get the idea."

"Thanks for your time, Mr. Harris," Baxter said, opening the door. "You might want to stay close in case your alibi doesn't check out."

Tyler pushed himself up out of his chair. "It'll check out. But please, can I count on your discretion? I gave you what you wanted, and I'd like for my private life to remain private."

Baxter replied, "I don't see a reason that this information should become public. Take care, Mr. Harris." After Tyler left the room, Baxter closed the door behind him and asked me, "What's your take on that weasel? Think he's telling the truth?"

"I think so. Once he knew we had him, he dropped his elite asshole persona. He didn't even hit on me on his way out."

"I agree. Next, I want to check out his boss. If you go with me, you can get some samples from his rock yard to test against the evidence we found at Eli Vanover's crime scene." Glancing at the name Tyler had written down, he added, "On the way, we can run down Harris's girlfriend, Ginger."

"Ginger? Is he dating someone's grandma?"

He laughed. "More likely she's someone's wife—someone with the connections to make sure he never works in this town again."

"Hmm. He seemed almost frightened to tell us about her. Old lady name aside, I'm thinking she could be some well-connected person's daughter. Just barely legal or even underage."

"Care to make it interesting?"

"Are you suggesting a bet, Detective?" I asked.

"Sure. Loser buys drinks at O'Loughlin's tonight after work."

"Deal."

19

"What do you think about George Cooper?" Baxter asked me on the drive to Powell Stone Supply.

"As a suspect or as a father?" I replied.

"Either. Both."

"Well, he's a sucky father, that's for sure. At the first mention of his son's involvement in the Marais murder, he ran the other way. Dr. Cooper said himself that he wouldn't be surprised if his dad disowned him over it."

"Cooper's mommy showed up for his arraignment, but daddy didn't. I'd say that sent a pretty clear message."

"No shit. You know, now that I think about that particular conversation I had with Dr. Cooper, I remember him mentioning to me that Vasti told him she'd had an affair with his father also."

"Damn, that girl got around," Baxter said.

"Dr. Cooper didn't believe her, though. He thought she made it up to hurt him."

"Every good lie has a grain of truth in it."

I raised one eyebrow at him. "Did you get that out of a fortune cookie?"

Chuckling, he said, "Haven't you ever noticed that anytime someone is accused of cheating, it eventually turns out to be true? People are horrible at keeping secrets. More often than not, one of the parties involved can't stay the hell quiet. And it's never the one with the most to lose."

"Does that mean you'd consider hauling George Cooper in?"

"Maybe, but not just yet. A man like him isn't going to stand for it. He has always seemed shady to me, and if he and Vasti Marais had an affair, it means he lied to me about not knowing her on the day we confiscated the rifle from his house. That isn't enough, though. I'd need to be able to place him at the scene. If we bring him in, even for questioning, I want to have enough to hold him. I doubt if we'd get a second chance, as powerful as he is. He could have my badge with one phone call."

"Yikes. Well, if you do decide to go after him, make sure it's Sterling's name on the paperwork."

Baxter smiled as he pulled into Powell Stone Supply. "I'll do that. Now, this guy Powell, he's a nobody. I think he used to be on the Hendricks County Council, but aside from that, he has no political clout at all. I don't mind rattling his cage."

Powell Stone Supply was in a huge industrial lot on the northwest side of Indianapolis. We parked beside a trailer that had an OFFICE sign over the door. The lot was lined with piles of all different kinds of bulk rock and gravel separated by short stalls constructed of concrete block. Forming a crooked wall of sorts down the middle of the lot was pallet upon pallet of large landscape rocks piled up and bundled together with wire, stacked three to four bundles high. Burly men driving forklifts and tractors were hard at work loading waiting trucks.

Upon entering the office, Baxter and I were greeted by a pleasant middle-aged woman. "Hello. How can we help you today?" she asked. I noticed that the nameplate on her desk read VICTORIA POWELL and assumed she must have been Mrs. Morris Powell.

Baxter flashed his badge. "I'm Detective Nick Baxter and this is Ellie Matthews. We're with the Hamilton County Sheriff's Department. We'd like to speak to Morris Powell."

Mrs. Powell smiled, but it didn't quite reach her eyes. "He's in a meeting right now."

"Mind if we take a look around the lot while we're waiting?"

"Um...sure. May I ask what you're looking for?" she asked, unease evident in her demeanor.

"Rocks," I said.

We left Mrs. Powell somewhat dumbfounded and went back outside. After retrieving my camera and a couple of pill boxes from my kit, we went in search of blue glass and pea gravel. It probably wasn't the brightest idea to traipse around this place without wearing hard hats. Once we got a ways into the lot, I became increasingly aware of how precarious the stacks of huge stones looked as they loomed several feet above my head. Lucky for us, we didn't have to venture too far to find what we needed. The fifth concrete stall was full of pea gravel, and in the next stall there was a big pile of the blue glass.

I studied the ground under my feet and snapped several photos. The entire lot's base layer was crushed limestone. The area in front of each stall was peppered with the type of rock each stall contained, I assumed from being dragged out or spilled during loading.

I had to raise my voice to be heard over the humming truck and tractor motors. "Anyone walking around in this area would have a combination of limestone, blue glass, and pea gravel on his shoes. Our killer has been here, but how do we know if he's an employee or a customer?"

"Or if he's a she?"

"Seriously? 'She' would have to be an Amazon with a women's size fourteen foot to fit into a men's twelve boot. *And* she'd have to be able to strangle someone nearly to death with her bare hands."

A smile played at his lips. "I thought you told me your friend Dr. Alessi could have done it."

"If we're sure it's the same killer for both murders, then no, it's not her." I frowned. "But if it *isn't* the same killer, I still wouldn't put it past Gianna to get rid of the girl who stole her boyfriend and then pin her crime on him. She's evil. She's always trying to get people into trouble, especially me."

Grinning full-on now, he said, "People either love you or they hate you, don't they?"

"Hey, I'm straightforward, I don't put up with bullshit, and I don't apologize for it. If people have a problem with that, they can go to hell," I huffed, crouching down to take a couple of closer shots of the rocks. When I got up,

I saw a man in a suit approaching us. I recognized him from his campaign ads—Morris Powell.

Walking toward us with a smile plastered on his face, Powell said, "What can I do for my local law enforcement officials on this fine day?" He extended a hand to Baxter and gave him an enthusiastic handshake. "Morris Powell." Turning to me, he shook my hand as well. He had that fake, larger-than-life politician quality to him that made my skin crawl.

"Detective Nick Baxter and Ellie Matthews. We need to ask you a few questions," replied Baxter.

"Fire away, Detective Baxter. I have nothing to hide." Anytime someone said he had nothing to hide, he definitely had something to hide.

"Let's start with your relationship with George Cooper."

Powell laughed, rocking back on his heels. "Oh, George. He's one tough customer. Good guy, though."

"Has there ever been an instance where either of you crossed the line with a campaign strategy?" asked Baxter.

"With Election Day approaching, his commercials have been getting more...catty, but I wouldn't say he's necessarily crossed a line. Mud-slinging is an age-old political tactic, but it's one I don't happen to participate in," Powell said, his expression as pious as a choir boy.

"I'm not talking about bad PR."

Cocking his head to the side, Powell replied, "I don't follow..."

Baxter got out a headshot of Vasti Marais that was taken on the slab at the morgue and showed it to Powell. Powell shrank back, horrified by the image. I didn't blame him—it was a graphic photo. Vasti's beautiful face was discolored and distorted from her body having been allowed to decompose outside in the heat.

"Do you know this woman?" Baxter demanded. I thought it was difficult to recognize her from the photo, but I was sure he was using this one in particular for the shock value.

"No," Powell breathed, his face white. "Who is she?"

"Her name is Vasti Marais. Does the name ring a bell?"

Powell wiped a hand down his face. "She's the woman George's boy killed. Such a tragic story."

I said, "A *perfect* story someone could use to damage George Cooper's political career."

Powell tried to muster his smile back, but faltered. "I...I haven't used the story against him."

"On the news yesterday, you weighed in on the situation," Baxter said. "I believe you said something about the apple not falling far from the tree. That maybe someone who raised a murderer shouldn't be trusted to represent our state in Congress."

Powell started backpedalling. "I might have spoken out of turn there—"

Baxter cut him off. "It seems awfully convenient that George Cooper's credibility took a major hit right before the election...and right when you were trailing him by a few points in the polls."

Trying to appear nonchalant, Powell waved his hand as if to dismiss Baxter's comments. "A few points is nothing. Polls have a wide margin for error. I'm not worried."

"Mr. Powell, I'm going to lay it out for you." Baxter gestured to the piles of rock we had been examining. "We found blue glass landscape rock, pea gravel, and limestone dust at Vasti Marais's murder scene and also at another crime scene. The killer was careful to leave enough evidence to point to Dudley Cooper, but maybe wasn't quite clever enough to realize he'd left behind something to incriminate himself."

"I sell a lot of rock, Detective. Many of the homes in the area have a combination of those rocks in their landscaping. It could have come from anywhere."

"I'm sure that's true, but you're the one with the motive," Baxter pointed out.

"I didn't kill anyone," Powell insisted, his demeanor changing from frightened to angered.

"Maybe you instructed Tyler Harris to do your dirty work."

"No!" Powell cried. "Tyler is a good kid. I would never ask him to do anything like that."

"Would you ask one of your other employees? Or hire someone to carry out the hit?" I asked.

"No!" Powell shouted, his face red. "I had *nothing* to do with that girl's murder, or any other crime for that matter! And I resent the fact that you've come to my place of business and accused me of such things." He narrowed his eyes at us. "Wait a minute. Are you on George Cooper's payroll? Did he have you come over here to question me to try to ruin my reputation?"

"No, sir. We answer to the Sheriff, not George Cooper," Baxter said, not at all ruffled by Powell's accusation. "We simply followed the evidence, and it led us to you."

"I hardly think finding a few rocks at a crime scene can link a murder to someone. I'll have to run that one past my lawyer." Straightening up to his full height, Powell said, "Speaking of my lawyer, if you want to talk to me again, you'll have to go through him." He turned on his heel and marched back toward his office.

I turned to Baxter. "Well, you certainly rattled his cage. What do you think?"

"I think he's another slimeball politician, but he's right—a few rocks are not going to tie him to either murder. Besides, he doesn't seem the type to get his hands dirty. Let's go talk to Harris's girlfriend."

Getting out the pill boxes I had brought, I said, "Hang on. I need to grab a few samples."

Baxter's phone rang, and he walked several feet away from me to take the call. I crouched down again and shined my flashlight on the ground. The stacked wall of stone opposite the bulk rock stalls had all but blotted out the afternoon sun in this area. I got out some tweezers, collecting samples of the blue glass rock, pea gravel, and limestone. For good measure, I also got out my scale and took a few more photos to document the size of the rocks.

The sound of a nearby tractor was practically deafening, but I happened to hear Baxter shout, "Ellie! Look out!"

Startled, I began to hop up, but Baxter crashed into me, pushing me back and tackling me. My breath whooshed out of me as we landed hard against the pile of blue landscape glass, the jagged stones digging into my back and bare arms.

He scrambled up and pulled me with him. "Are you okay?"

Wincing as I tried to straighten my aching back, I took a shallow breath and wheezed, "Ugh. Next time, buy me dinner first."

Rolling his eyes, he grumbled, "You're welcome."

"What the hell happened?" I asked, flicking off dirt and pieces of the blue glass that had stuck to my skin and clothing.

As we'd fallen, I'd heard a loud clattering sound. A white cloud of dust hung heavy in the air around us. When it cleared, we could see a pile of huge landscape stones spilling out of a broken cage in the place where I'd been standing seconds ago. I froze, a cold chill washing over me.

Baxter's face became ashen as he surveyed the mess of stones on the ground. He glanced up to the top of the stack from where they had fallen. His eyes flashed with anger. "Call me crazy, but I don't think that pallet fell on its own."

Bending over to try to finish catching my breath, but more so Baxter wouldn't see the terror I knew was all over my face, I took a good look at the stones. That load could easily have killed me if Baxter hadn't been there to push me out of the way. I shuddered. Someone was trying to send us a message, and it was pretty obvious who it was.

While I was trying to hold back a panic attack, Baxter took off around the side of the wall from where the rocks had fallen. Seconds later, he returned, a disgusted look on his face. "This part of the lot is suddenly deserted. What do you want to bet if I asked any of the workers if they saw anything, they'd all play dumb?"

My breathing still ragged, I said, "And if we asked Powell the same question, we'd get the same response from him. Let's just go."

We trudged back over to Baxter's SUV. I stopped Baxter before he got in, having him step on a big sheet of lifting tape to capture the limestone dust that was all over the soles of his shoes. For good measure, I swabbed his shoes as well, trying to take my mind off what could have happened back there.

Once we were on the road again and heading south, I felt Baxter's eyes on me. "What?" I asked. My hands were shaking, but at least I could breathe again.

"You look pale. Are you sure you're okay?"

"I'm fine." I crossed my arms so he wouldn't see my hands and changed the subject. "Where do we have to go to find Tyler's lady friend? Some old-money mansion on Meridian?"

He regarded me for a moment before replying. "No, she wants to meet at a bar east of downtown."

"East of downtown? I hate to be rude, but that's not exactly a classy part of Indy." A memory popped into my head. "Come to think of it, I lived there for about three months when I was a kid. I'm pretty sure my mom was dating a drug dealer at the time. I was little, so I had no clue what was going on, but I remember there were always people coming and going at all hours and lots of shouting. The drug dealer guy was nice, though. He bought me toys and he didn't hit me."

Baxter's eyes widened, but he didn't respond. After that, we didn't talk much on the way to our destination, only making stilted small talk about the weather and the Colts' upcoming home game.

The houses got smaller, older, and closer together as we neared our destination. On a particularly rundown street, we parked next to a small cinderblock building with metal bars on the windows. The neon sign next to the door had once said EASTSIDE BAR, but several letters had burned out. This did not seem like the kind of place where any friend of Tyler Harris's would hang out.

I moved to get out of the vehicle, but Baxter placed a hand on my arm. He said, "I'm sorry I clammed up earlier. You'd never said anything like that before, and it caught me off guard. I thought talking about it might upset you, so I didn't push it."

I studied his face. It radiated pity. That was one thing I didn't want, especially from him. "I didn't say it so you'd feel sorry for me. I was only making conversation. You're always complaining that I won't talk about my past, so I did. Trust me, living with a drug dealer wasn't even close to the worst thing that happened to me as a kid. It's not a painful story to bring up."

He sighed. "I'm not trying to pry. I just think if we're going to work together, we need to get to know each other and understand where each other is coming from. I want you to feel like you can talk to me."

"You know, you've always asked a lot of questions about me, but I've not heard you talk about yourself at all."

"Sorry, I guess that's the detective in me. What do you want to know?"

I changed the subject. "We should probably go inside before we get carjacked."

"Right," he said.

Out of the corner of my eye, I saw his face fall. In my opinion, we didn't need to get in each other's business. We worked together, and that was it. He did not need to know my entire life story.

We entered the bar, and the inside wasn't much better than the outside. The Eastside Bar must not have gotten the memo about Marion County's smoking ban, because the air was rank with cigarette smoke. The place was about half full—much too busy for a bar in the middle of the afternoon. Most of the people looked like they'd been here for a while.

Baxter stopped a weary-looking waitress and asked if she knew Ginger LaGrange. She pointed to a tall woman with long, red hair standing at the bar with her back to us. When the woman turned around, both of our jaws dropped.

20

I turned to face Baxter and murmured, "Given the fact that Tyler is so painfully hetero and conservative, do you think he realizes his girlfriend is transgender?" I whispered.

Baxter's eyebrows shot up. "I would hope he'd know the difference."

"Ha, ha. But seriously, maybe they haven't been intimate. Ginger is beautiful. I can see how a person could be mistaken."

"I agree, but since it was like pulling teeth to get him to give us her name, I'm betting he's trying to hide her to keep his secret."

I actually started to feel sorry for Tyler. "Oh. I guess now I get why he's always so over-the-top with the abusive flirting."

"In his line of work, it would be better to be known as a sleaze than a partner in a non-traditional relationship."

Ginger LaGrange was a gorgeous black person, tall and statuesque, with flawless makeup and an expensive auburn wig cascading down past her shoulders in silky waves. Her form-fitting dress looked like it had been made for her. She didn't look like she belonged in this dingy bar.

When we approached her, Baxter said, "Ginger? I'm Detective Baxter. We spoke on the phone."

"Hello, Detective," Ginger replied.

Baxter pointed to me. "This is my...partner, Ellie Matthews."

"Hi," I said. "Nice to meet you."

Ginger nodded. "You, too. So you're here to check out my baby Tyler's alibi?"

"Yes," replied Baxter. "Can you walk me through this past Saturday night, starting at about seven PM?"

"Tyler had to go to a big shindig his mother was throwing, so of course I wasn't welcome."

"Does his family know about your relationship?" I asked. It didn't pertain to the case, but I wanted to know.

"Of course not, dear. I don't know if we'll ever be able to go public as a couple, at least as long as he stays in politics." Ginger smiled, but there was a hint of pain in her eyes. "Anyway, he got to my place around eight forty-five, and he stayed all night."

"Do you have any proof that he was there?" asked Baxter.

"Just this hickey he gave me," Ginger replied coyly, holding back her hair to reveal a small, fading mark on the side of her neck.

Baxter blushed, and I had to bite my lip to keep from laughing. The man couldn't even discuss a hickey without getting embarrassed.

Ginger snapped her fingers. "Oh! I remember something. Tyler was so adorable in his little tuxedo, I simply had to take a picture of him. Will that work?" She flipped through some photos on her iPhone and after finding the one she was looking for, handed the phone to Baxter.

I looked over Baxter's shoulder to see Ginger's photo, and sure enough, there was a selfie of Tyler and Ginger, timestamped at 9:03 PM on Saturday night.

"Where do you live?" Baxter asked Ginger.

"Right around the corner."

After thinking for a moment, Baxter turned to me. "It's impossible that Harris could have made it all the way from Carnival Cove to here in twenty minutes, especially in Saturday night traffic. The coroner puts the time of death window between eight and ten that night, and according to Sellers, she was shot around 8:45. If Harris was in this area at 9:03, there's no way he could have killed her."

"I'd have to agree," I replied. I said to Ginger, "Thank you for your time, Ginger. You've been a big help."

"You're welcome, sweetie. I'd do anything for my Tyler."

Baxter and I left the bar and began the drive back to the station. He looked over at me. "I guess both of us lost the bet. Ginger is not the kind of wife or daughter we had in mind."

I nodded. "I did not see that one coming. So if neither of us won the bet, do we still get drinks?"

Back at the station, I headed to the lab to finish working on the fingerprints from the Vanover crime scene. Amanda was sitting at the AFIS computer, hard at work, and Beck was sitting at another computer, surfing the Internet.

"Hey, guys," I said, stowing my purse in the closet and putting on a lab coat. "Amanda, thanks for entering all those fingerprints. Have you been working on them this whole time?"

She glared at the back of Beck's head. "Yes, the *whole* time. I only have two left. As soon as I'm finished, I have some things to go over with you."

"Great. Thanks." I turned to Beck and asked in a fake sweet tone, "Beck, is there anything you worked on today that you can give me an update about?"

Not looking up from his gossip site, he said, "I give my updates to Sterling. If you want to know something, ask him."

I walked over and spun his chair around to face me. "I wasn't so much asking for an update as trying to find out if you'd done any actual work today, and it doesn't seem like you have. You know we have two active murder investigations here, and we only have one possible suspect? The evidence needs to be worked and processed as soon as humanly possible."

"Well, if you weren't out gallivanting around with your new boyfriend all the time and pushing the grunt work off on us—"

"Whoa, wait a minute," I said. "I've been out collecting new evidence and comparison samples, plus helping question witnesses and persons of interest. If I'm not at my real job or sleeping, I'm working this case. I'm helping you here, not the other way around."

He got out of his chair, trembling with anger. "You come in here and act like you own the place. Well, you don't. This is my lab, and *I'm* in charge."

I threw my hands in the air. "So do something. Be in charge."

Growling, he said, "I need a smoke," and stormed out of the lab.

Amanda smiled. "I thought he'd never leave. Now you and I can get some work done. Take a look at this."

I wheeled Beck's chair over next to her and sat down to study her screen.

She said, "The good news is I got hits on many of the fingerprints you lifted from the apartment. The bad news is that the only matches I got were Eli Vanover, Tristan Sellers, and Amber Corelli, the girl who found the victim. Other than that, there were several other contributors, but none of them popped up in AFIS. Sorry."

I thought for a moment. "Have Dudley Cooper's fingerprints been input into AFIS yet?"

"Yes, I entered them yesterday right after he was booked."

"That means none of these prints are his," I said, my spirits lifting.

"Correct," she said.

I dialed Baxter, and when he picked up, I said, "You and Sterling need to see this. We have the fingerprints finished from the Vanover scene, and Dr. Cooper's prints are not a match."

"We're on our way," he replied.

A minute later, Baxter and Sterling came striding through the door to the lab. Sterling pushed his way in front of Amanda and me, saying, "I want to see this for myself." After looking at the screen, he said, "Damn. Unless the DNA under Vanover's fingernails comes back as Cooper's, we don't have a case."

Baxter said to Sterling, "And the only hard evidence we have on Cooper is his print on the lighter from the Marais scene."

"Yeah, and I don't think that's enough. When we get back the DNA results for the cigar, it should help a little. At least it'll be another piece of evidence."

"What's up with the cigar and the lighter?" I asked.

Sterling turned to face me, scowling. "Oh yeah, I forgot you were in here. It's none of your business since you're not on that case."

"Come on. If you guys are so convinced that the two murders are related, and I'm working on one of them, I need to be kept in the loop about the other one. Keeping me in the dark isn't going to help either investigation," I pointed out.

Baxter sighed. "I agree. You need to know, so here it is. The bulk of the physical evidence we have is what we found at the spot where the killer was standing when he shot Vasti Marais at Carnival Cove. We recovered two spent cartridge casings that were fired from the murder weapon, a rifle we confiscated from Mayor Cooper's house. Next to the casings we also found an expensive lighter with Dudley Cooper's fingerprints all over it and the butt of a cigar."

Sterling said, "As much as I'd like to nail that preppy professor's ass to the wall, it seems a little staged to me that his fingerprints would be all over a lighter carelessly left at the scene but not on the murder weapon or the ammunition."

"I thought the same thing, but sometimes people do get careless in the heat of the moment," said Baxter. "Cooper is up to his eyeballs in motive. But even if the DNA on the cigar is Cooper's, it only proves he was at Carnival Cove at some point, not necessarily at the time of the murder. Since he owns Carnival Cove, his lawyers are going to say it's not damning that some of his personal effects were found there. We collected several of those blue glass rocks and some pea gravel from the grass where the shooter was standing but didn't think much of it until the same materials showed up at the other murder scene. We were hoping to be able to tie the two murders together so that the DNA under Vanover's fingernails would be the incontrovertible proof we needed."

I said, "We have the shoeprints on the pizza box and on the chair the killer kicked out from under Vanover when he was hanged." I asked Amanda, "Did you guys find any shoe impressions at the Marais scene?"

Amanda shook her head. "The grass was too thick and tall in that area. You could tell it had been trampled down, but there were no impressions."

"Are we sure there was nothing on Eli Vanover's murder weapon, the jump rope? No fingerprints or epithelials besides the victim's?" I asked.

Shrugging, Amanda said, "Beck processed it. He said he found nothing."

Sterling put his hands on his hips. "I wouldn't be surprised if that little prick screwed it up. Where the hell is Becky, anyway?"

"Smoke break," Amanda and I said at the same time.

Taking out his phone, Sterling made a call. "We need you in the lab, now." He listened for a moment and then barked, "I don't give a shit if you're on break, Becky. If you're not in here in sixty seconds, I'll come and drag your sorry ass in here myself."

An awkward silence filled the air until Baxter said, "We haven't been able to get any kind of confession out of Cooper for either murder. At this point, it's a waiting game to get the DNA results back from the blood and skin cells under Vanover's fingernails."

"It's ridiculous that it takes so long to get results back," complained Sterling. He nodded to me, "Hey, Matthews, why don't you go over to the state lab and offer the DNA nerds a special favor to speed up the process? It would be a better use of your time and talent."

As my response, I flipped Sterling the bird. I had seen a look of annoyance cross Baxter's face when Sterling was speaking. He didn't seem to be a big fan of Sterling. It made me wonder how tight their partnership was. It was likely that Baxter was the only detective nice enough to put up with Sterling's bullshit on a daily basis, so as a result, he got stuck with him.

Beck came back into the lab, his face red and pouty.

Sterling began, "Becky—"

"Don't call me Becky," Beck said through gritted teeth.

"Shut up," replied Sterling. "We want to know about the murder weapon in the Eli Vanover case. Are you sure you didn't miss something?"

A frown darkening his face, Beck went over to his desk and retrieved a file. He pulled out several photos and handed them to Sterling. "I found partial fingerprints belonging to the victim and to Tristan Sellers. However, most of those prints had been smudged, which would be consistent with the assumption that the last person to touch the jump rope was wearing gloves. That means no prints and no epithelials. Happy now?"

"Not really, because I've got nothing to work with!" Sterling hurled the photos at the nearest wall, succeeding only in scattering them across the floor. "I'm going to question our suspect again." He stomped out the door.

Baxter rolled his eyes. "I need to go play good cop." He put his hands together, pleading on his way out the door, "Get me some evidence, please, before Sterling kills someone."

While an indignant Beck picked up his photos, I noticed Amanda stifling a laugh. She cleared her throat. "You heard the man. What's next?"

I said, "I have clothing from the area of the struggle, a fingernail, hairs, and crap from the vacuum filter left to process. I thought I might go take a look at the hairs and the stuff from the filter under the new microscope in my lab at school. Plus I need to do my finished sketch of the crime scene, and I like my CAD program better than the one here. Would you two want to process the clothes and the fingernail?"

"Did you forget again that I'm in charge of this lab?" Beck snapped. "You don't get to hand out assignments."

Weary of arguing, I said, "It doesn't matter who's in charge; it matters that we get our jobs done. I'm taking the hairs and the filter trace, and for all I care, you can shove the rest of it up your ass." I grabbed my purse and hurried to evidence storage before he could shoot back an insult.

After I signed out the trace from the filter, the hairs collected at the crime scene, the sample hairs Tristan Sellers gave when he was questioned, and those Dr. Berg had collected from Eli Vanover during the autopsy, I headed for the sanctuary of my lab at Ashmore. There, I wouldn't have to deal with Beck or Sterling, or anyone for that matter. I was in charge of that lab, and I could kick out anyone I wanted.

It was late afternoon, and most classes were over for the day. That meant it was quiet in the science building, which was another plus for me. I decided to make the best use of my time by sorting the hairs recovered at the scene by length and color, hoping to make quick work of finding hairs that didn't belong to the inhabitants of the apartment. Tristan and Eli both had short, dark hair, so if I found any long blond or red hairs, for example, I would separate those out and give them special attention. Granted, everyone has color and length variations in their hair, so my plan wasn't foolproof, nor was it a scientific application. It was simply a fast way to wade through the evidence.

I sat down at the stereoscopic microscope, placing a strand of Eli's hair and a strand of Tristan's hair on the left side of its stage. I then took a pair of tweezers and began comparing each collected hair to the sample hairs one by one. Most of the hairs seemed to visually match my control samples, except for one long, blonde hair. I started to get excited, thinking I had found a clue, until I looked at the root end of the hair. There was no follicular tag, which meant the hair hadn't been yanked out—it had fallen out, therefore was not part of any violent struggle. Worse, no tag meant there was no DNA to be had. There had been follicular tags on a few of the shorter, darker hairs I had found, but I felt it was redundant and frivolous to have a DNA analysis run on hair likely belonging to the inhabitants of the apartment.

Needing a break from thinking about murder, I called my sister.

"Hey," Rachel answered in a hushed voice.

"What's up?" I asked.

"I'm with my study group. Why didn't you just text me? Is something wrong?"

Feeling bad for taking time away from her studying, I said, "No, I was bored and thought I'd call. I'll let you go."

"Are you sure nothing's wrong?" she asked, her tone suspicious.

"Everything's good. Go back to studying."

"Okay. See you later, then."

I had an idea. "Hey, do you mind if I pick up Nate from daycare and take him to dinner? I've been missing that kid this week."

"Knock yourself out."

After we hung up, I was in better spirits, even though I had the disgusting task ahead of me of sifting through the debris Baxter had vacuumed up from Tristan Sellers's apartment floor. I emptied the container onto a new piece of butcher paper on my work surface and began combing through dust, dirt, food crumbs, hair, fibers, and tiny bits of paper. There was nothing out of the ordinary here.

Once I was finished, I repackaged the evidence and used one of the lab's computers to work on my sketch of the crime scene. My CAD skills weren't the best, but it didn't take me long to rework my rough sketch into a finished version that was neat and precise and would be easy for jurors to understand. Forensic science is becoming more and more advanced by the moment, but at the end of the day, if the evidential findings cannot be presented in clear enough terms for a jury to understand, they can become practically useless. I saved my finished sketch to a flash drive and stored it in my bag with the other evidence. After closing up the lab, I headed across campus to pick up my nephew.

21

Ashmore College ran a daycare for employees' children, and I was able to get Nate in the program because he lived with me. He went there while Rachel and I were in class, which was perfect, because whoever was done first could pick him up on the way home for the day.

When I got to the daycare center, Nate was playing with his "girlfriend," Emma. They were adorable, playing chef with a kid-sized toy kitchen.

"Hey, kiddo," I said, kneeling down beside him.

He whined, "Oh, is it time to go?"

"Yeah, buddy. But I thought we could go somewhere for dinner on the way home."

Nate's eyes got as big as saucers. "Can we go to McDonald's? Can we? Can we?"

Groaning to myself, I said, "Yes, of course." McDonald's was the only place he ever wanted to go to eat. Rachel and I were sick of it, but we usually caved, since it was never a fight to get him to eat the food there.

Nate and I had a lovely time chatting over dinner. It did wonders for my mental state to disconnect from my rigorous schedule. When we left the restaurant, I picked him up to carry him across the busy parking lot.

Eye-to-eye with me, he asked, "Auntie Ellie, are you going to be doing your new job forever?"

I had just been ready to step off the sidewalk, but stopped so I could give his serious question my full attention. "Absolutely not. After I help the police figure out who the bad guy is, I'm done." I gave him a kiss on the cheek. "And then everything will go back to normal."

Nate smiled. "Yay. I don't like your new job. You have to stay out past bedtime."

I laughed. "That's right. Auntie Ellie needs her sleep, doesn't she?"

I hugged him to me and started walking across the parking lot. A moment later, an ear-splitting screech cut through the air, and I looked to my right just in time to see a bright yellow Volkswagen Beetle careening toward us, having to skid to a halt in order to avoid running us over. I screamed and jumped back, but if the car hadn't stopped when it did, Nate and I would have been on the way to the hospital.

Nate burst out crying.

My whole body shaking, I yelled, "Hey!" and slammed my hand down onto the hood of the car. "Watch where you're going, you—" I managed to stop myself in time from cursing in front of my nephew, who was clinging to me and trying to crawl up my shoulder. Stomping around to the driver's side window, I yelled, "You nearly ran us over! Didn't you see us?"

The girl driving gaped at me in horror. It was Maddie from my Intro to Forensics class, who was the girlfriend of our missing person of interest, Tad Ogelsby. Maddie's wild eyes darted from me to Nate and then around the parking lot, as if looking to see if anyone else had witnessed the incident.

"Maddie, I asked you a question," I snapped, trying to get her to respond.

She opened her mouth as if to speak, but then without a word she zoomed away, leaving Nate and me both still frightened and upset. He was whimpering, and I could feel his wet tears trickling down my shoulder.

I stroked his hair. "Shh, baby. It's okay. We're just fine."

"That was scary!" he wailed.

It was scary, but something about the way Maddie reacted bothered me. Now, however, I had to concentrate on taking care of my nephew. "I know, sweetheart. Auntie Ellie was scared, too, but it's over and we're safe."

Glancing across the street, I spotted the Marsh Supermarket. "Do you think a donut from Marsh would make you feel better?"

Donuts from Marsh were Nate's favorite. Rachel would probably kill me later for giving him McDonald's and donuts all in one evening, but this was an emotional emergency.

He brightened a bit. "Maybe. Can I have two?"

Smiling, I said, "I'll get two, but let's save the second one for breakfast tomorrow. How's that?"

"Okay," he said, putting his head back down on my shoulder and wrapping his tiny hands around the back of my neck in a vise-like grip.

After getting Nate his donuts, I deposited him at home with Rachel. Something had nagged at me since I came into contact with Maddie. I headed to the Sheriff's station, mulling over what had happened in the parking lot. I went to talk to Baxter about it and found he had run out to grab dinner, but Sterling was there. I hadn't worked much with Sterling on this case, even though he was as much a part of it as Baxter was. I figured it wouldn't hurt to clue him in to my information on Maddie since he was the one in charge of searching for Tad Ogelsby.

"Hey," I said, sitting down in a chair next to his desk.

"What do you want?" he growled, not looking up from his computer screen.

I sighed to myself. He was great at what he did, and if he were easier to work with, we could get a lot more done. I decided not to return an insult. "Have you found Tad Ogelsby yet?"

"No."

"Did you talk to his girlfriend?"

"We've reached out to her, but she hasn't returned our calls."

"She's a student of mine, and she didn't show up for my class yesterday."

Snorting, he replied, "So? It's college. No one goes to class."

"I'm worried something's going on with her. We had a test, which she knew about. She was the only student who didn't attend."

"BFD. Maybe she didn't study for the test or she felt like skipping," he replied. He was *not* working with me here.

"It's not like her to miss class. Just now, I saw her in the McDonald's parking lot over in Carmel, and she nearly ran me over."

"Good for her."

"Damn it, Sterling!" I exclaimed. "If we're going to work on this case together, we need to be able to talk like adults. Quit being such an ass."

Turning around to glare at me, he fired back, "I don't need you on this case. In fact, I don't know why you're even here, except Baxter thinks—"

"What does Baxter think?" asked Baxter, appearing beside me.

"Baxter thinks he better give me my dinner before I die of hunger," Sterling snapped, snatching a greasy paper bag out of Baxter's hand.

"If only," I said under my breath, getting up and following Baxter to his desk.

"I heard that," Sterling said.

Baxter sat down and got out his food. "You two can't have a civilized conversation, can you?"

"It would seem not," I said, on edge from my close call with the front end of Maddie's car and from having to deal with Sterling's attitude. "I'll tell you what he didn't want to listen to. Tad Ogelsby's girlfriend Maddie missed my class yesterday. I saw her about thirty minutes ago when she almost ran over my nephew and me with her car. She looked frightened when she saw me, and I have a feeling it wasn't because she was worried about cutting my class. I wonder if she's somehow involved with what's going on. Sterling said you hadn't been able to talk to her yet."

"No, not yet. I'll check up on her."

"Thanks."

I left Baxter and went back to the lab. Beck was nowhere to be found, again, but Amanda was there, hard at work examining a pair of pants under a stereoscope.

"Is Beck gone again?" I asked.

Amanda looked up from her work. "He went home for the day."

"You're kidding me, right?"

"I wish I were. He tried to get me to leave also, telling me if I didn't he'd write me up for insubordination." She let out a laugh, but then sobered quickly. "He can't do that, right?"

"No, he cannot." I walked over and looked at the pants she was examining. "Find anything useful?"

After taking off her gloves, she rubbed her eyes. "Not really. I found a combination of food stains, crumbs, random fibers, hair, and general dust and ick on the clothes from the struggle area. No blood or other bodily fluids, and none of the hairs had follicular tags. Oh, and everything reeks of pot and cheap cologne."

"Disgusting, but neither useful nor surprising. What do you have left to process?"

"These pants are the last of the clothes. Beck processed the fingernail and maybe one shirt, then got tired and went home."

I shook my head. "He's such a hard worker," I muttered. "Now that all of the evidence has been processed, I guess that means we get to start over."

"I always thought it was such a waste of time to have two people examine every piece of evidence that comes through." She snickered. "Then I met Beck Durant. I think they made that rule for him. I can't tell you how many times I've reprocessed something of his and found evidence he missed."

"Wow. Sounds like his lab skills got worse instead of better after I left. I guess we should get started."

Amanda repackaged the pants and followed me to evidence, where we retrieved the murder weapon, the pull-up bar, the clothes Eli was wearing at the time of his death, and the folding chair. She had already processed the pull-up bar and Eli's pants, so I gave her his shirt and the folding chair for examination and took the murder weapon, the pull-up bar, and Eli's pants for myself.

I placed the jump rope under the stereoscope for magnification. There was gray fingerprint powder on the black plastic handles from where Beck had dusted for prints. I would have to dust the handles again after I finished examining the jump rope to find any prints he may have missed. It was possible that I could find some prints with the help of a UV light, but only if whoever left them had been sweating or had another bodily fluid on his hands. I got out a UV light and some goggles, turned off the light above my worktable, and shined the UV light on the handles. There were no fingerprints to be seen, but there was a smear of blood, which appeared to have already been swabbed. I swabbed it again as part of my independent examination. The rope portion was of course covered in blood from where Eli had tried to claw it off his neck. Getting out a few more swabs, I moistened each one with a drop of distilled water and rubbed the smooth rope with them at several intervals, hoping to pick up some epithelial cells from the killer.

Finished with the UV light, I swiped fingerprint dust over the handles but didn't find any prints. Beck seemed to have done a good job at getting all the prints off the handles. Satisfied with my work, I processed the pull-up bar in the same manner, looking for any missed fingerprints and swabbing for possible touch DNA.

When I was done, I got the victim's shirt from Amanda and began studying it. It was a tattered T-shirt, a staple garment in the wardrobe of every college boy. This particular one, though, had bloodstains around the neck and a few blood smears across the front.

Turning around to Amanda, I said, "I can't help but imagine the last few minutes of Eli Vanover's life. I feel like this shirt should be able to tell us something. The murder was an intimate one, at least during the time the victim was being manually strangled. There has to be some kind of transfer on it, even though Beck didn't find anything."

She said, "Agreed. You were at the scene. How do you think it all went down?"

I thought for a moment. "There was likely some kind of a verbal exchange to start. A struggle ensued, during which the coffee table got shoved several inches over and a bong broke. The killer stepped on a pizza box, leaving behind a shoeprint and several rocks from his shoe treads. At some point, the killer grabbed Eli by the neck and choked him violently enough to break his hyoid bone, but not thoroughly enough to kill him. The killer also held a gun to Eli's head and pistol-whipped him, but we don't know if it happened before or after he choked him."

She wrinkled her forehead. "Probably before, right? I mean, if the killer broke our victim's hyoid bone, the manual strangulation was intense. Would the victim have even been conscious for the rest of it?"

"He was conscious for a time while he was hanging from the pull-up bar, because there's evidence he tried to get free, but I'd never thought of it that way. That's brilliant. And it means the killer would've had to hoist an unconscious or semi-conscious young man up onto a folding chair, which couldn't have been easy."

"How in the hell would you get an incapacitated person from the floor to a standing position on top of a chair, anyway? Wouldn't it be nearly impossible?" she asked.

"Let's find out. It's reenactment time."

After disposing of our gloves, we headed over to our office area, away from the evidence and expensive equipment.

Amanda said, "Lie down like I've choked you and you're unconscious." I did as she said, and she continued, "If it were me, I would move you like this."

She got behind me and put her hands under my armpits. Lifting my head and shoulders up, she then dragged me over to a nearby chair. Once I was propped against the chair, she stood over me, using the same underarm grab move to pull me up farther. This time we were face to face, in close proximity. She was able to hoist me into a sitting position on the chair, but then stood back, huffing and puffing.

"Whew! That was a workout, no offense, and I still don't have you in a standing position. Maybe the victim *was* conscious after all." Amanda brushed her hand across my shoulder. "Sorry, I got some makeup on your lab coat when I was lifting you."

"So this is what you girls do when you're alone in the lab," smirked Sterling, who had just entered the lab with Baxter. He turned to Baxter. "I don't know exactly what they were doing, but it was kind of hot, don't you think, Nicky?"

Amanda turned beet red, and I rolled my eyes.

Baxter ignored him and said to me, "I came to tell you that I made a few calls about Maddie Haynes. She packed up and left and hasn't been seen by any of her friends since Tuesday night, just like her boyfriend."

"Oh, that's not good," I breathed, fearing that sweet little Maddie was in way over her head.

"I'm willing to bet she and Ogelsby are shacked up somewhere and don't want to be found. You and I can dig a little deeper tomorrow." He gestured to Sterling. "Right now, we're tagging along on a drug bust, hoping to nab Eli Vanover's supplier. I'm not convinced the guy is going to show. It depends on whether or not he's heard about Vanover's death."

"Scumbags generally don't make it a point to watch the evening news or read the paper, so he's probably clueless," joked Sterling.

"Have fun on your drug bust. I'm heading home. See you tomorrow," I replied to them. Amanda gave them a shy wave.

After they left, I turned to Amanda and studied her for a moment. "So, which one of them do you have a crush on?"

Her face flamed bright red again, and she looked away. "I don't..." She cleared her throat.

"Is it Sterling?" I asked, wrinkling my nose.

Sighing, she nodded.

"I'm not trying to pry into your personal business or tell you how to live your life, but speaking from experience, Sterling might not be the best choice for a relationship."

"He said you told him he wasn't good enough for you once you got your professor job at the college," she said, her tone defensive.

I laughed. "*That's* what he's telling people? He pursued me for an entire month, and then when I finally got drunk and gave in, he lost interest. After we hooked up, he barely spoke to me. Of course, I told him what I thought of that, and he didn't appreciate it. Since then, we can't be in the same room with each other without fighting."

"Oh," Amanda said, frowning.

"But, hey, I'm far from qualified to give dating advice, so go with your gut." It was getting uncomfortable, so I changed the subject. "So about our little reenactment, it's likely there are plenty of epithelials on the victim's shirt, especially under the sleeves, right?"

"I think that's a safe assumption," she replied, beginning to shut down the office area for the night.

I went back to my worktable, tape lifted under both sleeves of the shirt, and set the sample aside to be sent to DNA. A lightbulb went off in my head as I glanced down at the shoulder of my lab coat where Amanda had smudged her makeup during our reenactment. I hurried over to a cabinet to retrieve a UV light and turned out the lights over my worktable. After donning a fresh pair of gloves, I shined the UV light on the shirt.

"Aha! There's something here on the shoulder. Could be sweat—the killer's sweat." I circled the area of the stain with a Sharpie, cut out a small piece of it, and placed the sample piece in a small manila envelope. "Perfect. That is, unless the victim made a habit of using his shirt to wipe his own face."

Amanda came back over to my table, yawning. "I'd say you're right on target. Good job."

"I think we should leave here on a positive note. Let's call it a night."

"You read my mind."

22

I was dreaming about being alone on a deserted Hawaiian beach, with no job and no worries. It was blissful and perfect until rocks started tumbling down from the cliff above me, coming straight down at me. I jolted awake.

"Ellie!" said Rachel, shaking my shoulder.

"What?" I groaned.

"Will you answer your damn phone? It's been ringing every few minutes, and it's driving me nuts."

She tossed my phone onto the bed beside me and flounced out my room. I had left my phone in my purse, in the kitchen, and as far away from me as possible. To say that I didn't want my sleep disturbed would have been a gross understatement. In hindsight, I should have simply turned the ringer off instead. I looked at the screen and found I had three missed calls and two voice messages from Baxter. Before I could listen to the messages, my phone rang again.

"What?" I griped, not bothering to say hello.

"Whoa. It's like I woke an angry bear," Baxter said.

"Did you call me for a reason, or did you just feel like bothering me?"

He laughed. "I need you."

"It's the middle of the night."

"It's only a little after ten."

I whined, "What could you possibly need that can't wait until tomorrow?"

"Besides a pat on the back for catching Eli Vanover's supplier, I need you to run his prints. I've got him on possession and dealing, but if I had a murder charge to throw at him, I might get him to talk about some of his fellow dealers."

"Like the third shooter from your convenience store case?" I asked.

"Exactly."

Sighing, I asked, "Why can't you call Durant or Amanda?"

"The department would have to pay them overtime if I call them back in. You, on the other hand, are getting a lump sum for your services."

"For the record, I'm not happy about this."

"Duly noted. See you soon."

I dragged myself out of bed and changed clothes, but couldn't even consider the thought of wrenching my eyes open to put in my contacts. I put on my glasses and headed back to the station. When I got there, Baxter was waiting for me, a ten-print card in hand.

I took the card from him. "Going old school?"

He nodded. "The live scan computer isn't cooperating. Personally, I like using the ten-print card. Something about getting fingerprinted the old-fashioned way rattles a lot of people. What's with the glasses?"

I had hoped no one would notice them, although they were rather large and had thick, black frames. "Someone woke me up, and I didn't feel like putting my contacts in."

"You look like a hipster."

"Call me a hipster again and see how many fingerprints I get done for you," I grumbled.

He grinned at me. "I'll be in Interrogation Room Three. Find me when you're done." He disappeared down the hall.

I trudged to the lab and scanned the fingerprints into our AFIS computer, taking my time in examining each print and plotting its individual characteristics. Baxter's suspect had an interesting double loop whorl pattern to his fingerprints, which was great because it made them that much more unusual and easy to visually distinguish. After I had the suspect's fingerprints entered, I sat back and let AFIS work on finding me some possible matches. In under a minute, I had proof that Baxter's suspect, Shawn Mayes, was *not* our killer—at least his fingerprints didn't match any we'd found at the crime scene. He was, however, involved in an unsolved liquor store robbery on the east side of Indianapolis from three months ago.

Armed with a printout of my findings, I headed toward the interrogation rooms. There were small windows in the doors, and I could see Baxter in Room Three, speaking with a young, rough-looking man with tattoos and piercings everywhere. I shivered. Normally, I didn't have to deal with too many unsavory characters, most of my work being done either at a secured scene or in the lab. When I worked as a criminalist, the only time I came into contact with suspects was in court when I would testify about my findings, and that too was a safe, controlled environment. It was a new experience to be working with Baxter, who seemed to want me involved in more aspects of the case since I knew most of the persons of interest.

I could see Sterling slouched in the corner of the interrogation room, his angry cop face securely in place. When I knocked, Baxter got up and came to the door. When he vacated his seat, Sterling took his place at the table and began grilling the suspect.

Baxter met me in the hallway. "What did you find?"

"Probably not what you're looking for," I replied. "Shawn Mayes's fingerprints didn't match any at our scene."

Baxter blew out a disgruntled breath. "This case is starting to piss me off."

"I do have some good news for you. I found one match for your guy's prints in AFIS on an unsolved liquor store robbery. It happened three months ago on the east side of Indy." I handed him my printout.

After reading it, he perked up. "This might help. Thanks. And thanks for getting out of bed to run the prints for me."

"You're welcome." As he turned to leave, I caught his arm. "Hey, um… thanks for pushing me out of harm's way this afternoon."

"I wondered when you'd get around to thanking me for saving your life."

I gave him a sheepish smile. "In case you hadn't noticed, I was a little freaked out by it. I was trying to keep my cool by not allowing myself to think about it."

"I figured as much. Bottling up your feelings is part of the job." He gave me a pat on the back. "Just don't bottle up too much. You'll end up like Sterling."

I woke up rested despite having had my sleep interrupted the night before. My morning classes went better than any of my classes had the entire week, and I was finally beginning to feel like my normal self again. In particular, I was thrilled about my lunch date.

After my class, I found Rob lounged against his SUV, waiting for me near the back door to the science building. When I approached, he drew me close and gave me a thorough kiss.

"Thanks for making time to see me," he murmured against my cheek.

"With a greeting like that, how could I refuse?"

Rob released me, smiling, and helped me up into his vehicle. "I thought we might head over to the City Center for lunch."

"Sounds good."

Truth be told, the Carmel City Center, an upscale new area of Carmel, wouldn't have been my first choice. Going there would be like hanging out at Dr. Cooper's fundraiser gala with the town's elite. It was not my scene, but I thought it best to go along with it and at least pretend to fit in. Rob had already seen enough of my white trash side.

We ended up at a Spanish tapas restaurant, and even though it was rather busy, we were seated immediately. He'd been there before, so I let him choose a few dishes for us to share.

"Did you finally get caught up on your sleep?" he asked.

"Yes. I could use more, but at least I'm no longer walking around in a fog like on Wednesday. I ought to be much better at conversation."

He laughed. "I thought you did just fine. It was nice to go on a first date and not feel like I'm at an interview. You were too tired to put on a false front. It was refreshing, actually." He took my hand. "It has to be difficult working two jobs at once. Do you do much consulting for the police?"

"No, this is the first time I've consulted. I was a criminalist for the county a few years ago, but I...was offered the teaching job and decided to make the switch."

"I'm sure it's better hours and a lot less stress."

"You have no idea."

"Why did you decide to go back and consult after all this time?"

"The Sheriff asked me as a personal favor. I've known her for years."

He smiled. "So are you rusty after not being out in the field for a while?"

I shook my head. "Not really. I've kept my certifications and my skills up. The hard part for me is dealing with the emotional side of crime. Sometimes a case can really get to you."

Squeezing my hand, he asked, "Did you know the kid?"

His touch was comforting. "Yes, sort of. Knowing the deceased adds a major dimension to an investigation. It's not as easy to disconnect."

My cell phone rang, and it was Baxter. I had little time to spend with Rob today, so I decided to ignore the call.

"Are you sure you don't need to get that?" Rob asked.

"No, it can wait," I replied.

He leaned over and brushed his lips against my cheek.

"Well," chirped a snippy voice. "It didn't take long for you to move on and go about your life once you turned my Dudley over to the police. Tell me, how *do* you sleep at night?"

My mouth agape, I looked up to find Judith Cooper scowling at me, her eyes red-rimmed from crying. Her sister, Vivian Harris, stood beside her, her face stony as well. Rob's expression was wary and his jaw was set, his body language suggesting he was ready to defend me. I thought I might need it.

"Mrs. Cooper," I began, trying to stay calm. "I don't think it's a good idea for us to discuss your son's case."

"Oh, you don't? Well, I guess we'll have to discuss it in court, then. I will have you know I'll be suing you for luring him into a trap. He trusted you, and you betrayed him!"

I knew she couldn't sue for something as stupid as that. She was angry, and she was trying to scare me. I didn't scare easily, but I also wouldn't put it past her to find a way to fire me from my teaching job. It wasn't smart to piss off the president of the college.

I said, "Mrs. Cooper, I'm working for the Hamilton County Sheriff's Department. This is not a personal matter of any kind."

"Very well, I'll sue the lot of you! You imbeciles have the wrong man. My Dudley would...would never hurt anyone." Tears spilled from her eyes. I truly felt bad for her. I could only imagine the pain she was going through.

I sighed. "I'm sorry things had to happen the way they did, Mrs. Cooper."

"I never understood why he insisted on befriending someone like you," she sneered, her voice like ice.

Flicking my eyes at Rob, I grimaced. "For what it's worth...I don't think your son is capable of murder."

She wailed, "If you're working with the police, then do something about it!"

"I'm not working that case. The detectives on his case are good at what they do, and the evidence will show the real truth. It takes time."

Evidently finished with me, Mrs. Cooper turned her wrath on Rob. "I'm shocked at your disloyalty, Mr. Larson. My husband will hear about this. Good day." She turned and stalked away, her expensive heels clacking on the wood floor.

Darting a furtive glance at her sister, Vivian Harris leaned toward me and whispered, "If you want to know the real truth, I suggest you look no further than George Cooper." Without another word, she hurried to catch up with her sister.

Dumbfounded, I watched them leave the restaurant, wondering what all that was about. Rob seemed as confused as I did. Our food came at that point, but neither of us made a move to eat anything. The tension from Mrs. Cooper's tirade still hung heavy in the air between us.

I murmured, "I'm sorry if being with me is going to cost you a job."

Rob shook his head. "Don't worry about it. He's a high maintenance client, and if I lose him, it won't hurt my business." He touched my cheek. "I'm not going to choose that asshole George Cooper over you."

Smiling, I said, "Thanks. Normally I'm a boring college professor. I wish we'd met a couple of weeks ago, before my life went to Crazytown."

"It doesn't bother me. I like a little excitement in my life."

"Um…I need to make a quick call." Grabbing my phone, I hurried to the hallway by the restrooms and dialed Baxter.

He answered, "Hey, not taking my calls? I thought you were on your lunch break."

"You know my schedule? That's a little stalker-like," I joked.

Chuckling, he said, "That hurts, Ellie. I called to ask you if you know the director of Fenton Hall, Tony Dante."

"Yes, unfortunately."

"Why 'unfortunately'?"

"He's a creeper."

Baxter laughed again. "Is that your professional opinion?"

"It's *everyone's* opinion. He hits on anything in a skirt. The younger, the better. Why do you want to know?"

"I ran across a big, unflattering story on him from a few weeks ago in the online version of the *Ashmore Voice*, along with a video of him getting angry with Eli Vanover over it."

"Right. He got moved from Harris Hall to Fenton Hall at the start of the school year. Everyone thinks it's because Fenton is an all-male dorm, which means no tail for him to chase. He's related to someone on the Board of Trustees, so that's why he got moved instead of canned. Why are you interested in him?"

"Because out of the sixty-seven idiotic videos I watched on that vlog, Tony Dante is the only person who had an altercation with Vanover *and* has an assault charge on his record. I think that makes him worth talking to."

"Knock yourself out."

"With you."

"No thanks." I changed the subject before he had a chance to try to talk me into it. "I thought you'd want to know I just got accosted by Judith Cooper, Dudley's mom."

"What did she want?"

"To rip me a new one for tricking her baby boy into getting arrested. I blame you."

"Sorry," he said, not sounding sorry at all.

"Anyway, her sister, Tyler Harris's mom, was with her. After Mrs.

Cooper was done berating me, Vivian Harris told me if I wanted to know the truth about Vasti's murder, I should look at George Cooper."

"Hmm. I wonder if she knows something or if she heard we questioned her son and is trying to throw the heat off him."

"That's your job to figure out. I'm just the messenger. I have to go."

"We'll take a look at George Cooper, too. We have lots to do today, so wrap up your date and get over here."

"How did you know I was on a date?" I demanded.

"I'm a detective, remember?"

"I have class until two. I can't skip again. I'll head to the station afterward." I ended my call with Baxter and hurried back to Rob.

"We're going to have to cut lunch short, aren't we?" he asked, his expression registering disappointment.

"No," I replied, covering his hand with mine. "This is important to me."

He broke into a stellar smile. "We're on the same page, then."

We ate our food in silence for a few moments.

Rob set down his fork. After hesitating for a moment, he said, "Mrs. Cooper mentioned that you lured Dudley into a trap. What did she mean by that?"

I didn't want to say too much, but I also didn't want him to think I was some siren who delighted in luring men to their doom. "I can't go into detail, but at the request of the Sheriff's Department, I agreed to meet with Dr. Cooper. They had a warrant out for his arrest, and I helped, um, facilitate his capture."

"That sounds dangerous. I thought you gathered evidence and processed it in a lab."

"I do. But since I was already involved, it seemed to be the simplest and safest way to apprehend him."

"Not for you," he said, his face creased with worry. "Besides, I thought you were working on the other murder case."

"I am, but...I help where I'm needed." I changed the subject. "This food is really great."

He wasn't ready to let the conversation go. "Sorry, one more thing. Vivian Harris mentioned Mayor Cooper to you in connection to that girl's murder." He shifted in his seat, seeming to wrestle with what he was about to say. "I've seen the girl before...at Mayor Cooper's place."

Goosebumps popped out on my arms. "Was she with Dudley or George?"

He blew out a breath before answering, "George."

"And what were they doing exactly?" I asked.

Looking away from me and shaking his head, he said, "I'm sure you can guess."

So Vasti wasn't blowing smoke up Dr. Cooper's ass when she told him about having an affair with his father. Baxter had been right about the "grain of truth." This was a little more than a grain, though.

Rob asked, "Are the murders connected somehow? If Dudley is a person of interest in your case, would that make George a person of interest in the cases as well, given his relationship with the dead girl?"

I shook my head. "I have no idea, and I really shouldn't speculate."

"Does that mean you still don't have a suspect in your case?"

Placing my hand on his, I smiled. "I'm sorry. I can't say any more. With switching over to teaching, I'd forgotten how difficult it is to talk to someone about your day and not actually be able to tell them anything about it. That's another tough part of the job—making sure you keep your mouth shut."

"I didn't mean to pressure you." He gave me a sheepish grin. "I was thinking of myself—wondering if I was going to have to end up testifying against one of my clients. That could be bad for business."

"You're right, it could. Sorry to crap on your day."

He shrugged. "I should have known better than to take on a politician as a client, right?"

We both laughed and went back to eating. Finishing soon after, we headed back to campus.

When Rob pulled up to the curb next to the science building, I said to him, "I hope all the nonsense at the restaurant didn't scare you away."

He gave me a dubious look. "Do I look like a guy who scares easily?"

Giving his solid bicep a squeeze, I replied, "Not at all."

"You know, I protect the good guys from the bad guys, too." He chuckled. "Or rather, I protect the rich guys from the bad guys."

I laughed. "And in some cases, the rich guys might *be* the bad guys."

Rob grew serious, placing his hand on my cheek. "I know I have no right to meddle in your life, especially since we just met, but...I like you, and I care about your safety. Please don't mess with George Cooper. He's well-*connected*, if you get what I'm saying."

I did, and it didn't surprise me to hear he had ties to organized crime. "I'll be careful. Anytime I'm out in the field, I'm with one of the detectives, and he looks out for me." I thought back to yesterday at the rock yard and stifled a shiver. "Besides, when this is over, I get to go back to being a mild-mannered professor with a lot of free time on her hands."

He grinned. "I'm looking forward to it."

23

When I got done with my final class for the day, Baxter was waiting outside my office.

"I thought I was meeting you at the station," I said.

"I wanted us to talk to Tony Dante together," he replied.

"And that was why I was going to meet you at the station—to get out of talking to Tony Dante. I've successfully avoided him for months."

"But you're the center of my evil plan. I'm going to let Dante get mesmerized by ogling you, then hit him with a bunch of tough questions. I figure he'll slip and tell me something he didn't mean to say."

"Unless he's decided I'm too old to pique his interest, the sick bastard. And for the record, I'm disturbed that you're using me as a pawn, *again*."

"I'll shoot him if he tries to get fresh with you."

I brightened at the thought. "Promise?"

From the science building, Fenton Hall was only a short walk across one of Ashmore's lush, green lawns. We found Tony Dante in the dorm's game room. Tony was a little man, thin and puny, making a pathetic attempt to grow a goatee. He was my age, but tried to dress like a college student, probably so he would seem accessible. Or, more likely, so he could blend in and hook up with girls before they realized how old he was. At this particular moment he was busy chatting up a young girl who seemed to want nothing more than to get back to a game of ping pong with her friends. He had her backed into a corner.

I gestured to him and said to Baxter, "See what I mean?"

"I'll handle this." Marching over to Tony, he put a hand on his shoulder and wheeled him around. "Maybe you should talk to someone more your own age, Mr. Dante." He flashed his badge.

Tony's eyes grew wide. "She's eighteen, officer."

"It's *Detective*. Detective Nick Baxter. We need to speak with you in private."

Relaxing a little and looking me up and down, Tony said, "I wouldn't mind talking to the lovely professor in private."

I had made it clear when I first came to Ashmore that his advances toward me were unwelcome. Maybe he needed a refresher. "Keep talking, assclown. Detective Baxter promised me he'd shoot you if you came on to me," I said.

Tony dropped the act and led us to his office. He gestured for us to sit down, still keeping a wary eye on Baxter's gun. Judging from his reaction, he might think twice about approaching me on campus ever again.

Baxter said, "Let's cut to the chase." He pulled a photo out of the folder he had brought and shoved it across the desk toward Tony.

Taking one look at the photo, Tony whimpered and shrunk back in his seat. I didn't blame him. The photo was a close-up I had taken of Eli Vanover's face and neck while he was still hanging at his apartment. Baxter wasn't wasting any time with this interview.

"Do you know who this is?" asked Baxter.

The color had drained from Tony's face, except for a little green. "It's hard to recognize him with the...with the—" Diving down next to his desk, he sunk his head into the nearest trash can and retched.

I flicked my eyes at Baxter, wondering if his crime scene gag reflex would be triggered at the sight and smell of someone else vomiting. He seemed to be fine, even going as far as to get up to go stand over Tony and demand, "Did you kill Eli Vanover?" Well, that was one way to interrogate a suspect.

Tony dragged his head out of the trash can and stared up at Baxter. "What? No," he croaked, wiping his mouth on his sleeve.

"Are you sure? Because I'm thinking maybe you got mad about the article he wrote about you in the *Voice*. Maybe his allegations about you getting friendly with female students hit a little too close to home and you wanted to silence him."

Tony made no move to get up off his knees. "No!" he cried. "I didn't kill him! I swear."

Baxter bent closer to him, growling, "But maybe you slapped him around a little and coerced him into hanging himself. I wouldn't put it past someone with an assault charge."

Tony was full-on crying now. "No! I didn't do anything to Eli. Yes, I have an assault charge, but...but that was from a bar fight I didn't even win!" He turned to me, pleading, "Aren't you going to do anything about this? Like at least play good cop or *something*?"

"Hmm..." Pretending to mull over his question, I rifled through the bowl of candy on his desk and came up with a mini Kit Kat. After popping it into my mouth and taking my dear sweet time to chew it, I looked up at Baxter and then back down at Tony. "Nope. I think he's doing a great job. You're just lucky he's not beating a confession out of you." I shook my head, enjoying the fact that Tony looked like he was about to puke again. "The last guy we talked to... Ooh. His face doesn't look so good anymore."

Baxter had to cough to cover up a laugh over my blatant lie.

Tony curled up into a ball on the floor.

"Where were you between noon and two on Tuesday?" Baxter asked him.

He lifted his head slightly. "Tuesday? I was...I was...having lunch at the coffeehouse across the street and...then I had a meeting at the Residence Life office."

"Can anyone corroborate your story?"

"Yes—Rachel Miller."

I stared at him. "My sister?"

He had the gall to smirk at me. "Yes. I had a lovely lunch with her—"

"You *what*?" I shouted, leaping out of my chair and lunging toward him. "You horny freak show, if you even *thought* about—"

"Whoa," Baxter said, holding me back by both arms. He whispered in my ear, "There has to be a good cop when we do good cop/bad cop."

Struggling to get free, I said between gritted teeth, "Give me your gun. I'll shoot him myself."

Baxter said to a still-trembling Tony, "I think we have what we need. You keep your nose clean, Mr. Dante." He collected the photo and his file and dragged me out of the room.

Baxter released me, and I stalked ahead of him down the hall. He muttered, "Damn. Remind me never to hit on your sister."

"Shut up."

He chuckled. "I'm kidding, of course. I have to say that up until you lost your crap, you played it perfectly. How in the hell did you manage to eat something with the stench of vomit in that room? I had to breathe through my mouth nearly the whole time."

My anger fading, I replied, "Nate is a puker, and it comes on fast. Many times, I have nothing to catch it with besides my own hands."

"That's disgusting."

"True, but it's made me immune to the smell. Honestly, I'm impressed you didn't join him."

"Ha, ha. Decomp is my only trigger."

"Why did you go for the throat in there? Did you think he was guilty?" I asked.

"Nah, I was just messing with him. I only needed his alibi, but it was fun to watch that douchebag squirm. Someone needed to bring him down a peg."

We were back outside now. I said, "I need to have a heart-to-heart with my sister before I head to the station."

"Take your time."

I looked at my watch. It was almost two-thirty. My sister was done for the day and would be picking up Nate soon, so I headed for the daycare building. I sat on a bench and waited, and after a few minutes I spotted her and a group of her friends walking my way. They were all so vivacious and happy, laughing and smiling as if they hadn't a care in the world. Sometimes I wished things would have worked out differently for my sister. Tonight, her friends would party and have fun into the wee hours of the morning. Rachel's college-aged fun, on the other hand, would end the minute she walked into the daycare building. From then until Monday morning, she would be a full-fledged adult mom. Granted, Nate was the best thing that ever happened to either of us, and I couldn't imagine life without him. But sometimes I wished she could be exactly like her peers, if only for a short time.

She stopped in front of me, and her friends continued on their way. "Why are you here? Is something wrong? Is Nate okay?" she asked, panic creeping into her voice.

"Nothing is wrong. I didn't mean to scare you. I need to talk to you for a minute." I patted the bench next to me.

Rachel sat down, a suspicious look in her eyes. "This isn't going to be a fun talk is it?"

"Not especially. I talked to Tony Dante this afternoon."

She shrugged. "And?"

I was hoping for something more along the lines of, "Why were you talking to that loser?" instead of her noncommittal response.

I said, "He told me the two of you had lunch this week."

"A couple of times, actually."

Shit. Tony Dante was Rachel's new guy. Now that I thought about it, she had never told me his name, and I had assumed he was a student. My stomach started churning, and I tried desperately to keep calm. "Is he the one you've been talking about? The guitarist you've been hanging out with?"

She turned toward me, her chin jutting out like it did when she would get angry as a child. "Yes. How is who I'm seeing a problem for you?"

My heart sank. I had to tread lightly here, otherwise my headstrong little sister would dig in her heels and never let go of this fool. "Normally, I'd be happy for you."

"But..." she said, her tone petulant.

"But, considering his reputation around here—"

"He's done nothing wrong."

"Maybe not legally, but ethically it's wrong to hit on students. And it's against school policy," I said. What was with these grown men around here who couldn't keep their hands off the female students? I had no interest whatsoever in my young male students—I saw them as children.

She waved her hand. "He's not hitting on students. He's just being friendly. Besides, he's not a teacher."

"He lives in a dorm full of students. That's worse."

She fired back, "He's in the all-male dorm. It's a moot point."

"Yeah, because they kicked him out of the co-ed dorm for making advances at the female students. He's a creepy, weird little man. I don't understand what you see in him."

"Oh, because *you* have such great taste in men!"

"So you're telling me that Tony Dante in no way has ever made your skin crawl? Not once?" I asked.

"No! He's nice and attentive."

"Right. I saw him being nice and attentive to a girl over at Fenton Hall just a few minutes ago. She didn't seem to appreciate it."

"Now you're just being a bitch."

"And you're being an idiot. He's my age!"

Rachel stood up. "I'm done with this conversation. You are *not* my mother, and you can't tell me what to do!"

"Fine!" I hopped up as well, fighting back tears from her stinging comment. "But don't come crying to me when he breaks your heart...or worse."

"Trust me, I won't," she replied, turning on her heel and stalking into the daycare building.

I stood there for a moment, silently cursing stupid Tony Dante for driving a wedge between my sister and me. I had to do something to break the spell he had over her, but I didn't know what.

When I got to the station, I was even madder than before, having stewed over my Rachel problem the entire drive. I headed straight for the lab, hoping to throw myself into my work and clear my head.

Beck was missing again, but I found Amanda sitting at one of the tables sifting through the vacuum filter mess collected from Eli Vanover's apartment. She looked up and said, "Hey, Ellie."

"Hey," I replied.

"Are you okay? You look...angry."

"Sister troubles," was all I said.

Amanda nodded. "I have two sisters. Drama queens, both of them."

"Ever wanted to murder one of their boyfriends in cold blood?"

She didn't bat an eye at my outburst. "Only all the time."

I smiled, feeling not so alone in my problems. I put on my lab coat and went to evidence to get the clothes that had been on the floor of Eli Vanover's apartment during the struggle leading to his death. Amanda had processed them already, but I needed to make a second examination. Setting the paper bags out on my worktable, I opened one bag and began to process the piece of clothing inside. I caught a whiff of the garment, even through my mask.

Turning to Amanda, I said, "You weren't wrong about these clothes. They do smell like pot and cheap cologne."

She laughed. "I don't know if college boys use toxic cologne to try to mask the pot odor, or if they actually think girls like the smell of it. Either way, it's not achieving the desired effect."

"You'd think they wouldn't be so clueless."

Amanda sobered. "Speaking of clueless boys...I have a date tonight."

"That's great."

She paused. "I thought I should tell you...it's with Jason."

I assumed as much, considering our conversation about Sterling last night. I felt her hesitation in telling me, so I wanted to set the record straight once and for all. "I don't want this to be weird. I shouldn't have stuck my nose in your business yesterday. I'm honestly happy for you guys."

She smiled. "Thanks. And you're sure you have no feelings for him, right?"

That was laughable, but I kept my amusement to myself. "I never did."

We both went back to our work, and soon after, I got a call from Baxter.

"Where are you?" he asked.

"In the lab."

"You didn't tell me you were here."

"Because I don't have to check in with you."

"You'd better be nice to me or else I won't tell you the big news."

"What big news?"

The doors of the lab burst open, and Baxter stood there, grinning ear-to-ear. He held up a file and announced, "I know who killed Vasti Marais."

24

My mouth dropped open. "Who?"

"Guess."

I thought for a moment. "Morris Powell."

"Guess again."

"One of Morris Powell's henchmen?"

Baxter chuckled. "I don't think he has henchmen."

"Right. Because that pallet of rocks jumped off the stack at me all by itself."

"Rocks?" asked Amanda.

Grimacing, Baxter said, "Ellie had a close call at Powell Stone Supply yesterday. A load of rocks mysteriously toppled down from a nearby stack and nearly hit her."

I added, "Luckily, Captain America here saved me."

Baxter rolled his eyes. "Anyway, because of that incident, we ran background checks on all of the Powell Stone Supply employees, but they came back clean. I'll give you one more try."

"Okay...George Cooper," I said.

His face fell. "How did you know?"

"I'm right? I was just throwing that out there to be funny."

"No, he's our guy. And, man, did we catch a lucky break. Preliminary

DNA reports just came back on the cigar we found at the scene. It wasn't a match to Dudley Cooper, but the DNA turned out to be a male familial match to him."

"That places George at the scene. Nice."

Amanda gasped. "That means Mayor Cooper let his son go to jail for a crime he committed. No way."

"It's true. Sterling went back over Vasti Marais's phone records and started looking into the calls made to the entire Cooper compound, not just Dudley's line. They have three landlines—one for the main house, one for Dudley's guest house, and one dedicated line for George Cooper's home office. You can probably guess which one we were looking at."

"She and old George really were having an affair," I said.

Baxter said, "We need better evidence of it, though."

"Oh!" I exclaimed, remembering something I had been meaning to tell Baxter since lunchtime. "I may have a witness."

Baxter wrinkled his brow. "How do you have a witness?"

"The guy I'm dating, Rob Larson—"

"The rent-a-cop?"

"I'm going to pretend I didn't hear that. Rob's firm provides security for George Cooper. After Mrs. Cooper accosted me at lunch today and her sister ratted out George, Rob told me he'd seen Vasti coming and going from the Cooper house, and it wasn't to visit Dudley."

"Do you think he'd testify to that?" asked Baxter.

I nodded. "I think so."

"Then you know what you have to do..." he said, trailing off with a frown.

I got a sinking feeling in my chest. "But I'm not working the Marais case."

His face softened. "We all know the two cases are connected. It's only a matter of time until we have enough evidence to prove it. You're involved up to your eyeballs in both cases as it is. You being in a relationship with a key witness could kill our chances in court. It sucks, but you know the rules."

I sighed, my eyes filling with tears. My bad luck with men had struck again. I had finally found a great guy, and now I had to dump him because of this damn job that I didn't even want to do.

"I'm sorry, Ellie," he began, but I pushed past him and out the door.

Stripping off my lab coat, I flung it onto the hallway floor without slowing down. I flew out the front doors and into the parking lot, only to realize I'd left my purse with my car keys in the lab. I couldn't even get the hell away from this place. That was the last straw. I sank down next to my car and covered my face with my hands, sobbing.

A few moments later, Amanda appeared over me. "I didn't think you'd get far without this." She handed me my purse. "Come on. We're going out for dinner."

Wiping my nose on my sleeve, I looked up at her. "But you have a date tonight with Sterling."

She shook her head. "Jason and Nick just broke their case wide open. Do you honestly think he's going to give our date a second thought?"

"Probably not."

"Nick said they're waiting for the arrest warrant to come through, then they're picking George Cooper up. They'll be busy all night, and they don't need us, so we're going out." She held her hand out to me. Grateful for her empathy, I took her hand, and she hauled me up off the ground.

Amanda drove us down to Fishers to a new sushi place. Once we had ordered our food, she said, "I'm so sorry you have to break things off with the man you're seeing because of the job."

Playing absentmindedly with my chopsticks, I muttered, "Me, too."

"It's hard enough to find a nice guy out there, and even harder to find a guy willing to go out with a woman who has anything to do with law enforcement."

I nodded. "I had the same problem when I was working for the department. We must intimidate them or something. Like they think we're going to arrest them at any moment. We couldn't do that if we wanted to."

"I had a date tell me once that he thought women shouldn't be allowed in any facet of police work because we're too emotional and our menstrual cycles cloud our judgment. You can imagine my response."

"Wow. Did you get 'emotional' and slap some sense into him?" I joked.

Amanda chuckled. "No, but somehow I managed to spill a full glass of water in his lap."

Throughout dinner we traded stories about our sisters and our ruined relationships. It was nice to get to know Amanda away from the lab. More importantly, it was nice to have someone I could vent to about the murder case. Baxter was easy enough to talk to, but a lot of times I felt like he didn't get me. After Amanda and I finished our food and lingered over a pot of tea, I was ready to go back to work.

When we got to the station, the parking lot was packed with news vans. Amanda barely found a place to park, and the media circus at the front door was so crazy we opted for slinking in through the back entrance. On the way to the lab, we heard shouting coming from the main lobby.

"What the hell is going on out there?" I asked.

Amanda said, "I don't know, but I'm dying to find out."

Bypassing the lab, we continued down the hallway, stopping short of the lobby. We weren't the only ones who had come to eavesdrop. Half of the department was standing either just inside the lobby or in the connecting hallways. We had to push our way through to be able to see who was making the commotion. Mrs. Cooper was standing in the middle of the room, screaming at Baxter, who didn't seem to be fazed by her verbal abuse.

"You've already taken my son, and now you've taken my husband! You have *nothing* on either of them! I demand that you release them both *this instant!*" she cried, her face bright red and her entire body trembling.

Behind her stood several men in suits, either George Cooper's lawyers or political campaign staff—all of them looked equally weasel-like to me. I craned my neck around the corner a couple of inches more and froze. Rob was standing off to the side, his posture rigid. I could tell he was stressed out, poor guy. When he saw me, his eyes locked on mine and a slight grimace passed over his face.

Pressing myself back against the hallway wall, out of his sight, I murmured to Amanda, "This could get awkward."

"It's already awkward," she said, gawking at the show.

Baxter was speaking quietly to Mrs. Cooper, trying to calm her down, but it wasn't working. She was still yelling.

I said, "See the guy out there who doesn't look like a lawyer?"

She raised her eyebrows. "The hot one?"

"Yeah, that one. He's the one I have to dump."

Aghast, she said, "It would kill me to have to let that guy get away. Now I *really* understand why you're so upset."

Peering back around the corner so I could see Baxter and Mrs. Cooper going at it, I heard Baxter say, "Mrs. Cooper, you're welcome to sit in our conference room until your husband is available for visitors." She started to speak, but he held up a hand to silence her and continued, "Mr. Larson, we'll need to take a statement from you. Legal team, you may meet with Mayor Cooper in Interrogation Room Two." Before anyone could disagree, Baxter turned and ushered Mrs. Cooper and Rob into the other hallway, toward the conference rooms. The lawyers followed a deputy to the interrogation room.

The small crowd dispersed, and Amanda and I headed for the lab. Actually, Amanda headed for the lab, and I made a detour to the break room.

"Where are you going?" she asked.

"Tonight is going to require a shitload of chocolate."

"You just had dinner."

"It's either this or I go find a fifth of vodka."

She smiled. "I'm coming with you, then. I wouldn't want you to have to drown your sorrows in chocolate alone."

When I was on my fourth candy bar and beginning to feel queasy, Baxter came into the break room for a cup of coffee. "Working hard?" he asked, gesturing at the pile of candy bar wrappers between us.

Amanda held up her half-eaten candy bar. "We're toasting the demise of Ellie and her hot guy's relationship. Want to join?"

"As fun as that sounds, I'm going to have to pass. Sterling and I are about to start our interrogation. Now that we have probable cause, I need you guys to go to the Cooper house and search for the Timberland boots we found prints of at the Vanover scene. I'll get Deputy Martinez to drive you over. Amanda, can you grab a kit and meet him at the back entrance? And...um, Ellie, can I speak to you in private?"

Amanda nodded and headed out of the room, leaving me alone with Baxter.

"I told Larson to wait in one of the conference rooms. You need to go talk to him. Now that he's part of this case, you can't be seen with him in public."

The candy bars in my stomach were threatening to come back up, but I managed to fire back, "And what if I refuse to break things off with him?"

He seemed sympathetic to my situation, even though he was the one pushing me to do the thing I didn't want to do. "I get that you're unhappy about this. I would be, too. But you know there's no other way. Do you want the Sheriff and the DA coming down on you?"

"Not especially."

"Get it over with now, and it won't be a problem. I do have some good news for you, though."

"Oh, yeah?" I replied, unimpressed.

"When Sterling was looking through the phone records of the Cooper compound, another number popped—Eli Vanover's."

"You're kidding."

Smiling now, he said, "Everything is falling into place to nail this guy. I think we did it."

I nodded and stood, trying to muster a smile.

He threw an arm around my shoulder, guiding me out of the room and down the hall. "Drinks are on me tonight." When we got to the door of the conference room where Rob was waiting, Baxter gave me a pat on the back. "Let me know if you find the shoes. Good luck."

I took a deep breath and tried not to feel sorry for myself. When I opened the door, Rob stood and rushed over to me, taking me into his arms and hugging me tight to him.

"You're a sight for sore eyes. All hell just broke loose for me," he said. "The Coopers are beside themselves. George insisted I drive Mrs. Cooper over here, and she proceeded to rip me a new asshole the entire way. She thinks you and I are working together to pin this on her husband."

It took all I had to push away from him. "That's why I came in here to talk to you." Running my hands through my hair in frustration, I said, "Rob, I'm being forced to break things off with you. It's not my decision. Our relationship could hurt the case against George Cooper."

He stared at me, dumbfounded. "Why? I didn't think you were working the girl's murder case."

"The two murder cases are connected, and besides, I found Vasti Marais's body. Like it or not, I'm involved in the entire mess. And now that you're going to be a witness for the prosecution and I'm working for the prosecution, we can't be seen together in public."

He frowned. "So we'll keep our relationship a secret. I don't want to walk away from what we have, Ellie."

Shaking my head sadly, I said, "Too many people know about us already—most importantly, Mrs. Cooper. Her lawyers will have a field day with this as it is. We have to make a clean break because we'll have to answer for it in court. I'm not going to lie on the stand. It could jeopardize every case I've ever testified for. I'm sorry."

"You don't sound very sorry," he said, his eyes showing hurt.

"This is killing me, and I'm trying so hard to hold it together," I whispered, a single tear escaping down my cheek. "I have to get back to work. Goodbye, Rob."

As I made a move to leave, Rob grabbed me and kissed me like he'd never see me again, which was likely. I kissed him back, tears flowing from my eyes. When I couldn't take it any longer, I pulled away and rushed out the door. Wiping the tears from my face, I hurried to the back door and out to the waiting cruiser.

Amanda had taken the front seat next to Deputy Martinez. I was fine with that, happy to sit in the dark in the back seat with my undoubtedly blotchy, red face. The two of them were in a heated discussion about whether or not the Colts could beat the New England Patriots during Sunday's game. I concentrated on their banter, hoping to occupy my thoughts with nonsense instead of my own troubles. No matter how hard I tried not to think about it, the look on Rob's face haunted me. Just as disconcerting was my growing concern that I was sure to be fired from my real job when Judith Cooper found out I was barging through her home trying to find further evidence to convict her husband of murder. Fortunately for me and for my sanity, Amanda and Martinez argued back and forth the whole drive to the Cooper house.

Deputy Martinez got out of the vehicle and said to us, "You wait here. I'll serve the warrant and clear the house."

"I thought all three of the Coopers were either at the station or in jail," I said.

Martinez shook his head and snickered. "The butler is home."

"They have a butler?" Amanda said.

Sure enough, when Martinez rang the bell, a pompous-looking man dressed in a sleek suit answered the door. They conferred for a moment, and then Martinez entered the house. After a few minutes, he came out again and said, "All set."

Amanda and I entered the house, and the butler showed us to the master bedroom. After he made himself scarce, she and I headed for the closet. When we opened it, we both gasped.

"This closet is bigger than my apartment," breathed Amanda.

"Wow. I've never seen so many navy suits," I said, looking at dozens of what appeared to be the same suit hanging in George's side of the closet.

Drooling over Mrs. Cooper's shoe collection, Amanda said, "She has designer heels in every color of the rainbow."

I set our case down, put on some gloves, and handed a pair to Amanda. "We should quit ogling their closet and get to work. We're looking for a pair of Timberland boots."

She started at one end of the closet and I started at the other, inspecting each pair of shoes to rule them out. After looking at a few of the shoes, I said, "Wait a minute. All of these are size ten. What about the ones you've looked through?"

"All tens here. Why?"

"The Timberland shoeprint was a twelve, easily."

"What are you thinking?" she asked.

"I'm thinking we're not going to find the boots here. And that Sterling and Baxter will probably both have an aneurism when we call to tell them."

She frowned. "Let's keep looking."

After we had checked every pair of shoes in the closet, we still had nothing.

"What now?" she asked. "Start in the bedroom and work our way through the house?"

"I guess. Did you check Dudley Cooper's guest house for the shoes?"

"Yes, Beck and I went out there yesterday afternoon and searched. We didn't find them there."

Sighing, I said, "Then we better start scouring this place. I'll take the first floor if you want to take the second."

"That works. See you when I see you."

I headed downstairs. The whole house was gorgeous, and it reminded me quite a lot of Tyler's mother's home. The memory of meeting Rob there flashed into my head, and sadness overtook me again. I trudged out to the garage, figuring it would be an ideal spot to store boots. I found several pairs of boots, but none of them were Timberlands, and none were larger than a size ten. I started going through bins, drawers, and cabinets, but again had no luck. I went back inside, searching the mudroom and kitchen. With everything so impeccably neat and tidy, I couldn't imagine finding a pair of shoes just sitting out somewhere. I had an idea. The butler would know where everything was, because he would have been the one to put it away.

I went outside and found the butler pacing in the driveway. Martinez was watching him with an amused expression on his face, but neither man was speaking. I approached the butler.

"Hi, I'm Ellie Matthews with the crime lab. I have a couple of questions for you. Your name is...?"

He stopped pacing and stood tall. "My name is Geoffrey Church. And I don't have to answer any of your questions, ma'am." With his clipped British accent, he sounded even more pompous than he looked.

I ignored him. "I'm looking for a pair of Timberland boots, size twelve or thirteen. Do you know if Mayor Cooper owns a pair of Timberlands?"

Church regarded me for a moment. "The Mayor doesn't own anything in the Timberland brand. He prefers a more expensive shoe. And the Mayor wears a size ten."

I had always thought Timberlands were rather high-priced, being a couple hundred dollars a pair, but evidently they weren't good enough for George Cooper. I took Church's answer with a grain of salt. The shoes could still have been here, and he could have been covering for his employer.

"Thanks for the information, Mr. Church," I said, going back to the house.

Amanda was coming down the stairs when I got into the entry hall. "Did you find them?" she asked, her expression hopeful.

"No, and according to the butler, Timberlands aren't expensive enough shoes for George Cooper to put his feet in. He assured me we would find no Timberlands here."

"Damn. Have you finished the first floor?"

"No, I've only done the garage, kitchen, and mud room."

"We can divide up the rest. I'll take the dining room and the living room."

I said, "I'll take the other living room and his office."

Why the Coopers needed more than one living room was beyond me. I looked in one of them, and aside from a curio cabinet filled with expensive-looking figurines, there was nowhere to hide shoes. I went to George's office, which was where he kept his gun collection. It was an impressive collection, all kept behind lock and key in glass-front gun cabinets. Some of the firearms were ornate and looked quite old. My warrant didn't cover me touching any of them, so I kept my hands to myself and began looking through file cabinets that would have been large enough to hide shoes in. Most of them were locked, probably containing sensitive paperwork, but I didn't figure I could stretch my power so far as to get the butler to open them for me. Again, my search turned up nothing.

I met Amanda in the entry hall. She looked disgusted. "I can't believe we didn't find anything. Jason and Nick are not going to be pleased. Maybe you should handle calling them. I don't want to ruin my chances with Jason before we get to go out on our first date."

"You have a point. I wouldn't put it past Sterling to shoot the messenger. I'll call Baxter." I took my phone out and dialed his cell, hoping for his voice mail. I was surprised he answered, figuring he would be still hard at work interrogating George Cooper.

"Tell me you found the shoes," he said, his voice sounding weary.

I hesitated. "I'm sorry, but no. We turned the place upside down and found nothing. Besides, George Cooper wears a size ten, so it's unlikely he could even keep a pair of twelves on his feet."

"Son of a bitch!" he growled.

I winced. Amanda, who'd been listening to my side of the conversation, made a sympathetic face.

He continued, "Sorry. We have enough to hold him on the Marais murder, but without the shoes, we have nothing to tie him to Vanover. That is, until the DNA comes back on the blood under Vanover's nails."

I was beginning to think George didn't have anything to do with Eli's death. I didn't see him as the type who would kill with his bare hands. "Does George have any defensive wounds on him from having been in a scuffle with Eli?"

"He's got a few scratches on his arms, but he says they're from brushing against tree branches when he went deer hunting earlier this week."

"Well, at least you have him for the one murder."

"Barely. Those lawyers gave us a run for our money. They even rattled Sterling."

"Wow," I said, impressed. Nobody got the upper hand on Sterling in an interrogation.

"Which is why I need a drink. You heading back now?"

"We're on our way."

"I'll wait for you."

I ended the call and said to Amanda, "They have enough to hold George Cooper for the Vasti Marais murder, but not enough to tie him to Eli Vanover. And to warn you, his legal team managed to get Sterling flustered. Your boy may not be in the best of moods if you try to talk to him tonight."

"Ooh," she said, the corner of her mouth pulling into a smile. "Maybe I can provide a shoulder for him to cry on, then."

Laughing, I said, "It's worth a shot."

As we turned to leave, lights flashed through the leaded glass insets of the front door. Someone had pulled up, and I was really hoping it wasn't Mrs. Cooper. I didn't want to have another altercation with her, but I was afraid it would be inevitable after finding me in her home. I made Amanda go outside first. Mrs. Cooper was already out of the vehicle and screaming at Deputy Martinez.

"What are you doing here? Isn't it enough that you people have ripped my son and my husband away from me? Now you're invading my home?" she cried, her shrill voice cutting through the quiet night.

Nothing ever seemed to bother Deputy Martinez, including Mrs. Cooper's tirade. He handed her the warrant and replied, "Ma'am, we have a warrant to search your premises for a pair of your husband's shoes." He glanced over at us. "Looks like we're just leaving."

Mrs. Cooper followed his gaze and locked her eyes on me. "You! You've been trying to tear my family apart this whole time! You're...you're fired! And you'll never teach anywhere in this country ever again!" She flew at me, but before she could get to me, I saw Rob coming my way out of the corner of my eye. He threw himself in front of me just as Mrs. Cooper was raising her hand to strike me, ready to take the brunt of her rage.

Just as quick, Martinez caught her flailing arms from behind. He said, "Mrs. Cooper, you don't want to do that. The Sheriff's Department won't hesitate to file an assault charge on you for touching one of their employees."

Mrs. Cooper stopped resisting and stood there trembling. Narrowing her eyes at me, she seethed, "Get off my property. Now."

Martinez ushered Mrs. Cooper inside. Rob moved away from me, refusing to meet my eyes. He headed toward the front door. Between getting fired and seeing the hurt look in Rob's eyes again, I was at the end of my rope. I tried desperately to keep the tears at bay.

"Rob?" I choked out.

He turned around to face me but said nothing.

"Thanks," I whispered.

Giving me only a curt nod, he turned on his heel and disappeared into the house.

25

I should have known from experience that going out with Baxter for "one drink" loosely translated to "Ellie gets hammered," especially after the day I'd had. We went to O'Loughlin's Bar again, and everyone and his brother began buying us drinks after the news got out that Baxter had brought down Mayor Cooper for murder. Countless cops, young and old, came over and clapped Baxter on the back, congratulating him on his work.

"Admit it," I said, my words slurring together. "You came here for the attaboys and the free drinks."

Baxter could hold his liquor better than I could, so he wasn't quite as drunk as I was. "I don't see you turning down any free drinks, either."

"That's because I can't afford any drinks myself. I got fired, you know," I lamented, draining my glass.

He rolled his eyes. "I'm telling you, like I have the last fifty-three times you've said that, Judith Cooper can't fire you from your job at Ashmore because of the work you do while employed by the Sheriff's Department. Everything you've done has been legal and above board, so she has no leg to stand on. The department has your back. They have lawyers for this kind of thing." He reached across the table and gave me a light punch on the arm. "Now quit talking about yourself. This is my night, remember?"

"Right. Sorry."

He peered around at the crowd. "I thought for sure that Sterling would be here. He wouldn't pass up the chance to lord a high-profile arrest over all the guys here."

"I think he had a better offer."

"Oh yeah?"

"Amanda. They had a hot date tonight." I slapped my hand over my mouth, belatedly realizing that information might not have been for public knowledge. I whispered, "Oops. I don't know if I was supposed to tell or not."

Smiling, he said, "I already knew. He's been acting less like a jackass today, so I made it my business to find out why."

"And you didn't tell me?"

"You didn't tell me either," he pointed out.

"Touché."

"You and Amanda seemed to have hit it off. Does it bother you that she's going out with Sterling?"

"Why would it bother me?" I didn't know why everyone insisted on thinking I carried a torch for Sterling.

"Because you two..."

"What? Had thirty magical seconds back in the bathroom?"

His eyebrows shot up. "Thirty seconds?"

"You know how efficient he is..." After taking a look at Baxter's appalled face, I burst out laughing.

He joined in my laughter. An old and crusty retired detective came over to congratulate Baxter and buy us another round of drinks. I began to lose track of how many I'd had, but our conversations were getting funnier and funnier, so I didn't worry too much about it.

"Okay, okay," I said, trying to quit giggling long enough to give him the next category. We were trading our most ridiculous work stories. We had covered the categories of Dumbest Suspect, Worst Boss, and Funniest True Alibi. I said, "Worst co-worker."

We both said at the same time, "Beck," and dissolved into laughter again.

"I've got one," Baxter said. "Grossest thing you've seen."

Still laughing, I choked out, "You barfing at the Marais murder scene."

He waved his hand, spilling a little of his drink on the table. "Oh, come on. That can't be it."

A sudden image flashed through my head of decomposing body parts in garbage bags. The room started to spin, and I lost control of my inner monologue. I blurted, "When we found a body hacked up and left in garbage bags and...it turned out to be my mother." I squinted at him. "Do you think the room's spinning? Because I think the room's spinning."

At my horrific revelation, Baxter's mouth hung open. After a moment he shook his head as if to clear it and said, "Oh, shit. You're gonna puke." He dragged me out of the booth and half-carried me to the ladies' room, getting me to a stall just in time. As I retched over the toilet, I could feel him pulling my long hair back from my face and holding it for me.

Once I was finished, I sprawled out on the grimy floor and leaned my head against the stall wall. He handed me a couple of wet paper towels so I could clean myself up. When I looked up, I saw that his face was a mix of emotions.

"Hey, thanks for holding my hair. Only your best girlfriends will do that for you," I croaked.

"You're welcome, I guess," he said, seeming confused by my comment. He hoisted me up off the floor. "Let's get some coffee in you."

Two cups of coffee and a basket of greasy fries later, I was feeling marginally sober. I propped my head up with my hand. "My head is starting to hurt. I think I need to go sleep it off."

"I'll walk you home."

This time, I didn't protest.

Once we were outside and heading for my house, he ventured, "I can't get something you said earlier out of my head."

"I say a lot of stuff, especially when I'm drunk. What was it?"

Hesitating for a moment, he said, "About your mother. Was she murdered?"

The alcohol had brought my defenses down enough that it didn't seem so difficult to admit the truth, and it all came tumbling out. "Yeah. I'd been working the case for nearly a month and had no freaking clue who the victim was. We ran DNA, but they were backed up, and it was taking forever even to get preliminary information. The sick son of a bitch who killed her kept making anonymous phone calls to give us the location of the bags, one by one. First came her feet. Then her legs. Then her arms. Then her hands, but her fingertips were missing. We got her torso in two pieces. Her head came last."

Baxter put his hand on my arm and stopped me. "You don't have to tell me this if you don't want to. It has to be hard to dredge everything back up."

"It's okay, Nick. I don't mind that you know." After all we'd been through the past week, I trusted him enough to tell him. I started walking again, and he followed. "It was late August, and she'd been dead for a month before we got hold of the first bag. The bags had all been left outside, so you can imagine the rate of decomp, not to mention the smell. I didn't even recognize her face. My own mother."

Saying nothing, he reached out and put his arm around my shoulder.

I laughed mirthlessly. "You know how I finally ID'd her? Her earrings. I remembered them because...they were the first present I'd ever bought for her." I wiped a tear from my eye. "I was seventeen and had my first job. I was so proud of those earrings because I'd bought them with my own money for her birthday. They were unusual, from a trendy store in Carmel that sold handmade jewelry. When I gave them to her, she was drunk, which wasn't out of the ordinary, but that night she was especially mean for some reason. She took one look at them, flung them across the room, and accused me of stealing them. We got into a huge fight. I figured she'd tossed them in the trash because I never saw her wear them...not until I opened that last bag." My voice broke, and Baxter stopped me to envelop me in a tight hug.

I allowed myself to be comforted by him only for a moment before pulling away.

"I had no idea. That case was what caused you to leave the department, wasn't it?" he asked, his eyes sad.

I couldn't handle his pity, so I stared at the ground. "Yes, it was. Needless to say, when I realized it was pieces of my mother in the bags I'd been processing, I lost it. I went to Jayne and resigned on the spot. She tried to keep me, but she understood why I had to walk away." I looked up at him, admitting, "I blamed myself for my mother's death. I thought if I hadn't cut ties with her...if I had tried to get her the help she needed, maybe things would have turned out differently."

"Ellie, you can't blame yourself for what happened to your mother. The only person to blame is her killer. Don't put it all on you."

"Nick, it is on me." Tears started pouring from my eyes. "When I found out she was turning tricks for drugs with my pregnant little sister in the house, I went and took Rachel away from her. I called my own mother a crack whore and told her to go to hell. That was the last thing I said to her. A year later, she was dead. I could have helped her walk away from that world. I just didn't. I decided she wasn't worth the effort."

Baxter's eyes got misty at my painful confession, and he again pulled me close to him. I let myself give in and cried against his chest.

After a few minutes I was able to compose myself. Taking a step back, I wiped my eyes on my sleeves. "I bet you'll think twice about taking me out for a drink again. You always learn way too much about me," I joked, trying to lighten the mood.

He smiled down at me. "Next time, I'll tell you my life story. Then we'll be even."

"Deal." We started walking again, soon arriving in front of my house.

He turned to face me. "Can I ask you something?"

"Sure, although I don't think I have any secrets left to tell."

"Did your mother's case get solved? Who killed her? You left that part out."

"Can't turn your detective brain off, can you?"

Giving me a sheepish grin, he said, "No."

"The case was unsolved. She died of blunt force trauma to the head, but her body was so degraded there was no evidence to tie anyone to her death. The garbage bags were in terrible shape—either covered in mud or shredded by animals—so I couldn't get prints off them. Plus, the primary crime scene was never found."

He wrinkled his forehead. "I'm so sorry. It must be terrible to have no closure and always wonder who did it."

"Oh, I know who did it," I said, bitterness welling up inside me. "Marcus Copland. Rachel's father."

"Rachel's father? Did the police investigate him?"

"They would have, but they couldn't find him. It was like he vanished into thin air."

"Has he tried to contact your sister?" Baxter asked.

"No. She hasn't heard from him since he disappeared."

He stroked his chin, deep in thought. "He either killed your mother and ran, or he's dead as well. I could—"

"No," I said, cutting him off. "I know that look. I appreciate that you'd like to take a crack at solving the case, but please let it be. Rachel and I have been through enough. I don't care whether that sadistic bastard is dead or in hiding as long as I don't have to see him or think about him ever again." I got my keys out and paused at my door. "Hey, congratulations on catching a murderer. You're pretty good at what you do."

Smiling, he said, "Thanks. Don't forget we have a meeting tomorrow at ten with the brass to go over our next move for the Vanover case."

I sighed. "Just what I wanted to do with my Saturday."

Even though I got to sleep in the next morning, thanks to my overindulgence last night, I woke up with a horrible headache. I popped some Advil and headed straight for the coffeepot. I could hear Rachel and Nate talking in the kitchen as I approached and felt a stab of apprehension. She and I hadn't spoken since our fight yesterday. After my feelings about how I'd treated my mother resurfaced last night, I had resolved not to make the same mistake with Rachel. Nothing was worth ruining our relationship over. I didn't know how I was going to stomach the fact that she was dating that douche Tony Dante, but something had to give for us to be able to repair our sisterly bond. I had to squelch my stubborn streak and let her make her own choices even if I thought they were idiotic ones.

Rachel and Nate were sitting at the table having breakfast when I came into the kitchen. "Hey, guys," I said quietly.

"Auntie Ellie!" yelled Nate, flinging his arms up so I could hug him as I passed his chair.

I winced as his loud cry shot additional pain through my head. "Good morning, sweet boy," I said, giving him a hug and a kiss.

Rachel was concentrating on her cereal. I could tell by the set of her jaw that she was still angry. Nate went back to eating his breakfast, unaware of the palpable tension in the room.

"Hey, Rach," I said.

"Hi," she replied, not looking up.

"Can we talk outside?"

She shrugged, but got up and headed for the back door. Young adulthood had to be tough for her—being old enough to have her own child and be responsible for him, yet still young enough that she was expected to take direction from her teachers and sometimes from me.

When we got outside, she plopped down on the nearest lawn chair. "What do you want to talk about? Who else I can't date?"

Ignoring her snappy tone, I said, "I want to tell you I'm sorry. It was wrong of me to try to control who you see."

Her posture relaxed a bit. "You're apologizing? But Ellie Matthews never admits that she's wrong."

I smiled. "I know. It's something I think I should work on. Look, you love who you love, right? It's not my place to make that decision for you. I might not agree with your choices, but it's your life. I only want you to be happy. That's all I wanted in the first place—I just didn't say it right."

Rachel's mouth dropped open. "But you hate Tony. You've said that since you met him. That's why I didn't tell you about our relationship. I can't believe you've suddenly changed your mind."

I hadn't changed my mind about him, but I didn't think it was wise to bring it up. "This is about us. I want us to be okay."

She got up and gave me a tight hug. "We *are* okay." After we broke apart, she stepped back and studied me. "The question is, are you okay? You seem...off."

Nothing got past her. "Well, without revealing any details of a murder case, it turns out Rob is a witness to a certain...piece of the puzzle. And I'm knee deep in puzzle pieces. I had to break things off with him, otherwise the fact that we're in a relationship could get tricky for us once the case goes to court."

She pulled a sympathetic face. "Sorry. That sucks. I know you liked the guy."

"I did. I still do." I heaved out a sigh. "It's complicated. Oh, and I got fired."

"What? From the crime lab?"

"No, from school."

"Shit!" she exclaimed, horrified. "How?"

I shrugged. "Mrs. Cooper flew off the handle at me because of my involvement in the murder cases. Something about deliberately targeting her family. According to Baxter it's wrongful termination and she can't legally do it."

"I hope he's right. What a mess. You need something to take your mind off it. Why don't we take Nate to Forest Park today?"

"That sounds perfect. I have to go in for a meeting this morning at the Sheriff's office, so how about we meet at the park around noon?"

"I'll bring lunch."

26

When I arrived at the station, most of the seats in the conference room were taken. Present were Jayne, DA McAlister, Sterling, Baxter, and Amanda. Beck should have been there, but he was conspicuously absent. I slipped into the seat next to Amanda.

Leaning over to her, I whispered, "So? How did it go last night?"

She tried to contain her smile. "Great," she replied, blushing and stealing a glance at Sterling. "We'll talk about it later."

Baxter came over next to me and leaned against the table. "Well, did you manage to avoid the dreaded hangover?"

"I'll be fine as long as no one starts yelling," I said.

He chuckled. "I'll probably piss off the DA before it's over, so watch out."

Jayne said, "Everyone, let's get this meeting started." She looked around the table. "Where's Beck?"

Amanda cleared her throat. "I haven't seen him yet this morning, Sheriff."

Rolling her eyes, Jayne went on, "Detectives Sterling and Baxter, before we discuss the particulars of the two cases, I want to say congratulations from the department for solving the Marais murder. It took a great deal of investigating as well as determination to find enough solid evidence to hold a powerful man like George Cooper, but you two came through. I also want to thank the rest of you as well. Without the tireless work of this entire team, it wouldn't have been possible. That said, we still have another murder to solve. Detectives, I'll turn it over to you."

Sterling stood up and flicked the lights off so we could better see the projector screen on the wall. "To recap, we're currently holding former Mayor George Cooper for the murder of Vasti Marais. His arraignment will be first thing Monday morning." He swiped the tablet he was holding to scroll through the evidence photos in his presentation as he spoke about each one. "We recovered the murder weapon, a Blaser K77 Imperial Grade seven millimeter hunting rifle, from the suspect's private gun collection at his residence."

When the photo of the ornately engraved rifle came onto the screen, DA McAlister whistled. "That gun's easily worth twenty grand. Who the hell spends that kind of money on a murder weapon?"

Jayne said, "The kind of person who has enough money to pay a team of lawyers to keep him out of jail. We need to have our ducks in a row if we're going to make this conviction stick. Continue, Detective."

Sterling said, "There were no fingerprints found on the murder weapon. It seemed to have been wiped clean. At the crime scene, located on the premises of the former Carnival Cove Water Park currently owned by the suspect's son, Dudley Cooper, we found a discarded cartridge casing with a partial print belonging to the suspect's nephew, Tyler Harris. Harris has a solid alibi for the time of death window, and he explained that his fingerprint could have been on the casing from when he used his uncle's firearms and ammunition on a recent hunting trip. We also recovered a silver cigarette lighter with the initial 'C' engraved on it. It belongs to George Cooper, but Dudley Cooper's prints were found on it, which, in addition to the fact that he had a sexual relationship with the victim and no alibi, was the reason we had him in custody originally."

Jayne asked the DA, "Where are we on releasing the son?"

DA McAlister replied, "The paperwork is already started, but he'll have to remain in custody until a judge dismisses the charges. Are you people absolutely sure Dudley Cooper had nothing to do with this murder? Maybe father and son were in cahoots."

That thought hadn't entered my mind. I looked over at Baxter.

He said, "We feel confident that George Cooper acted without his son's knowledge. We interviewed Dudley Cooper again after his father was brought into custody, and his reaction seemed genuine when he heard the news of his father's arrest." I could imagine the hurt in Dr. Cooper's eyes when he found out his father had allowed him to take the fall for his own crime.

Sterling said, "Also recovered from the scene was a partially-smoked cigar. Preliminary analysis suggests that the DNA found on the cigar is a male familial match to Dudley Cooper. He has no brothers and no living uncles or grandfathers, so that gave us probable cause to obtain our suspect's DNA."

The DA cut in, "Like I told you last night, if you chuckleheads have not been one thousand percent by the book with any aspect of this investigation, Cooper's lawyers will find it. And then they'll keep chipping away at it until the entire case unravels."

I felt the tension in the room increase exponentially. Baxter and Sterling both stiffened at the word "chuckleheads."

Jayne's jaw clenched. "I can assure you, Wade, that my detectives have this case nailed down tight. There won't be any surprises." She gestured for Sterling to continue.

Sterling said, "George Cooper was also in a relationship with Vasti Marais, evidenced by phone records and texts. We found a pre-paid cell in his home office, which he used solely to text message the victim. The only piece of evidence we haven't definitively tied to the suspect is the handful of rocks we found where he was standing during the shooting. They are two types of landscape rocks, and at this point, they're our only physical evidence that could tie the Marais murder to the Vanover murder."

"I get why George Cooper would have killed his mistress, but I can't for the life of me figure out what connection he would have with the other victim. What's the motive here?" asked the DA.

Baxter replied, "Best we can figure, it comes down to Tristan Sellers. He was present when Vasti Marais was shot, but he swears he didn't see the shooter. Eli Vanover was at Tristan Sellers's apartment when he was killed, so one theory is that the killer was trying to tie up a loose end and mistook

Vanover for Sellers. We had some leads on other persons of interest, but none of them panned out."

"That's it? That's the best you've got? I can't possibly take the Vanover case to court with rocks as the only evidence and mistaken identity as the motive! I'll get laughed out of the building," DA McAlister cried.

Baxter replied, "I know, but it's worth noting that the blue glass rock, the pea gravel, and the limestone dust that were found at both scenes can also be found in the same area at the Powell Stone Supply yard. Morris Powell is George Cooper's opponent in the Senate race. It's possible that George Cooper could have visited Morris Powell at his business, and that's how the evidence ended up on his shoes and was tracked into the two scenes." Baxter glanced at me and grimaced. "There's also something about Morris Powell that doesn't add up for me. When Ellie and I went out to his rock yard, a pallet of stones fell and landed practically on top of us. It didn't seem like an accident—it felt like a threat. Morris Powell is hiding something. He clearly didn't want us nosing around his place."

"That's all good investigating, but there's no smoking gun for the Vanover case," said Jayne.

Baxter said, "We hope to have our smoking gun soon. We're waiting on the DNA analysis of the blood and epithelial cells under Eli Vanover's fingernails." He added, "And hoping he managed to scratch his attacker in the scuffle before his death."

"Are we supposed to sit around with our thumbs up our asses while those jokers in DNA take their dear sweet time? Do you really have nothing else?" griped the DA.

Jayne's face was stuck in a frown. "I'd feel a lot better if we didn't have to rely solely on possible DNA evidence. If it doesn't match George Cooper and we don't find any matches in CODIS—or worse, if it belongs to the victim—we're back to square one."

Sterling said, "Even though there was a lot of evidence collected at the Vanover scene, none of it has turned out to be too useful. None of the fingerprints came back to anyone except the inhabitants of the apartment and the girl who found the body. There were two shoeprints collected, which we at first assumed belonged to the killer, but we found out last night that George Cooper wears a much smaller shoe than the prints we found. Most of our evidence for the Vanover case might not be evidence after all."

I didn't like what he was saying. "Wait a minute," I said. "A size twelve Timberland boot was used to knock the folding chair out from under Eli Vanover when he was hanged. I'm sure of it. There's a dent in the side of the chair where I found the print. I don't want to discount your George Cooper theory, but his foot didn't push that chair." When I noticed Sterling, Baxter, and DA McAlister all staring daggers at me, I added, "Sorry."

Jayne nodded, deep in thought. "I see your point, and I also haven't been able to let go of how strikingly different the two murders were in the way they were carried out. I have no problem believing that George Cooper could have shot his mistress. He did it from such a distance it made the whole thing impersonal, and he didn't even have to get his hands dirty. The Vanover murder, however, was messy. There was a struggle. The killer abused and manually strangled the victim before he killed him. As much as I think these two crimes are connected..." She stopped and sighed. "I'm not convinced we're looking at the same killer."

In the silence, Amanda cleared her throat and said quietly, "Maybe George Cooper had help on the Eli Vanover murder. Maybe he wasn't acting alone."

Jayne said, "That's an interesting theory. Go on."

Amanda glanced at me. "Well, um, we know from the autopsy that there was a gun pointed at the victim's head at some point, so that would explain how someone could coerce him into getting on top of the chair in order to be hanged. However, when Ellie and I were processing the victim's clothes, we started discussing the fact that he was strangled with enough force to break his hyoid bone before he was hanged by the jump rope. We weren't convinced that he was conscious at the time he was strung up. She and I recreated the act of trying to get an injured, semi-conscious person from the floor onto a chair, and it was nearly impossible for one person to do. Also, the victim had to have been in a standing position on the chair to have been hung with that short length of rope. George Cooper is older and doesn't look terribly brawny, so..." She took a deep breath. "I don't see how he could have done it by himself."

Sterling snapped, "It would have been nice for you to share this with the class a little sooner in the investigation."

She fired back, "It didn't click for me until this morning, but thanks for berating me in front of everyone."

Baxter and I shared an amused look. I had been worried that Sterling would wear the pants in their relationship, but it seemed like Amanda would have no trouble holding her own.

"Okay guys, that's enough," warned Jayne. "Let's go with Amanda's theory for a moment. Where would George Cooper turn to get help with murdering someone?"

I remembered something Rob had said about him. "This is hearsay, but I've heard the former mayor has mob connections."

"It wouldn't surprise me," grumbled DA McAlister.

"That shouldn't be too difficult to figure out. Have you gone through his financials yet?" Jayne asked the detectives.

Baxter shook his head. "Haven't had a reason to until now. While we're spitballing here, what if he simply paid some thug with a size twelve foot to kill Eli Vanover? I think a big guy would be capable of manhandling our scrawny victim into a noose, conscious or not."

Jayne nodded in agreement. "That sounds plausible. Detectives, compile a list of George Cooper's staff, colleagues, and any mob associations you can dig up. Cross-reference them against any substantial payments he's made lately. If you come up with nothing there, take a harder look at Morris Powell and his employees."

"Will do, Sheriff," said Baxter.

Jayne glanced around the table. "If there's nothing else, we can adjourn."

Everyone started gathering their things and leaving the room. I waited for Baxter.

"It looks like you're going to have a mountain of work to wade through," I said.

"Offering to help?" he asked.

"Not on your life. My work here is almost done. I have a few more items to process as a second examination and then I'm out of here. Today should be my last day, barring any new evidence on the case."

Baxter's face fell. "Oh, I didn't realize that." He shrugged. "With how crazy this case has been, you never know. We might have you back in here before you know it."

"I hope not." When I saw the disappointment in his eyes, I added, "Not that it hasn't been fun working with you, but I need a break."

"Right." He hesitated. "There's something I want to talk to you about. Are you free for lunch?"

"No, sorry. I'm meeting my sister and Nate at the park. We made up after fighting over the Tony Dante thing. Now I have to go and pretend I don't care that my sister is dating a complete loser."

"Will you be able to do that? You don't exactly hide your feelings about most things..." he joked.

I smiled. "I'm working on it. We'll talk later, okay?"

"Okay."

I found Rachel pushing Nate on the kiddie swings at Forest Park.

Nate spotted me when I walked up. He yelled, "Watch me, Auntie Ellie!"

When the swing came forward, he jumped out of the seat, causing Rachel and me both to scream, "No, Nate!" and rush toward him. He had landed on his knees, and I originally thought he was crying based on the way his shoulders were shaking. When he lifted his head up, I realized he was laughing, proud of himself for making the dangerous jump as well as for scaring the crap out of his mother and me.

"Nate, I told you not to do that," scolded Rachel. After Nate ran off to play on the slide, she said to me, "I hate it when he says 'Watch me.' It's the toddler equivalent of 'Hold my beer.' It usually ends in disaster."

I chuckled. "True. I think he enjoys freaking us out."

"So, how's work?" she asked, walking over to a nearby picnic table. She handed me a sandwich out of a bag and took one for herself.

"Good, actually. I think after a few more hours, I'll be done with my part of the case."

"That's great!" she exclaimed. "I bet you'll be happy to go back to being a boring teacher." Her face fell. "Oh, I'm sorry. I forgot you might not have a job to go back to."

"Yeah," I muttered.

We ate in silence for a while, watching Nate as he played on every piece of playground equipment in this section of the park. He had found another little boy to pal around with, which was no surprise. The kid could make friends with a tree trunk.

"Um...now that you're free, sis, would you consider watching Nate for me tomorrow night?" Rachel asked, uncertainty in her voice.

I could see right through her. She had a date with that schmuck Tony Dante. I mulled over whether watching Nate would constitute acceptance on my part, but pushed my feelings aside. "I'd be happy to watch him. I've missed him this week."

"Thanks, because Tony and I—"

"You know what? Let's leave it at the fact that you have plans, and you don't need to run them by me. Okay?" In this situation, I figured ignorance was bliss. I didn't want to make my skin crawl by thinking about what they'd be doing.

"Um, okay."

After our stilted exchange, we continued to watch Nate in silence.

Several minutes later, my phone rang. It was a number I didn't recognize, but since I was no longer being hounded by the media, I decided to answer it.

"Hello?" I said.

"Professor Matthews?" asked a tentative female voice.

"Yes. Who is this?"

"It's Maddie Haynes."

27

I hurried out of Rachel's earshot. "Maddie?"

"Yes, you know, from your Intro class?"

"Right. I know. Are you okay? I haven't seen you around school for a while."

She hesitated. "Uh, well, I've had things... Professor Matthews?"

"Yes?"

"I need a favor. I know you're, like, tight with the cops and stuff..."

"What can I do for you, Maddie? Name it," I said, hoping she'd open up to me. If I could get her to tell me where to find Tad Ogelsby and get him to talk, Eli Vanover's murder might finally make sense. If Tad was a witness to something, it could blow the whole case wide open.

"Um...Tad and I are seriously tired of hiding out. I think I finally have him convinced—I mean, I think he wants to talk to someone, but he's afraid to talk to the cops because they're looking for him. He's worried they're going to arrest him or something. He could talk to you, though."

My breath caught in my throat. The break we needed had just fallen into my lap. "The cops are not going to arrest him. They only want to talk. He has nothing to be afraid of."

"I told him that, but since you're not a cop it would be easier for him to talk to you," she said. "Can you meet us?"

"Sure. Where?"

"Um, you have to, like, promise not to tell the cops where we are."

My heart sank. I had to tell someone eventually, but I supposed I could meet with Tad and try to talk him into working with Baxter. "I won't tell them."

"I'll text you the address. Can you come now?" she asked, sounding relieved.

"I'm on my way."

The address was in Sheridan, a tiny town northwest of Noblesville. The place was out in the middle of nowhere, a rundown house on an old country road surrounded by trees and other rundown houses. I recognized the vehicle in the driveway—it was the same yellow Beetle Maddie had been driving when she nearly ran over Nate and me in the McDonald's parking lot a couple of days ago. I had the right place.

Taking a deep breath, I walked up to the door. I had called Baxter on the way over to let him know what I was doing. He got angry when I wouldn't tell him where I was going and made me promise to record my conversation with Tad so he could hear everything we discussed. After starting my phone's recorder app and silencing my ringer, I placed my phone in my purse, making sure the mic was facing up. I knocked on the front door, and a moment later Maddie appeared.

She poked her head out the door, darting her gaze around to the driveway and the street. "You came alone, right?" she asked, her voice shaking a bit.

"Yes," I replied.

Backing up, she held the door open for me, and once we were inside, she closed the door and locked it behind us. We were standing in the living room of the house, such as it was, with its peeling 1970's avocado green wallpaper, filthy shag carpet, and mismatched, broken-down furniture. Tad was nowhere to be seen, but I could hear the sound of water running in another room.

"Do you want to sit down?" Maddie asked, awkwardly offering me a chair.

I sat down, placing my purse on the messy coffee table between us. She perched on the arm of the tattered couch, and she kept glancing toward the back of the house. She seemed on edge. It was understandable, considering she and Tad were holed up here, possibly fearing for their lives. However, I thought there was still something more to it, especially given our conversation over the phone. She had been vague about whether Tad had agreed to speak with me.

"Maddie, does Tad know I'm here?"

She bubbled out a nervous laugh. "Well, he's kind of in the shower right now, so...no."

"I mean, did you tell Tad that you asked me to come over here, or is this all your doing?"

Maddie's face crumpled, and tears started flowing from her eyes. "I can't stand this. I can't stand hiding." She gestured at the room and made a face. "And I can't stand living *here*. This place is my uncle's nasty rent house. I think we have rats." Her whole body shuddered.

Giving her a sympathetic smile, I said, "I'm sure this must be difficult for you, Maddie. Can you tell me why the two of you had to disappear? Does it have to do with Eli?"

Sniffling and lowering her head, she nodded.

When she said nothing else, I prompted, "Does it also have to do with a story Eli wanted to run in the *Voice*?"

Snapping her head up, she said, "How do you know about that?"

"I spoke to the staff. What's so important about this story?"

Her eyes widening, she said, "It will *ruin* Ashmore College."

More than anything, curiosity was getting to me. I had heard for days about this earth-shattering story, and I was speaking to someone who seemed to know all about it. However, Maddie and Tad's safety was first and foremost. It was my job to get them to agree to talk to the police and to agree to be placed in protective custody if necessary.

"Do you know for a fact that Eli was killed over this story?"

"Tad thinks so."

"Did Eli record something he shouldn't have? He seemed to get into trouble for that a lot."

Maddie nodded. "Tad and Eli were walking to class one day when they overheard this weird conversation between..." She looked back toward the rear of the house and grimaced. "...a man and a woman. Eli of course whipped out his phone and started recording. The guy saw Eli and came after him and Tad, threatening them if that video ever surfaced, they'd be dead. They managed to outrun him, at least that day. After Eli died...Tad went crazy. He packed up and packed me up, and my uncle let us hide out here."

"Does Tad think the man who threatened him killed Eli? Does he know who the guy is?" I asked.

Maddie opened her mouth to speak, but Tad entered the room, his hair wet and a bath towel tied around his waist.

Upon seeing me, he spat at Maddie, "What the hell is she doing here?" He added between gritted teeth, "I thought we agreed not to tell *anyone* where we are."

She got up and hurried over to him. "I know, but...you know when we talked about being sick of hiding, and...I said I thought...maybe you should consider talking to someone like Professor Matthews?"

"I didn't agree to talk to anyone," he growled.

Shaking her head, she said, "Look, I can't do this anymore, Tad. I love you, but I'm so freaked out right now. I want this nightmare to be over."

"It won't be over until the cops catch the guy who killed Eli," he said.

"Did you hear they brought in George Cooper for Vasti's murder? They think the two deaths are related," I said.

Tad stared at me. "George Cooper, like the Ashmore president's husband?" He shook his head. "They've got it all wrong. *She's* the one they want."

My mouth dropped open in disbelief. Before I could reply, there was a loud banging at the front door.

Flashing a panicked look at the door, Tad whispered to me, "Were you followed here?"

"No, I don't think so," I breathed. "No one knew where I was going."

The three of us stood motionless, hoping whoever was out there would go away. The blinds were pulled, so it was impossible to see who it was, and the person wasn't saying anything. The banging started again, and we all stepped back farther from the door. I began to sweat. If it had been any type of law enforcement, they would have identified themselves. The banging stopped, and then we heard footsteps crunching the dry grass outside.

Tad murmured, "They're going around back."

"Is the back door locked?" I whispered.

He set his jaw. "Yes."

From where we were standing in the living room, we could see through the kitchen to the back door of the house. The knob began rattling, but held fast.

A knot formed in the pit of my stomach. "I think we should call for help," I said, heading for my purse.

Suddenly the door burst open, the aging doorframe exploding in a flurry of splinters as the wood around the deadbolt gave way. A man stepped into the house. Tad, Maddie, and I froze. He was a big, imposing man, wearing all black, his face partially shielded by a baseball cap and dark sunglasses. More troubling, he held a large caliber handgun—a .45 by my guess. He looked familiar, but I couldn't put my finger on how I knew him.

His mouth curling in a menacing sneer, he stalked through the kitchen and into the living room like he owned the place, not that Tad, Maddie, or I were in any position to stop him. He turned to Tad. "Are you Tad Ogelsby?" he grunted.

Tad nodded warily, tightening the grip he had on his towel.

Without uttering a word of warning, the man leveled his gun at Tad and pulled the trigger, shooting Tad square in the chest. Amid the deafening reverberation of the gunshot, Maddie let out a guttural screech as Tad fell back and dropped to the floor, blood spurting from the hole in his chest and forming a pool underneath him.

My heart seized and twisted as I screamed, "NO!"

Maddie collapsed on top of Tad's still body, sobbing uncontrollably. My ears were ringing from the boom of the shot and my head was spinning from the shock, but my only thought now was how to get Maddie and myself out of this alive. I had to struggle with every ounce of my being to keep my wits about me.

The man gestured his gun at me. "Who are you two?"

My voice trembling, I replied, "That's Maddie. She's Tad's girlfriend. And I'm Ellie." I swallowed the lump in my throat. "I'm her teacher, and I came here because I was worried about her missing class. We have no idea what Tad had himself mixed up in. We certainly don't want any trouble. Please."

He didn't respond for a moment, causing me to break out in a cold sweat. He finally said, "Did he tell you anything about a video?"

"No." It was the truth—my conversation with Maddie had been interrupted before we got to any specifics.

The man raised his gun and shot the TV three feet away from me. I flinched and bit my tongue to keep from crying out, my ears stinging again from the blast.

He pointed the gun at my chest, growling, "Sure about that?"

I put my hands in front of me defensively, palms facing him. I tried not to focus on his gun as I choked out, "I know Tad was hiding because of what was on some video, but he wouldn't tell anyone about it. Not even Maddie." I lied about that fact, but I was only trying to keep Maddie alive.

The man nudged Maddie, who was still on the ground whimpering, with his foot. "Is that true?"

When she didn't answer him, he kicked her in the ribs. She cried out in pain.

I snapped, "Hey, you just killed her boyfriend. Leave her alone. I told you she doesn't know anything."

He reached me in two strides and clocked me across the temple with the side of his gun. Pain shot through my head. I fell to my knees, disoriented. He said, "Shut the hell up. I give the orders around here."

Struggling to think clearly with the excruciating throbbing in my head, I said, "There's no reason to kill us. Maddie is beside herself, and I probably have a concussion now, so we couldn't pick you out of a line-up if we had to. We don't have a clue as to who you are, so please, just go. Don't make this worse than it already is."

He started to reply, but was interrupted by someone else banging on the front door. "Randy! Randy, are you in there? I know you're here. Your truck is out front. I heard a shot. Open the door," called a voice I'd recognize anywhere. Rob Larson.

The man, Randy, cursed under his breath and shouted back, "Robby, this is none of your damn business. Get out of here."

"It's over, Randy. I know you've been trying to track down that other kid. Open up," said Rob, his voice sounding strained.

"I said for you to get the hell out of here, or my next bullet comes your direction. You hear me?" Randy said.

Like the back door had, the rotting wood around the front door's frame splintered in every direction as the door crashed open. Rob stepped inside, his eyes zeroing in on Tad's lifeless body on the floor. Maddie still lay on top of Tad, covered in his blood and continuing to cry hysterically, the rest of the world blotted out for her. Rob didn't notice me crouched near the wall. His jaw clenched, and he slowly turned his murderous stare on Randy.

"You killed another kid, Randy? How could you? After what I went through the last time for you..." Rob shook his head, his face bright red with anger. "Not this time. I'm not helping you cover this one up."

"Like hell you're not. If I get caught, you get caught. You'd never let your precious reputation get tarnished. I own you."

"Not anymore. I'm coming clean, and I'm going to make sure you never do anything like this again."

Randy laughed, pointing the gun at Rob. "Big talk from the guy who's not holding the gun. What are you going to do, tell Mom on me?"

I gasped. No wonder Randy had looked so familiar to me. I could see the family resemblance in the two brothers' jaw lines and noses.

Rob finally looked in my direction when I gasped. He did a double take, his face a mixture of confusion and horror. "Ellie? What are you doing here?"

Their conversation took a moment to click in my addled mind. When it did, I felt sick at the realization that Rob knew all along who'd killed Eli. "You lying bastard!" I cried, my head hurting too much to come up with anything more biting to say.

Grinning, Randy said, "Oh, do you two know each other?"

Still gaping at me, Rob didn't respond.

Anger boiled inside me. "You do realize that you didn't simply help your brother cover up a murder," I spat at Rob, hauling myself to my feet and taking a few steps toward him. "You helped him kill Eli Vanover. Eli wasn't dead when the two of you strung him up."

Rob's eyes went wide. "How did you know that?"

"Oh, come on. It was obvious that Eli's death wasn't a suicide. You two geniuses didn't cover your tracks at all."

Randy scoffed, "Then how come the cops haven't picked us up yet? They don't have a damn clue." He regarded me for a moment, then his face twisted into a scowl. "Wait a minute. Robby, is this your new cop girlfriend you told me about?"

Rob frowned at me, ignoring his brother. I glared right back at him.

Randy began pacing around, shaking his head. "This is a problem, Robby. Your lady here lied to me earlier. She told me she was a teacher, not a cop. And now you've shot off your damn mouth about what we did." He stopped pacing and gestured to me. "The bitch knows too much."

As Randy pointed his gun in my direction, Rob leaped in front of me. A shot rang out. I screamed as Rob groaned in pain and fell back, knocking me to the floor with him.

I heard Baxter's voice yell, "Hamilton County Sheriff's Department! Put down the gun!"

I looked up in time to see Randy swivel around to point his gun at Baxter, but he was too slow. Baxter put three shots into the middle of his chest, and Randy dropped to the floor.

Rob shouted, "No!" He rolled off me, grunting in pain as he crawled across the floor toward his brother.

Sterling and a wave of deputies and EMTs poured into the tiny house. Baxter hurried over to me. Picking me up off the floor, he asked, "Are you okay? Are you hit?"

Overcome with emotion, I couldn't speak. I shook my head.

He held me in a crushing hug. His voice tight, he said, "Next time, you tell me where you're going. I almost got here too late."

"I'm sorry," I choked out, burying my face in his chest and squeezing my eyes shut to keep the tears from flowing.

28

Baxter led me outside and sat me down on the tailgate of his SUV. He sat next to me. We didn't speak for a while as we watched Sterling gently guiding a shell-shocked Maddie out of the house and toward one of the ambulances.

"How did you know to come out here?" I asked Baxter.

Looking away, he said, "I had your cell phone tracked."

I was a little miffed at his admission, but thankful for the outcome. "But how did you know to bring the cavalry with you?"

"Long story, although lucky for us the pieces fell together fast. After our meeting, I had a message waiting for me from Tristan Sellers. Evidently, Vanover did have a stash, and he hid it in Sellers's rollerblades. When Sellers went to put them on this morning, he found the stash. There were some drugs, but more importantly, he found the flash drive with the video we'd been looking for."

"Finally. What was on that video?"

"An exchange between Judith Cooper and Randall Larson. Here." He started the video on his phone and handed it to me.

The video showed Randy and Mrs. Cooper sitting on a bench on Ashmore College's front lawn.

Her voice terse, Mrs. Cooper said, "I told you not to come here."

"I wouldn't have to if you'd pay me what you owe me," Randy replied.

"I told you it would take me another week."

Randy shrugged. "Change of plans. I want it now."

"As I said before, you'll get it. I don't want to raise any suspicion with my husband by withdrawing such a large sum at this time."

"That's not my problem, Mrs. Cooper. If I happen to let it slip to anyone about our working relationship, it would seriously damage your credibility around here. You wouldn't want anyone to find out you put a hit out on some poor innocent girl."

"Poor innocent girl?" Mrs. Cooper let out a bark of laughter. "You have some gall asking for your money early, considering the shoddy job you did planting the evidence—I hear the police are looking at my son, not my husband. If my son is blamed for this, you might not get your money at all."

"I'd be careful if I were you. If I don't get my money, I'll start with ruining your life. You won't like where it goes from there."

"Who do you think anyone is going to believe—some thug or me?"

Randy leaned toward her. "I can be very persuasive."

"Are you threatening me?"

"You catch on fast, Mrs. Cooper. You're a smart cookie."

She gave him a cold stare. "You'll get your money."

"I'll be back for it tomorrow. Pay it or else."

Mrs. Cooper stood up and stalked away from Randy. Randy turned his head and seemed to zero in on the camera. Getting up slowly, he began walking closer and closer. The camera angle started jiggling, and a young man's voice said, "Shit! I think he saw us." After that, the video cut off.

I handed the phone back to Baxter and stared at him in shock. "Mrs. Cooper was the mastermind?"

"Scary, huh? After we watched the video, we arrested Mrs. Cooper and persuaded her to tell us who the guy was. Turns out Randall Larson handles a lot of George Cooper's business for RZL Security *and* he works on the side for none other than Morris Powell."

"You're kidding. He's the connection to Powell Stone Supply."

"Right. He also has a rap sheet a mile long, mostly assault and domestic. When we couldn't locate him at home or at work, we tracked his cell phone. When I realized he was heading in your direction, that's when I mobilized the entire county."

I nodded, trying not to think about what might have happened to me if Baxter hadn't shown up when he did. "So Mrs. Cooper did all this—had three kids killed and framed her husband—because her husband cheated on her? Did she forget that she married a politician?"

Shrugging, he said, "Hell hath no fury like a woman scorned."

"You and your fortune cookie sayings. At least you've quit with the bad puns." I laughed, but then winced and grabbed my temple as a shooting pain coursed through my head.

Baxter's expression grew concerned as he took my chin and turned my face toward him to inspect the area where I'd been hit. "What happened?"

"Randy pistol-whipped me. It hurts like a bitch."

"You need to get that checked out."

"I'm fine. I—"

I stopped suddenly as I saw the EMTs wheel Rob out of the house on a stretcher. There was a large bloody bandage covering his right shoulder. It must have been where Randy shot him while he was trying to save me. I wondered what he was feeling right now. He had fought bitterly with his brother, only to watch him die seconds later. Part of me wanted to go to him, to comfort him and thank him for saving my life. But another part of me was so angry it overshadowed my feelings of gratitude. Rob had helped his brother commit murder. Maybe Eli had been unconscious at the time they strung him up and Rob mistook him for dead. But when Eli started clawing at the noose and trying to get away, Rob shouldn't have stood by and let him die. That was one thing I could never forgive.

"Don't do that," said Baxter.

Breaking out of my thoughts, I asked, "Do what?"

"Blame yourself for not knowing your rent-a-cop was a scumbag."

I closed my eyes. "It's my job to find teeny, tiny specs of evidence and to be able to think like a criminal. I'm supposed to notice everything. How did I *not* notice I was dating a murderer?" I even wondered if Rob had led me on in hopes of getting case information out of me, or worse yet, if he'd intended to try to convince me to alter my evidence to ensure he didn't get caught.

"It could happen to anyone," he said.

"That is such bullshit, and you know it."

Baxter chuckled and got to his feet. Holding out his hand to help me up, he said, "Don't take this the wrong way, but it's time to get your head examined. Literally. Your ambulance awaits."

I could feel the swelling and pressure spreading its way across the side of my face, so I didn't argue. Before I could reach out and take Baxter's hand, he dropped it to his side. I followed his worried gaze to the police vehicle that had just arrived. A stern-looking man in a rumpled suit got out and started making his way toward us.

"You're going to have a shitty week, aren't you?" I asked.

He blew out a breath. "That's an understatement. IA doesn't waste any time after an officer-involved shooting. I'll be tied up for a while, but I'll be in touch. Feel better, okay?"

"Good luck."

I watched as Baxter handed his gun over to a deputy and was whisked away by the IA officer. I didn't envy the coming days for Baxter. He would be put through the ringer—his competence, ethics, and judgment all called into question. And it was all because I tried to handle a situation on my own.

My head started pounding again as my mind replayed the events of this afternoon in a distorted, never-ending loop: Randy gunning down Tad, Tad bleeding out on the floor, Maddie weeping over Tad's body, Rob getting shot protecting me, and Baxter shooting Randy. In a numb fog, I walked to the ambulance, wishing to pass out from the pain so the horrible images I'd witnessed today would quit flooding my thoughts.

I was diagnosed with a mild concussion, so I took a week off school to rest and recover. Mrs. Cooper's firing of me didn't stand. Since she was in jail for conspiracy to commit murder, she was no longer in charge of Ashmore College. The vice president had taken over her job and deemed my termination unfounded because she'd fired me over a personal issue and in a fit of rage. I still had a job, and I considered myself lucky for that.

After being briefed about what happened, Jayne came to the hospital to check on me during my seven-hour stint in the ER. Even though I tried to hide my guilt and depression from her, she saw right through me and put me in therapy for an hour a day with the county's psychologist. The psychologist and Jayne both insisted that none of the events that had occurred were my fault. Jayne said Randall Larson had been tracking Tad and Maddie for days and had finally caught a break on the day I happened to visit them. She stressed to me that everything else that happened was a result of the bad choices Randy had made. The therapy helped somewhat, but I couldn't manage to get the graphic images of the events of that day out of my head.

The following Saturday I went to school to work on the fingerprint lab I had planned for Monday's classes. I was retrieving the last fuming chamber from the forensics storage cabinet when Baxter called me.

After I answered, he said, "I hear you're back to the land of the living."

"I suppose." I felt better physically, but emotionally I was still a wreck.

"Want to meet for coffee? I can tell you all about my week from hell."

"Coffee? What, no drinks at O'Loughlin's?"

"I figured you were on pain meds or something and couldn't drink."

Fiddling with the latch on the door of the fuming chamber, I said, "Oh, right... I'm not supposed to drink for a while."

Baxter and I made plans to meet later in the afternoon, and I went back to assembling the items I needed for my lab. When I was finished, I headed back to my office. As I rounded the corner, I bumped into someone coming the other way.

"Oh, excuse me," I said automatically before realizing who it was.

Dudley Cooper stared down at me, his expression a mixture of surprise, hurt, and anger. "I didn't expect to see you here," he said quietly.

"I was, um...getting a lab together...for Monday." I broke out in a sweat. I hadn't spoken to Dr. Cooper since I lured him to his arrest.

"I'm leaving."

My mouth dropped open. "Leaving? You mean you're leaving Ashmore?"

"I'm leaving town."

"Why? You were exonerated. I don't underst—"

He waved his hand and cut me off. "It's not about that." His expression was hard. "My father was quick to assume I was guilty of murder and disowned me. And worse, my own mother allowed me to be accused of a crime she paid someone to commit."

"I know you're hurting, but what about your career? What about your research facility?" I asked.

Dr. Cooper let out a bark of mirthless laughter. "You think I could work day in and day out at that place after what happened there? Besides, who would help me run the facility?" Looking pointedly at me, he added, "My friends and colleagues *all* turned their backs on me and believed the worst. I can't stay here."

I closed my eyes, unable to meet his. "I'm so sorry for what I did to you. I didn't have a choice. I was working for the Sheriff's Department, and there was a warrant out for your arrest. They knew you'd been contacting me. If I hadn't cooperated, I would have been charged with obstruction and put in jail myself."

"So you chose to put *me* in jail instead."

His words stung, but I didn't defend myself. "Yes. And I'm sorry. I don't know what else to say."

"I do. Goodbye, Ellie." He brushed past me and stalked down the hall.

I didn't think it was possible for me to feel any worse about what had happened, but after talking with Dr. Cooper, I did. I trudged back to my office and fished around in my bag for my "water" bottle. I downed a swig and took sick pleasure in the way the clear liquid burned all the way down.

Later that afternoon, I met Baxter at a coffeehouse on Noblesville's town square. He was already there when I arrived. I noticed he'd grown a beard during his time off. I thought it suited him—it made him look less baby-faced. I got some coffee and a chocolate bar and sat down with him.

He eyed my chocolate. "You've been off work for a week. What could possibly be stressing you out?" Even though he'd only known me a short time, Baxter knew my vices well, at least some of them.

Ripping off the wrapper and taking a big bite of the chocolate, I mumbled, "I ran into Dudley Cooper earlier."

"That must have been awkward. Have you not seen him since..."

I shook my head and took another bite of the chocolate.

"Was he mad?"

"Um, *yeah*," I said sarcastically. "He's leaving town."

Baxter shrugged. "I can't say I blame him."

"I guess not." I studied him for a moment. "You seem pretty together after everything that went down. What's your secret?"

"I won't deny that it bothers me to have taken another person's life. But at the same time, I feel like my actions were justified. The guy killed three kids, he tried to shoot you, and then he turned his gun on me. If I hadn't stopped him, well...I think you know what could have happened."

"I know. But don't you feel...guilty? In the back of your mind, where things don't always make sense?"

"Sometimes I have those thoughts, but I talked to the county shrink. A lot of cops think therapy is a crock of shit, but it was helpful to me." He stopped, staring at me for a moment. "Wait. Are *you* feeling guilty about what happened? Is that why you're bringing this up?"

I pretended to be engrossed in shredding the empty candy wrapper and didn't meet his gaze. "No. I was just making conversation."

"Liar. What's wrong?"

"Nothing."

"You're not acting like yourself," he said, concern in his voice.

"I have a concussion, you know."

"No, there's something else."

I snapped, "I said I'm fine. Leave it."

Baxter held up his hands in defeat. "Okay. Moving on. I talked to Sterling, and he said the DNA came back on the blood and epithelials underneath Vanover's fingernails. It's Randall Larson's. His DNA was already in CODIS from when he was arrested for beating the hell out of his girlfriend last year."

I sighed. Rob had told me that one of his brothers often fought with his girlfriend and got kicked out of the house. That would explain it.

"The DNA from the sweat stain you and Amanda found on Vanover's shirt is a male familial match to Randall Larson, so as soon as we have confirmation it belongs to Rob Larson, we'll have enough evidence to put him away. We have your audio recording of him admitting what he did, plus he entered a guilty plea, so being able to physically tie him to Vanover makes it a slam dunk. Good job."

I closed my eyes. The recording I made on my phone was originally intended to only consist of my conversation with Tad Ogelsby. However, it ended up being a complete audio documentation of Tad's murder, Rob's confession, Randy's intention to shoot me, and Baxter's order to Randy to put down his gun. My recording helped prove that Baxter followed protocol in the situation, but it also was damning evidence against Rob—as was the DNA I found during my overly thorough job of processing the shirt Eli Vanover was wearing when he was killed. I felt conflicted over the fact that my work netted the evidence to jail someone I'd slept with. The court would probably feel the same way, so I was in store for a nasty trial experience.

Baxter said, "Judith Cooper either didn't bother to or didn't know how to cover her tracks. We have phone records, emails, and money transfers all linking her to Randall Larson. Even with her team of lawyers, she's going down."

"That's good. She deserves it," I said. I was ready to change the subject. "So what's up with the beard? Did you take a break from grooming yourself, too?"

He chuckled and stroked his beard. "I thought it would make me look tougher."

"It does. So what else did you do during your administrative leave?"

Baxter hesitated. "Well, since I had plenty of time on my hands, I did some research. Now, I know you said you weren't interested in reopening your mother's case, but I think I might have the beginning of a trail on Marcus Copland."

My heart dropped into my stomach, and my body went numb. "Nick, I told you not to dredge this up. I can't handle it...especially right now." My throat tight, I fought back tears as I whispered, "How could you?"

His face fell, and his shoulders slumped. "I...thought it would help you to get some closure. I never meant to upset you."

"Was I not clear before about my feelings?" I stood up, trembling. "Let me be crystal clear now: *I don't want my mother's murder case reopened under any circumstances.* Do you understand? I don't want any attempt made to locate or contact the psychopath who killed my mother. Rachel even changed her last name from Copland to Miller to make sure he couldn't find her. Don't put my family at risk because you always have to be the hero."

Without a backward glance, I stormed out of the coffeehouse. I only made it a block down the street before Baxter caught up to me and grabbed my arm.

"What the hell was that?" he demanded.

I struggled to keep my emotions in check. "That was me being done with a conversation."

"Well, I'm not."

I wrenched my arm free. "Tough shit. This is my life, and you don't get to meddle in it. Don't worry. With the investigation over, you won't be seeing me anymore anyway. You can move on to your next charity case."

He stared at me, dumbfounded. "You think you're a *charity case* to me?"

Throwing my hands up in the air, I said, "I can't imagine what else I'd be."

"You're the best criminalist I've ever worked with. We make an amazing team."

"I never wanted to be part of the team. I told you that from the beginning. I'm done."

He wouldn't let it go. "But think of all the good we could do. How can you just walk away from that?"

"Watch me." We were near my car, so I hurried over and wrenched the door open before he could stop me. Before I got in, I added, "Nick, you don't know me like you think you do. I'll disappoint you. It's what I do."

I got in my car and sped away. When I got home, I locked myself in my room and drowned the pain until I no longer saw Baxter's disappointed face every time I closed my eyes.

AN EYE FOR AN EYE
Book #2 of the Ellie Matthews Novels

A string of targeted kidnappings launches criminalist Ellie Matthews into the midst of a shocking case.

After surviving the brutal ordeal of her last investigation, Ellie Matthews just wants to return to teaching, and put her nightmares behind her. But fate has other plans. It isn't long before the reluctant investigator finds herself drawn back into the field.

And once again, tragedy strikes close to home...

Ellie's mentor, Sheriff Jayne Walsh, reaches out to her with a desperate plea for help. A series of women have gone missing. Each victim is a family member of a law enforcement professional. And each one has turned up dead. Now, the latest victim is Jayne's niece...

Struggling to piece together a series of cryptic poems left by the killer, Ellie must work hand in hand with her old partner, plus a combative FBI agent who seems to butt heads with her at every turn. But when the trail leads to a cold case from Ellie's past, she quickly discovers the killer's vendetta may be even more personal than she thought.

Now time is running out, and the murderer is poised to strike again...

Get your copy today at
severnriverbooks.com/series/ellie-matthews

ABOUT THE AUTHOR

Caroline Fardig is the *USA Today* bestselling author of over a dozen mystery novels. She worked as a schoolteacher, church organist, insurance agent, banking trust specialist, funeral parlor associate, stay-at-home mom, and coffeehouse owner before she realized that she wanted to be a writer when she grew up. When she's not writing, she likes to travel, lift weights, play pickleball, and join in on vocals, piano, or guitar with any band who'll have her. She's also the host of a lively podcast for Gen Xers called *Wrong Side of 40*. Born and raised in a small town in Indiana, Fardig still lives in that same town with an understanding husband, two sweet kids, and three exhaustingly energetic dogs.

Sign up for Caroline Fardig's reader list at
severnriverbooks.com/authors/caroline-fardig

Printed in the United States
by Baker & Taylor Publisher Services